'There she is!' Lange panted.

Lotte had reached the canal. She reeled onto the bridge and grasped the railing for support. Then she turned to face her pursuers. The pistol trembled in her hand as she levelled the barrel at her own head. Kempe stopped in his tracks immediately and grabbed hold of Lange.

'Lotte!' roared Lange, 'Put that thing down! No true-blooded German woman would do what you're doing!'

Lotte's lips tightened and her smile died. Her face convulsed with misery as she looked at the two men. They wanted to rob her of the chance to put all her losses behind her, wanted to rob her of her right to die. . . .

She pressed the trigger.

LEBENSBORN

WILL BERTHOLD

SPHERE BOOKS LIMITED
30/32 Gray's Inn Road, London WC1X 8JL

This novel is based entirely on facts
arising from the documentation of the
Nürnberg trials, from declarations made by
Lebensborn members and mothers whose
children were conceived in Nazi stud farms,
and from reports made under oath by people
directly concerned with the racial policies
of the Third Reich.

'I let it be understood, unofficially at first, that Lebensborn was there to help the unmarried woman who desperately wanted a child, but had no immediate prospects of motherhood. The SS would adopt her child and take care of its upbringing and education. I realised the revolutionary nature of this idea . . . but, as you can imagine, we were intending to use only men of the greatest integrity and racial purity as studs . . . We shall only really begin to use the full potential of Lebensborn when the war is over. Then we shall make it a matter of the honour of every German woman who has not had a child by the age of thirty to use the Lebensborn facilities. Gradually, people will get used to the idea, and the time will come when we need no longer leave it up to the conscience of the individual, but can enforce it by law. . . .'

HEINRICH HIMMLER, leader of the SS, 9 May 1943, to his doctor and biographer, Kersten.

Chapter One

It was May and spring was in the air. It had rained that sultry afternoon and mist hung captive in the trees. Lazy drops fell from the leaves. The first moths danced through the damp air towards the milky lights of the ornate street-lamps.

Only scrunching footsteps on the gravel broke the silence of the evening. In the distance a clock struck the hour. Doris nestled against her man and felt the pressure of his hand on her arm. She knew that this sensation would be with her long after their parting : the strong and silent pressure of his hand.

'Klaus,' she said softly.

The moon's disc emerged from the clouds and its light touched the face of the young flying officer. He was tall and slim and strongly built. The leathery colour of his skin suited his white-blond hair as little as the stern set of his jaw suited his full young mouth. Klaus Steinbach was twenty-four years old and the hollows in his cheeks were the result of at least twice as many air battles.

'Klaus,' whispered Doris, 'this holiday . . . have you enjoyed it ?'

He stood still. His smile stole away the lines from his face and he became once more the carefree young man whose deep eyes and sensual mouth created such a stir amongst the girls. The young lieutenant was more than good-looking – he was the Germanic ideal, built on the clear, strong lines idolised by the Nazis. But as yet he knew nothing of that. He had faith in the life he lived in that year of 1941, and he lived by that faith . . .

'Yes,' he answered. 'It was wonderful . . . It is wonderful.'

'And tomorrow you must go back,' said Doris.

'I can do nothing about that.' He spoke more harshly than he had meant to.

'But you'll come back again . . .'

'Back to you, yes,' he replied.

Doris touched him lightly on the cheek. Her hands were long and slender – sometimes Klaus thought they were her best feature. But then her legs were so long and shapely too. When Klaus thought about her in this way, he always came to the conclusion that everything about her was beautiful: the almost unnaturally large blue eyes, as changeable as the sky; the delicate little ears nestling decoratively amongst her curls; the mouth which seemed to pout and smile at the same time. So kissable. But there was something else about her face which filled Klaus with a kind of shyness: the strong, clear profile, the lofty brow. It was at once the face of a girl and the face of a woman – the woman of Klaus' dreams.

'What are you thinking?' asked Doris. She stood on tiptoe and stroked an unruly strand of hair from his eyes.

He shivered, as he always did when she touched him, partly because of the desire she aroused in him, partly because he was too clumsy and awkward and shy to show it. Doris didn't notice anyway. He looked into her eyes; they were dark blue and merged with the night sky. The unreal light of the moon silvered the golden down which grew below her hair line. It was all he could do not to take her there and then.

'What's the matter?' she asked softly.

'Nothing.' He tried to shake away the thought of living without Doris. They had done so much together this holiday. Every day they had played tennis or been on the river or visited each other in their parents' homes. They had grown so close.

But there was something missing – he knew it when he kissed Doris, and he still kissed her as though he was a schoolboy. Always the tide of passion that rose in him was stemmed by some invisible barrier – he could feel Doris silently pulling away every time he held her to him. But he wasn't a schoolboy any longer, he was Lieutenant Steinbach,

8

and he wasn't going to be stopped by any invisible barriers.

That was how he had felt at the beginning of the holiday – now here he was at the end of it with nothing accomplished. Tomorrow it was back to the war. Suddenly in the silence of the park the young officer heard the drone of aeroplane engines, the roar of the aircraft cannon, the thud of the bomb, the whine of a plane hurtling through the air in a nose dive . . .

They walked on. Klaus was jealous of the darkness which wrapped itself around the girl's slender body. The gravel crunched under his boots. He felt his palms growing hot and clammy. He searched in vain for the right words.

'Is it – something to do with us?' asked Doris.

'No,' he said roughly.

She linked her arm through his. The sultry night held no ambiguities for her. Suddenly she laughed quietly to herself.

'Do you remember?' she murmured, pointing beyond the tree-lined walk to the children's playground, where a see-saw stood out clearly in the moonlight. 'Do you remember that little boy who wanted to knock down my sandcastles, and you punched him and chased him off?'

'Mmm. I think so,' he answered distractedly. 'But we can't always play at sandcastles, you know.'

'Pity.' Doris laughed. Then she noticed his expression. His eyes were not on the playground – he was frowning into the distance. The girl looked sideways at him. Dear Klaus, she thought. When we were six he had eyes only for my toys, at ten it was my plaits – he used to pull them terribly – then at fourteen he was too shy to even look at me. At sixteen he started to follow me everywhere, and two years later our eyes really met for the first time – and that was that – we never want to lose sight of each other again.

They had reached the end of the park where the path forked. They took the left fork which led to home. Doris would have liked to walk further, the night was so balmy, but Klaus led her on with urgent steps.

'Doris,' he said hoarsely, 'why don't you come and have something to drink at my place?'

He had got to get over this dreadful shyness. Just uttering

9

those words had made him feel as though he was being caught red-handed.

'That would be nice,' said Doris easily.

Suddenly something snapped inside him and he began to talk compulsively to make the walk go faster. He was afraid that she might change her mind. But Doris wasn't even considering it – she understood his motives as little as he understood her feelings. That's why they each regarded the other's feelings as a mystery, a miracle.

In the house all the lights were out. Klaus led the way, avoiding floorboards that creaked and hushing Doris at every step. Doris was puzzled – stealth was so unnatural to her. They crept up the stairs and stole into the attic room that had belonged to Klaus ever since he was a baby.

It wasn't the first time that Doris had been there, but she felt strange somehow. The young officer shut the door carefully behind them, then stood there for a moment, looking as if he was about to take root. He stared at the girl, fixing his eyes hungrily on her temptingly-parted lips. His gaze wandered to the golden down on her bare arms which automatically crossed themselves under his scrutiny. His eyes roamed to the modest neck of her light summer dress. Doris was looking at him in bewilderment. He avoided her eyes.

'Sit down,' he said awkwardly, and putting his arm around her shoulders he pushed her roughly on to the couch and fell on top of her, nuzzling up to her clumsily, rubbing his face and mouth against her neck.

Doris stiffened and laid a restraining hand on his shoulder. He was trying to force something which should come of its own accord, and in its own time. When he noticed her reluctance he lay quite still, stunned and ashamed and defeated.

'Oh, Klaus,' she sighed. She ran her fingers absently through his hair, round his ears. But her eyes, blue as summer seas, looked past him. Through her tears she gazed at the dear familiar room – the patterned carpet, the home-made desk with its gaudy ashtray – that had been a present from her – the comfy armchair that used to live downstairs, that they were always being shooed off as children in case they scuffed its leather upholstery, and on the wall, in the place of honour over the bed, the portrait of Hitler and a broken propeller blade – a souvenir of Klaus' first crash landing.

The tears welled up and spilled down her cheeks. This room was home and she was afraid that his impassioned behaviour had robbed her of it for ever.

'Klaus,' she pleaded, while he hid his face against her shoulder. 'If you would only try to understand . . . we must save that for, well, later – after the war. It will soon be over.'

The young officer was silent.

Doris went on in a little voice: 'It would be just like everyone else . . . so cheap.'

He raised himself up on one arm and buried his face in his hand.

'Tomorrow you're going to the front and so this evening you want . . . ' she choked back a sob and turned away her head. 'It is so cheap,' she repeated. 'It would seem unnatural, and I'm afraid of anything like that.'

'Yes,' said Klaus bitterly. 'You would call it unnatural.' He paused. 'I don't suppose it has occurred to you that I might not come back, that I might . . . ' he stopped, horrified at the barbarity of his own thought. He had wanted to say: and that I have a right to some happiness before I get killed.

He broke away from her, stood up unsteadily and reached for the brandy bottle. He poured himself a glass and downed it in one.

Doris got up and smoothed her rumpled dress. They went downstairs together and he turned to face her on the door-step, torn between shame and anger.

Doris leaned her head against his chest and he could feel that she was trembling too. She tried to kiss him, but her lips were ice-cold and his pressed tightly together.

'Come back to me, Klaus,' she whispered. Then she turned quickly and was gone.

Klaus stared after her.

* * *

The Messerschmitt touched down gruffly on the landing

strip in northern France. Its propeller turned another couple of times and then stopped. The engine cut and flight engineers swarmed like ants over the fighter plane, clambering over the wings and opening the cockpit to help their Commodore unstrap himself. NCOs, mechanics and officers of the flying squadron pounded over the tarmac to congratulate their chief. Before he landed he had dipped his wings three times – each dip an enemy aircraft.

Lieutenant Colonel Berendsen waved off the congratulations as he heaved himself out of the cockpit.

'Forget the fuss – just give me my cigar,' he shouted good-humouredly.

He looked down at the blue smoke of the Havana that they always had ready for him in the hope that he would come back alive and then squinted into the sun, towards the site of his recent battle.

'See you later,' he said, touching his cap in a lazy salute.

His men stood back to let him pass and he sauntered off towards the barracks.

He was a short man, stockily built, with broad, heavy features and a jaw that looked as if it had been carved out of mahogany. His men liked and respected him. Happier in the air than sitting at a desk, he liked his drink strong and his women dark and sultry. His life was simple – he worked hard, and he played hard. The politics of the war didn't concern him, but he lived to fight, to fly, to die if necessary.

The thunder of the rest of his squadron following him in was deadened as he entered the barracks. Berendsen kicked open the door of his room in his usual fashion and went in.

Captain Albrecht, the adjutant, stood to attention.

'Well,' asked Berendsen, 'what's the situation?'

The adjutant had the portfolio at the ready.

'Look, don't bother me with papers – just tell me what's happened to the second squadron.'

Captain Albrecht looked down at the desk. It would have been psychologically better for the Commodore if he'd been able to keep that part of his report until last. He began to sweeten the pill: 'Captain Wernecke has reported two fine kills – ' The adjutant's voice dropped and he went on gloomily: 'But Lieutenant von Bernheim has been shot down –' Berendsen grunted. 'And Staff Sergeant Rissman was seriously injured when his plane crash landed . . '

The chief was pacing up and down his office, as he always did when bad news clouded his vision of the glorious life of the fighter pilot. War had yet to teach him fear, and in 1941 he still believed that the 'hero's death' was caused by avoidable ineptitude.

'Is that all?' he asked gruffly.

'For the time being,' answered the adjutant carefully. 'The third squadron has yet to make its report.'

Berendsen pointed to the portfolio. 'Let's have a look at that then.'

The captain produced a sheaf of papers: lists of reinforcements, inventories, orders to the squadrons, applications for leave, reports.

The Commodore stood and scratched the side of his head with his pen and didn't look at any of them. Captain Albrecht was shuffling the papers and stacking them in order of importance.

'Load of rubbish,' growled Berendsen.

'And here's another enquiry from Berlin. They want to know if we'd like a theatre at the front.'

Berendsen snorted. 'What – with the same old crowd of tarts as last time?'

'No, sir, new ones.'

'In that case, you don't need to ask me.' The Commodore stopped his ceaseless pacing in front of the desk, got a bottle of brandy out of one of the drawers, and filled two glasses.

'Anything else?' he asked.

'Yes,' answered the adjutant. 'A circular from the SS. They've got some sort of organisation going and they're looking for members.'

Berendsen picked up the secret document absently. 'They want people from here?'

'That's right,' confirmed Captain Albrecht. 'Lebensborn, it's called. Every German can join. Costs one mark a month.'

The chief puffed at his cigar. 'What's that? Lebensborn – sounds like some sort of kindergarten. What sort of Arian crap are they dishing up to us now?'

The adjutant took the letter out of his hand. 'May I?' he

asked deferentially, then began to read in a droning voice: 'A nation which neglects its most valuable possession, its children, is ripe for destruction –'

'Cut the theory, Albrecht,' Berendsen broke in impatiently. 'Just tell me what they want.'

'Members,' said the adjutant laconically. 'The circular is signed by Himmler himself. Only tall, fair-haired men – classical nordic types – will be considered. And of course they have to be true National Socialists.'

The Commodore's face remained impassive. 'True-blooded Nazis, eh?' he growled. 'Well, we can't afford all this absenteeism, somebody's got to stay and do the dirty work. Get one of the younger officers to volunteer for it.'

Captain Albrecht frowned. 'Nordic . . . I wonder?'

'What about Steinbach,' suggested the Commodore. 'He looks as though he's just escaped from Valhalla. Why don't you ask him?' He topped up the adjutant's brandy glass. 'What do you think of the leader of the SS, then, Albrecht?'

'I'd sooner have you than Himmler, sir,' said the captain carefully.

'Good. Let's drink to your excellent taste.'

Before they had chance to drain their glasses, the door flew open and an NCO from the radio station marched in and stood stiffly to attention. Berendsen looked at him with irritation.

'What's up?'

'Report from the first squadron, sir. Lieutenant Steinbach has been shot down.'

'Shot down,' repeated the Commodore mechanically. He gulped his brandy and went over to the window.

Captain Albrecht spoke almost bitterly : 'Should I nominate someone else for Lebensborn then, sir?'

The Commodore turned slowly and walked out of the room.

* * *

Lebensborn was Himmler's brainchild. Even before war was declared in 1939 Heinrich Himmler had estimated that millions of German men would perish. If they died without fathering the next generation of soldiers, the future strength of the Reich would be severely diminished.

What Himmler wanted to replace the war dead was a master race – a race of tall, strong, athletic men and women, with pure nordic features, clear blue eyes and blond hair, and pure Arian blood in their veins.

Himmler decided to produce this élite of warriors and childbearers by a procedure of unnatural selection. He dubbed this procedure Operation Lebensborn. When Lebensborn was launched in 1939, Himmler announced that it was an organisation designed to support mothers of large families. To his listeners that seemed like a sensible and enlightened idea and when he invited those in favour to become members, donating a monthly subscription to the cause, the response was enthusiastic.

Later, Himmler generously extended the support of Lebensborn to unmarried mothers. Later still, he announced to a select audience that Lebensborn would organise the systematic breeding of illegitimate children – children who would be produced like chickens in a poultry farm. Roll like cars off a conveyor belt. Lebensborn was one gigantic stud farm.

Recruits would not be taken from the couple of hundred thousand standing members, who merely handed over their subscriptions and knew very little about the actual purposes of the organisation. But Lebensborn officials with well-oiled tongues would visit the various branches of the League of German Girls, inspire them with fervour for the Führer's cause, and when emotions had reached a high, call for volunteers prepared to prove themselves in the service of the Fatherland. The response, predicted Himmler, would be enormous.

Each volunteer would be examined by a team of medical experts and, if the results were positive, she would be sent before she had time to ask any questions to one of a dozen or so hostels dotted all over Germany. There she would meet the tall, blue-eyed soldier who had been sent to do his 'biological duty' on her – according to Himmler's plans, no blond-headed Arian would be laid to rest under the birchwood cross until he had become a father.

15

To keep up a semblance of respectability, the men and girls would be made to attend a series of lectures on 'race hygiene', but in reality all they were required to do was to get into bed and get at it. Twenty-five men were given three weeks to get twenty-five girls pregnant.

Conceived in lovelessness, the infants would be torn from their mothers at birth and taught to box instead of to pray; to hate instead of to love. They would be truly Hitler's children.

Chapter Two

Seconds before his plane exploded, Klaus had flung himself from the burning cockpit. As he pulled the rip cord, his whole body was jerked violently to the left and he looked up in horror to see that one of the cords had pulled a hole in the white silk of his chute. He was plummeting to earth twice as fast as he should have been, and without any control over his steering.

He looked down at the world heaving dizzily below him. A spinney. A pylon – directly underneath. He began to drop like a stone towards death on the high voltage wires. He pulled helplessly at his cords, then braced himself for the end.

Suddenly the crash came. Branches slashed his face and his hands and he fell heavily on one ankle only yards from the pylon.

When he realised he was still alive, he tried to stand up, but the stabbing pain in his leg was too intense – all he could do was crawl, dragging the injured leg behind him.

After a couple of hundred yards he gave up, flopped down exhausted on to his back and let the warmth of the September sun seep into his body. The last thing he remembered was staring up into the cloudless blue sky of Normandy – then he must have lapsed into unconsciousness, because when he woke up it was late afternoon, he was famished, and his body was too stiff even to crawl.

He lay there hour after hour. His flying suit stopped clinging to him – his body lost all feeling. As night fell, he grew numb with cold. He had not seen a soul all day, and if somebody did come and find him there was no guarantee that he wouldn't slit his throat.

His ankle was throbbing – it seemed to be the only part of his body still alive. He looked up at the stars in the clear night sky and searched automatically for the Great Bear, the Little Bear, the Pole Star. Perhaps Doris, who had now also left home to serve her country in the League of German Girls, would be looking up at the stars too and thinking of him, just as he was thinking of her.

The cold and pain racked him severely. He drifted into delirium and a procession of distorted figures floated into his head – there was Doris, she was naked in his arms, her body warm and scented under his touch. But as he bent his lips to hers, he saw with horror that she was no more than a little girl – he let her fall away from him, her mouth open for a silent scream. Away she fell, her body tumbling through space, tumbling towards the glittering high-voltage wires. There was a brief bluish flare. The pain shot through Klaus' body. He woke covered in sweat with Doris' name on his lips.

An icy shiver ran through his body, and he realised for the first time just how close he had been to death.

The next morning, soon after Klaus awoke, stiff and cold, he spotted a farm truck passing close by. He shouted and waved to the driver, who stopped and, horrified at his blood-streaked face and tattered clothes, helped him to climb aboard. Klaus knew that he was saved – with the help of this man he'd get into the town hall, make a phone call, and his problems would be over.

An hour later he had adjutant Captain Albrecht on the line. 'You're lucky to be alive, Steinbach,' he said. 'Tell me where you are and I'll send a car for you.'

Klaus was 150 km away from base, but the ride was bumpy and it seemed much further with his injured ankle, which was throbbing painfully, although the French doctor who'd examined it had said it was merely sprained. The lieutenant hoped to be in the air again within a fortnight.

When he arrived, his colleagues had already celebrated his return to the living, and the only one who wasn't completely drunk was the Commodore, who had actually consumed the most. He slapped Steinbach on the back.

'I'm glad,' he said, 'I'm bloody glad you're back.' He turned to the adjutant, who was standing next to him. 'There was something else we had to tell Steinbach, wasn't there?'

'That's right, sir – Lebensborn.'

Berendsen sat down and motioned to Klaus to join him. 'Listen,' he said confidentially, 'how tall are you?'

Klaus smiled. '1.82 m.'

'Couldn't be better!' the Commodore lowered his voice: 'Hitler Youth Movement?'

'Yes, sir.'

'Leader?'

'Group leader, sir.'

'In the party too, are you?'

'Of course, sir.'

'Member of anything else?'

'The Nazi Flying Association, sir.'

'Well, I'll be damned. You qualify hands down!'

'What for, sir?'

'They're looking for a confirmed National Socialist – well, they're two a penny,' the Commodore grimaced. 'But he's got to be tall and blond and Christ knows what else. Do you want to do it, Steinbach?'

'Whatever you say, sir!'

'Ah, but it's not what *I* say, you've got to volunteer!'

'Well, I'll volunteer, then!'

'That's the spirit! Now drink up and later we'll go and sign the papers.'

And so the young lieutenant, burning to serve his Führer and his Fatherland, signed the declaration for active membership of Lebensborn.

He didn't suspect for a moment that what he'd signed was a blank cheque for his own flesh and blood ...

* * *

The girls were working like slaves to get the camp scrubbed for tomorrow's inspection. They were using up immense resources of water and nervous energy, for it was a time of greatness, and therefore they were required to march, scrub, and sing in unison, all at once.

When they gathered for assembly that evening the camp

leader ranted and raged because one of the rubbish bins still hadn't been emptied and the Führer's portrait hadn't been dusted.

A hundred members of the League of German Girls hastily assumed expressions of guilt, either because they shared their leader's fear of the imminent visit, or because they didn't understand her fastidiousness over the preparations.

Amongst the young women present was Doris Korff, who had joined the League four months ago and in the stuffy, cramped quarters of the camp she had quickly learned to forget the flower-scented air of her parents' roomy villa. But she had made the exchange gladly to serve her country in its hour of need. In a way, she thought of it as helping Klaus. Her father had tried to dissuade her, but she had received plenty of encouragement from her mother, who had been able to boast to her political friends at her next coffee morning that her only daughter had enlisted in the service of the Fatherland – if only with broom, hoe and potato peeler.

Doris swung her broom as though it were her dancing partner and she wore the coarse brown League uniform like the most elegant evening dress. She wielded the hoe with a fury that would have weeded out all Germany's enemies. She gave up perfume and make-up, spoiled her delicate white hands with hard work and cut short her blonde locks in the service of Führer and Fatherland.

Already, after two months, her enthusiasm had fallen off, but after four it was rewarded. She was called out of the ranks and made a leader and sent on a special training course. And now she was waiting for tomorrow's inspection up in the room which she shared with two other girls, Erika and Lotte.

'I wonder what the old sods will be like this time?' said Erika, snuggling down into her pillows for the night.

Lotte lay stiffly on her bed staring hard at the ceiling.

'Listen, I'm tired,' said Doris, sensing a quarrel in the air. 'Why don't you put the light out?'

But Erika kept on talking. 'So much fuss about nothing,' she grumbled. 'The whole camp has to be turned inside out just because a couple of old crones are coming to visit. What's the point? All they ever look at is our legs, anyway.'

Lotte sat bolt upright in bed bristling with hairpins. Her pigtails were fastened to the top of her head for the night and added to her shocked appearance.

'I can't stand it!' she screamed at her two room-mates. 'How can you be so disrespectful when you're speaking about your leaders!'

But the leaders, and the visit, turned out to be almost as Erika had predicted – almost.

Erika had a very realistic outlook on life and she had only joined the League because she didn't mind buying her freedom, as she called it, with temporary hardship. She had applied to be one of the leaders because the air was healthier in the upper echelons than in the lower. Meanwhile, she stuck pin-up pictures of men all over her locker and when she had time, she wrote home that everything was fine.

Not until they were all lined up in the assembly room did the girls realise that this was no ordinary inspection – their visitors were headed by a top SS official. There was a respectful hush as the girls stood to attention and he was introduced.

The SS officer mounted the swastika-hung podium, which was decorated with the sort of greenery usually found in a butcher's shop window.

'Cheeky bugger,' pouted Erika under her breath.

'My friends – ' shouted the officer to the back of the room.

Lotte lowered her pale head almost reverently. Bright red patches appeared on her cheeks, making her look as though she was branded with the Nazi emblem.

'It is a pleasure to come here and speak to you today,' trumpeted the man in the black uniform. His short-cropped hair stood up excitedly, as if at the sight of the brown-clad charmers seated in front of him. 'We are all fighting for one idea, towards one goal: a victorious Germany. You girls, you young women have been chosen to set Germany on its path to greatness, and I have come to tell you that the Führer is very moved by the personal sacrifice each one of you is making for him.'

The slick Party language permeated the air like a syrupy mist and the girls did not stop to ask themselves how Hitler could have been moved by hundreds of tons of potato peelings. Instead, their hearts were beating faster at the thought of their leader's soulful eyes, at least, so the SS officer hoped.

His voice rang out again. 'I know what your answer will be when I ask you girls if you are loyal Party members. Your answer will be yes. But I want you to be honest with yourselves. Ask yourselves whether you are committed heart and soul, with every fibre of your being, for your whole life?'

An animated whisper ran through the lines of listeners and a fervent chorus of clear girlish voices answered yes. A strong soprano rang out above the others – it was Lotte's.

The SS officer's face remained unsmiling, but he lowered his head as if to hide the urgency of his feelings.

'But when I ask you,' he said, raising his eyes thoughtfully to the back of the room, 'when I ask you which of you would be prepared to make the Führer a *real* sacrifice, to give him a unique and intensely personal birthday present, I wonder which of you would be prepared to do it? Who would volunteer then?' His voice rose in a crescendo to fill the room.

A hundred hands shot up simultaneously. The little speech had worked. The officer smiled at last and dismissed the wave of hands. Modulating his voice, he explained carefully to the girls what was at stake – without making them any the wiser.

'You shouldn't be so eager to rush headlong into something you know so little about,' he said patiently. 'Your eagerness does you credit, but you must be fully aware that you will be asked to make a great sacrifice – the highest that a German woman can offer. Consider it carefully!' He egged them on subtly: 'You all have the freedom to decide for yourselves.'

Again the young faces burned with the desire to serve, yet not one of the girls had the slightest idea what the speaker was talking about. His apparent openness was nothing but a cloak for lies.

A few hands wavered and fell like timid flames. Then a few more. But there weren't many who could summon up the courage to be cowardly in front of all their friends. This was something the speaker had cleverly taken into account. Standing drumming his fingers on the lectern, the SS officer wore the fixed smile of one who can sit back confidently and wait for the outcome.

Doris' hand was still up. It wavered for a second and she felt a tingling in her fingertips, but her neighbour, Lotte, was searching out all those who backed down with scornful eyes.

'Shame on them!' she hissed. She found it incredible that a German girl could refuse the Führer anything.

So Doris kept her hand held high and resolved to stand by her decision. The Führer couldn't ask anything of her that wouldn't be right to give, she thought. They probably wanted volunteers for hospitals at the front. She would be near Klaus – she owed him that.

An official counted the hands and then made up the birthday list. The trap snapped shut. But nobody heard it and they were all swept blindly on towards their doom.

While the officer had been speaking, his invisible helpers had been setting up desks and writing equipment in three adjoining rooms. It was here that the girls were sent after they had given in their names at the podium. Doris read the word 'Lebensborn' on a folder on the desk. It meant nothing to her, or to the other four girls gathered in the first room.

Suddenly she was confronted by two doctors in white coats with military boots sticking out below them and SS collars above.

'Looks like the Führer wants a bit of our insides for his birthday,' whispered Erika, pointing to a spectacular array of medical instruments.

The doctors moved quickly and without uttering a word. Measuring devices danced in front of the girls' eyes. Calipers were placed against the backs of their heads. Peculiar wooden laths were pressed against their foreheads. The men in white coats read the figures off their instruments and mumbled them to the clerk who was taking them all down.

Doris tried to look the doctors in the eyes. But she met only the blank looks of experts whose interest was in the size of her head rather than what was going on inside it. Only her skull seemed important – and this was measured and felt for minutes at a time, as if it were an article up for sale.

'Definitely nordic,' confirmed one of the doctors with satisfaction.

'A good head,' commented the other. But it wasn't a compliment – Doris felt as if he were discussing a filly at a horse fair instead of a human being.

'Into the next room, please,' said the clerk.

The second lot of doctors was female. The girls were asked to undress and given a long and thorough examination.

Finally, they all stood, fully clothed again, in the hall. Then a list of names was called out – these girls had passed the test and been found fit for service. Lotte let out a sigh of relief : 'Thank God I've been chosen!'

There were fourteen other girls whom the commission had deemed worthy to make a sacrifice for the Führer in the name of German womanhood. They looked at each other questioningly. They little suspected what lay before them.

'Good Lord!' said Erika at once. Her eyes darted from one girl to the next. 'The gentlemen prefer blondes, do they? Tall, blue-eyed blondes . . .

The girls stared at each other and jumped involuntarily like kittens who had caught sight of themselves in the mirror for the first time.

'Well, what a coincidence!' Lotte smiled blandly.

The following day they were still guessing, but after a while they gave up and got back into the routine of scrubbing floors, shelling peas and peeling potatoes.

A week later Erika rushed into the room where Doris and Lotte were sitting.

'They've tricked us!' she cried, beside herself with fury. 'Do you know what we're supposed to be giving the Führer for his birthday, you idiots?' Her voice broke. 'A baby, that's what – a baby!' Erika stared wildly at her room-mates' astonished faces. 'It's true – I read it with my own eyes in the office.'

Doris shook her head in disbelief.

'We're all going to be sent for three weeks in some hostel or other – the men have already been laid on – and then –' her voice rose to an ugly pitch, 'and then – to bed! Have fun. We're nothing but *breeders*, that's what we are!'

'Shut up!' screamed Lotte.

'I don't believe it,' said Doris quietly. 'It's inhuman.'

During the next few days she managed to shake the

thought from her mind and persuade herself that it was nothing but idle rumour.

Until Colonel Westroff-Meyer, one of the pioneers of Lebensborn, arrived at the camp and called the fourteen chosen girls, all blonde, all blue-eyed, all over 1.70 m tall, into the assembly hall.

The chosen few sat in a row like frightened hens after a storm. Their eyes darted from the floor to their visitor's face and back to the floor again. They were wearing coarse, ugly coloured skirts and white, sleeveless blouses, from which their brown arms drooped helplessly. In the front at the right sat Lotte: devout, almost entranced. Next to her was Doris: wide-eyed with fear at what she was going to hear, whereas Erika, next to her, was cheerful, almost daring the truth to come out. Then came the other eleven girls, tall, blonde, idealistic – all grist to the Nazi mill.

'My friends,' began the Colonel, 'I have come from Berlin to convey to you the Führer's personal thanks for your unique sacrifice.'

Their pride wrestled with their uneasiness. They listened and hoped, stomachs fluttering, yet heavy with dread.

'The time has come for you to serve, and I am here to try and explain to you the nature and importance of your service.'

Westroff-Meyer fixed his sharp little eyes on each of the girls' faces in turn. His slack mouth tensed and he gripped the lectern to emphasise the importance of what he had to say. The girls sat as though hypnotised in their chairs.

'Starting tomorrow you will follow a special course of instruction. You will meet men who have already proved themselves in action and whom we have established to be as racially pure as yourselves. You should be rightly proud that you belong to such an élite – the cream of the German race.'

Doris had switched off, letting the treacly words flow over her unheeded. She was thinking of Klaus. He had been right, that last evening – she ought to overcome her reticence and shyness, because they belonged together, for always. The next time he came home on leave, she would tell him …

Suddenly Westroff-Meyer's tone had changed and Doris was brought back to the present with a jolt. The flow of hollow, sentimental rhetoric had dried up. There was nothing for it – Westroff-Meyer had to take the plunge and reveal to these fourteen innocent young girls the monstrous experiment in which they would be taking part. He bared his teeth sharply for the attack, like a rat driven into a corner.

'It is the Führer's dearest wish, it is the wish of the whole nation, that the noble young men who will be your colleagues on this course should become your partners.' He took a breath. 'I will not conceal from you that Lebensborn expects children from these unions.'

There was a sharp intake of breath from his listeners, but at once he raised his hand as if to ward off objections. 'We should of course prefer you to enter into marriage with these men. But we cannot leave the matter of population growth to chance, and this is why we must begin on a large scale, on a very large scale, to select suitable parents for Germany's next generation. Sometimes marriage will not prove possible, but let me assure you that every active member of Lebensborn will always enjoy the full protection of the Nazi movement.'

He cleared his throat and resumed his soft and pleasing tone. 'And you will no doubt ask: what part does love play in all this? And I can promise you that nothing would please us more than if you were to find love with your chosen partners. We must stamp out the permissiveness with which the Jews are polluting our society; we must replace their filth with purity; we demand responsibility instead of permissiveness! Your children will not be chance conceptions, they will be the future pillars of the German Empire!'

The fourteen girls were paralysed with horror. Even Lotte had registered shock and her smile was pale and false. But then her eyes widened and the look of devotion returned to her face with a rush of blood. She was the first to give her decision: she was ready.

Erika simply shook her head. Irene cast her eyes downward and stared at the floor. She wanted to be a League leader: she would have to do what was asked of her.

Doris had shut her eyes tightly to stop the room from spinning about her. Her whole soul revolted against the idea.

They sat in silence, sweating from every pore. There was

the occasional nervous cough. They didn't dare look at one another – they needed more time in order to be able to sort out their own feelings.

'I must stress,' the Colonel went on, 'that everything is entirely voluntary. Once you're on the instruction course, you won't be asked to commit yourselves to anything you can't possibly go through with.' His eyes sought to reassure them. 'You have been chosen as pioneers. Be proud of the fact that you are the cornerstone of the great German Empire.

'I realise that your parents will perhaps be too deeply rooted in the past to understand the nature of your sacrifice, and there might be other personal reasons why you wouldn't wish it to be made public.'

He lowered his voice : 'The births of your children will not be recorded in the public register; what is more, they will be brought into the world in one of the Lebensborn hostels specially equipped for the purpose, where they will be brought up to be good Germans and loyal National Socialists – the élite of the next generation.

'The state will even relieve you of the burden of caring for them – neither your conscience nor your pocket will suffer, and you should not feel morally bound to your partner – we are expecting far greater things of you : we are hoping you will marry and become mothers several times over – but the first child shall be for Adolf Hitler !'

He went on speaking for ten minutes, his words a strange mixture of incitement and reassurance – the usual Party formula. He exploited the girls' confusion. He lashed them with words and caressed them with phrases. He didn't allow them time to consider.

And then he called them one by one into the next room, where he began to pressurise them individually.

Thirteen girls remained behind, saying nothing. Gradually they broke up into groups and whispered amongst themselves.

'What do you say to that?' asked Erika.

'Incredible,' answered Doris numbly.

'A child!' enthused Lotte, caressing it already with her words.

27

'You'll probably have twins, you bloody fool,' said Erika harshly under her breath.

Lotte didn't hear her. She had a new gospel and she was ready to follow it blindly. 'We are fortunate to belong to this élite.'

'Naturally,' mocked Erika. 'The purer the breed, the weaker the brain. Anyone can see that from pedigree dogs.'

Before she could think of a reply, Lotte's name was called. She hurried off as if she feared she might be too late.

As for the other girls: they had grown up in the Nazi movement to believe that black was white and white black, so that despite their natural feelings they hesitated, confused, or else they were too cowardly to withdraw. The few who did resolve to say no were soon persuaded otherwise when Westroff-Meyer cast his evil spell over them again.

To everyone's surprise, even Erika threw in her lot and signed the agreement – she knew that she was strong enough to stop any man fooling around with her, and she admitted that she was filled with sheer curiosity to see exactly how far the Nazis would go in pushing through their preposterous plans.

Doris was the last but one to go in. Up to now, Westroff-Meyer had been able to persuade every one of the girls that it was in their interests to join – he wasn't going to let his record be spoiled by this one.

'I shall not sign,' she declared.

'Why ever not?' asked Westroff-Meyer civilly.

'For personal reasons,' she replied. 'I am engaged to be married.'

Westroff-Meyer nodded his head understandingly. 'The most important factor for those who join is the series of lectures,' he explained. 'The other thing, well, that will sort itself out once you're there.' His tone suddenly became more intimate. 'My dear, I don't believe a little education would hurt you.'

Doris shrugged her shoulders unhappily. Westroff-Meyer put a friendly hand on her arm. 'Are you a National Socialist?'

'Yes, of course,' said Doris uncertainly.

'And you believe in the Führer?'

'Yes,' she agreed weakly.

'Well, there we are then,' he said, slapping his hand on his thigh. 'No problems at all!'

He handed her a printed form, pointed to section three, which underlined the voluntary aspect of the project, pressed a pen into her hand and worked on her for a further five minutes.

The young girl looked up at him, her large blue eyes clouding over like the sky before a storm.

The Colonel went through his entire repertoire. He coaxed and threatened, cursed and wheedled. In the end he gave Doris three minutes to think it over.

Meanwhile he called for Herta, the last candidate, who signed immediately.

'Are you going to be the only one not worthy of the name of German womanhood?' Westroff-Meyer asked Doris, and his words seemed to hang in the air like poisonous gas.

Her hand trembled as she awkwardly formed her name, burning with resolve not to do anything which might endanger Klaus. She wrote in capital letters, with long, shaky strokes, not bothering to read the document she was signing.

Soon a time would come when she would need to decipher each point and learn it off by heart, so as to be able to negotiate the snare of each clause to which she was irrevocably bound.

Chapter Three

The vast house in which the turbulent events of the following weeks played themselves out was situated in Warthegau, 8 km from the nearest small town. Lebensborn had fitted the building with central heating, as if the blooms of the German race needed to be forced in a hothouse.

Originally, the home was a sanatorium for the treatment of nervous disorders – a fitting background for the Nazis' present scheme. It was surrounded by woods and grass meadows. In the garden the trees rustled their dry leaves in the warmth of the evening and the sinking sun gilded the dahlias which thickly lined the gravel paths. The tall french windows stood open on to the terrace where the late summer air was hung with threads of gossamer which seemed to dance to the sounds floating out from the house: the tinkling laughter of the girls, scraps of conversation, the deep voices of the men, the clatter of cups and saucers.

On the other side of the french windows a coffee party was going on in the dining room, where Colonel Westroff-Meyer was at present sitting amongst his guests, his hands resting on the table as if he had to force himself to keep from rubbing them together in satisfaction. His mouth opened and shut as a harmlessly cheerful flood of conversation issued forth. A portrait of the Führer stared heroically over his shoulder at the heavily laden coffee table. It seemed as though there was a look of hunger in Hitler's eyes.

A colourful collection of people sat round the horseshoe-shaped table. Some of the girls were wearing civilian clothes, but the men were without exception in uniform, most of them wearing the insignia of the SS. It almost seemed that the Iron Cross was the minimum entrance charge – and the insignia were second in importance only to the size of their wearers' skulls.

Three seats were still unoccupied : these were reserved for the guests who had been invited from the Luftwaffe. The fastest of the armed forces was late, as usual.

Doris was sitting half way down one side of the horseshoe. At first she hardly dared look around. Her palms were clammy and she was trembling. The ersatz coffee tasted of turnips and the Viennese cream cakes of saccharine. She wore her YW League Sunday-best blouse like a sacrificial robe.

The man on Doris' right was wearing the uniform of a battalion leader with practically every distinction the war had to offer pinned over his heart. He was a tall, burly fellow and he felt conspicuous and awkward in these genteel surroundings.

Three days ago he had been still leading a pioneer battalion against the Russians – and they had fetched him away. He took the order with the fatalism of every officer at the front who can take anything so long as he still has his cigarettes. He would much rather have stayed with his men. When he found out why they had called him away he had cursed and smiled wryly to himself. It was a bloody funny idea to try and make a father out of him when he'd got two children at home and a third on the way, but if they wanted him to spend three weeks chasing pussy, then who was he to refuse ?

He turned to his left and peered at the place-name that stood by Doris' plate.

'Doris,' he read. 'That's a pretty name.'

Doris shrugged her shoulders.

'You're not shy, are you ?'

'A bit.'

'Well, my name's Horst. Horst Kempe. It's a funny set up they've got here, don't you think ?'

Doris nodded. He looked at her profile. She was a pretty one – he'd noticed her as soon as he came in. Kempe struggled with his feelings – he wanted to say something nice and searched for the words, wrinkling his brow. He swallowed a curse, thought of his unit and flicked the cake crumbs off his jacket, 'accidentally' touching her hand.

31

Doris jumped as though she had received an electric shock.

'Oh, sorry,' said the battalion leader flushing crimson and turned to his right to where Lotte was sitting, wearing a holiday expression on her face. Since she had known her purpose at Lebensborn, Lotte had undergone a transformation. Her mousily average appearance had grown almost pretty. She wore her thick blonde plaits wound round her head like a crown.

'Have you just come from the front?' she asked.

Kempe replied that he had.

She pointed to his Iron Cross. 'What did you get that for?'

'I don't know,' said Kempe honestly. 'I was the only officer in the battalion who hadn't got one already.'

Lotte looked at him in bewilderment. 'But you must have done *something* to earn it?'

'Of course,' answered Kempe smiling broadly. 'I stayed alive, didn't I? Have another piece of cake?'

Westroff-Meyer was looking anxiously at his watch when an orderly stepped in front of him and stood stiffly to attention.

'The officers from the Luftwaffe have arrived, sir.'

'Well – bring them in, then,' snapped the Colonel.

Doris looked up absently to the door through which the three officers were making their entrance. So the Luftwaffe are in this too, she thought. A captain strode into the room and stood easily to attention, followed by a young lieutenant who unselfconsciously sized up the female company before he presented himself to the Colonel. Behind him was another officer who kept his face turned awkwardly away.

He looks like Klaus, thought Doris idly. Suddenly she looked up and a wave of fear and nausea swept through her as she recognised him. It was Klaus.

* * *

Four days ago Klaus had fought his last air battle. He had risen to captain of his squadron and needed only three more kills for the Knight's Cross. But his luck had turned: either the enemy got away, or he had to instigate a retreat himself,

32

or else there were no enemy aircraft over Normandy. So he was frustrated day after day, because the sky had become his world.

Then Berendsen had sent for him. 'It's not worth your staying here at the moment when there's so little going on,' he said.

Klaus looked at him inquiringly.

'You've been called away.'

'Where to, sir?'

The Commodore gave a hearty laugh and pointed to a letter on his desk. 'Lebensborn,' he answered. 'You lucky swine, you're going to be a sort of kindergarten worker as far as I can gather from that.'

Klaus sighed impatiently. 'How long must I be away?'

'Three weeks. First you have to report to Berlin and they'll send you on from there. Have a cigar? Brandy?'

The Commodore puffed smoke rings into the air, poured the usual dram of his usual tipple into two tumblers and handed one to his officer.

'Prost!' he said. 'I can't vouch as the SS do in this letter that the whole of the German nation will be indebted to you for your Lebensborn service, but I can tell you that the squadron is grateful you are going as its representative.'

Neither of them knew what Berendsen was talking about.

So Klaus left for Berlin and presented himself at the Lebensborn HQ. What he learned there shook his belief in himself, his Führer, his God and his ocupation for the first time in his life.

A major who was noted for his ability to call a spade a spade had been asked to speak to the men who were to be sent to the Warthegau hostel. There were about nine officers of different ranks in the room, representing a cross-section of the armed forces.

'I shall speak openly to you as man to man,' said the Lebensborn official. 'You have been chosen to sire the next generation of Germans.' He paused and looked round at the astonished faces of his listeners. 'Suitable partners have been selected for you and you will be introduced to them within the framework of a course of instruction. Not that you'll need anyone to instruct you,' and he leered at them knowingly.

A tall, thin infantry captain with a Knight's Cross dangling on a ribbon round his long, skinny neck shot to his feet.

'What does that mean?' he asked harshly.

'That you will do your duty, captain.'

'What duty?'

'The duty to propagate your race.'

'What evil nonsense is this? Do you want to degrade our women like this and call it duty? What sort of women would give themselves in this way? And what sort of children do you expect from such ... such mating?'

'You will be so kind as to leave that to us. The operation has been arranged scientifically. I am only here to encourage you to carry out what is required of you in an honourable fashion.'

'Then you can count me out,' answered the wearer of the Knight's Cross. He walked up to the major as if he was going to spit in his face. Then he left the room, slamming the door so hard behind him that flakes of plaster fell from the ceiling.

'We'll manage without him,' said the major between his teeth. He cast his eyes over the row of officers in front of him. 'Any more traitors?' he asked sharply.

Klaus shuddered. He wasn't a traitor, but he certainly wanted no part in this affair. Before he had chance to consider his position, the major had launched his attack.

When it was all over, Klaus' thoughts and emotions were in a turmoil – he felt his whole world crumbling about him. He had pledged himself to Doris and since the shame of their last evening together, he had tried to suppress his instincts and content himself by dreaming of the time when they would be married and all her reluctance would fall away.

And now he was being ordered to do the very thing that he had found so hard to renounce with Doris with some strange woman, some slut chosen by the SS with a view to propagating the race.

On the other hand, he had grown up in the Nazi movement, given his life to prove himself in its service, believed infinitely in its aims. If he refused what it was asking of him now, his whole life would be wasted. He would be betraying himself as well as the Party. To take such a momentous step, he had to first have concrete evidence that he was doing the right thing. He had no alternative but to go and find out.

The next thing Klaus knew was that he was sitting in a jeep with two other officers from the Luftwaffe, heading for Warthegau. He looked out of the window: trees, houses, cars, all flew past, but always in front of his eyes was Doris.

When they arrived at the one-time sanatorium, he remained enveloped in thought, impervious to the laughter, the ripple of conversation. For a second he stood as though blinded in the doorway, not daring to look around him, then he walked on legs like Viennese creams to his appointed place and sat down.

Westroff-Meyer had now begun to speak. 'Our members are now complete and it is my pleasure to welcome you to Lebensborn and to declare this course open. Ladies and gentlemen, no alcohol will be consumed on these premises and we beg you also to refrain from smoking. Discipline is the order of the day.' He smiled ingratiatingly at them. 'If you have any problems I hope you will bring them to me. I hope you will think of me as your godfather.'

It's a madhouse, thought Klaus. The girls must be insane to let themselves in for something like this – they're insane, or else they're lost souls.

Suddenly he became strangely indifferent to everything. He raised his head and looked around openly taking in the parade of faces: there was Erika, who was looking at him with obvious approval; there was Irene, fluttering her eyelashes at a squadron leader; there was Lotte with her Germanic crown of plaits. He pulled a face. Next there was . . . something inside him petered out when he saw Doris smiling weakly up at him and something vile and bilious took its place.

Doris kept stealing covert glances at Klaus, but he would not catch her eye. From the stubborn and disgusted look on his face she was left in no doubt as to what he was thinking. At first she was annoyed, and then she understood and her spirits sank. I shall go to him, she thought, and explain everything. He loves me – he must trust me . . .

All at once a shudder ran through her body. What is Klaus

35

doing here? she asked herself. What has he come for? Surely he couldn't have involved himself in anything as depraved as this?

Klaus stood up and walked over to the window. His uniform sat uneasily on him, looking as though it was rubbing against his naked body. He had his back to the company, as if they were nothing to do with him. Abruptly turning round, he fixed Westroff-Meyer with mean, narrowed eyes.

At that moment Kempe, who had given up with the girls, sauntered over, hands in pockets. 'What's the Luftwaffe up to these days?' he asked.

Klaus shrugged his shoulders.

'I wanted to be an airman too, but the SS got at me first.'

'So I see,' said Klaus mechanically. Kempe smiled and offered his hand. 'The name's Horst, and if you're a man after my own heart you'll come and have a few beers.'

Klaus looked glumly out of the window and said nothing.

'Hey, I meant you,' said Kempe, giving him a friendly punch on the arm. 'What's your name?'

'Klaus Steinbach.'

'I understand how you feel. Let's get out of this hell hole and go and get pissed.'

He turned to go and Klaus followed behind indifferently, just as Doris had mustered the courage to speak to him.

'Klaus,' she said timidly and gave a frightened smile.

But he walked straight past her.

* * *

They got drunk in silence.

'This is the stuff of life for veterans like us – it's what makes us fight,' gasped Kempe in between draughts. 'Knock it back and you'll be fit for anything.'

It tasted of gall, but it went down easily enough.

'Let's have it,' said Kempe. 'What's the matter?'

'My fiancée is there – my former fiancée, I mean.' Klaus corrected himself quickly.

Kempe caught on immediately. He whistled through his teeth.

From then on a silent understanding grew up between

36

them and oblivious of the others around them, they gave themselves up to the warm embraces of the soldier's oldest mistress: alcohol.

After a while, Klaus was as sick as a dog and Kempe left him in the garden holding his head between his hands and staggered back to the hostel. The alcohol had given him the courage and the desire and the Nazis had given him the permission. He'd go back and see how far he could get with Lotte, since Doris belonged to that other poor sod.

He reached the heavy wrought-iron gates and paused to look before going through. Dusk had fallen and light spilled from the windows of the big house on to the lawn. From somewhere inside came the sound of a gramophone playing ancient dance music, interjected with volleys of high-pitched laughter and shrieks of excitement. Kempe nodded to himself with satisfaction and drew a deep breath of warm autumnal air. It was just the night for love.

He fumbled with the catch and swung the gate shut behind him with a force that sent a stray cat streaking in fear from the rhododendrons. He scrunched up the gravel to the house and went in.

The air in the big downstairs common room was thick with smoke, despite the ban on cigarettes and a group of people crowded round the table at the far end of the room, pushing and jostling, their empty cups held high over each others shoulders for a taste of the schnapps and brandy being shared out by two young officers whose cropped heads were just visible above the fray. In the middle of the room a girl in a green dress was dancing wildly to the raucous recording of a gipsy violin. She had sent her shoes skidding across the polished floor and was kicking her legs high in the air, showing a large expanse of bare thigh to her glassy-eyed partner, who was wheeling round her grinning stupidly.

Kempe tore his eyes from her heaving bosoms and looked past the bobbing blonde heads to the other side of the room, to where a lot of screaming and laughter was coming from a mass of struggling arms and legs on a prim-looking sofa. Next to the sofa was a high-backed chair, and on the chair sat Lotte, hands clasped tightly in her lap, with a look of deep offence on her face.

37

Kempe surged through the crowd towards her 'What's a pretty girl like you doing all on her own?' he asked, swaying slightly on his feet as he stood in front of her.

She flushed, but continued to stare straight ahead, her lips tightly pressed together into one thin line.

'How are you settling in then?' persisted Kempe, squatting down on the floor beside her.

Lotte looked down at her hands. 'I feel quite at home in any place where my presence is required,' she answered primly.

Kempe nodded and narrowed his eyes to get her into better focus. 'You're all screwed up,' he said.

She turned a shocked face towards him. 'What do you mean?' she stammered.

'I mean you're all screwed up. How about you and me getting together?' He smiled up at her encouragingly. 'After all, we're here to do our duty, you know.'

'Yes – yes we are,' said Lotte, blushing furiously.

'And when are we going to start?'

'When we are told to,' she said in a high-pitched voice.

'Let's go outside for a breath of fresh air,' said Kempe. He stood up and looked hazily into her wide staring eyes.

As they were walking through the garden he put his arm around her and pulled her towards him. It was the first time in all her modest experience that she had ever been touched by a man. It was strange and unnerving, but somehow exciting.

'Have you had much experience?' breathed Kempe, beer fumes fighting with the sweet night air.

Her worried eyes met his. 'I haven't had any experience at all, and I don't think I want any – not like this.'

'Not like this, and yet you've come here?' He looked hard at Lotte and she cast her eyes down in confusion. He shrugged his shoulders. 'Well, why should I care?'

Then he stood still and pulled Lotte roughly to him. She made herself as stiff as a doll and tried to think of the sacrifice that she was here to make. It's going to be very difficult, she thought. But I shan't be doing it for myself, it'll be for the others, for the movement that chose me to do it, the movement that will lead the people from darkness into light.

'Come,' said Kempe softly. 'Let's go upstairs.'

Lotte nodded as if her life depended on it. She was afraid of the sacrifice, but her time was up.

Somehow, Kempe steered her back into the house and Lotte turned her face aside with shame while cheers and lewd comments were flung after them as they climbed the stairs. To her disgust Kempe laughed crudely and joined in the shouting, squeezing her so hard about the waist that they stumbled and nearly fell.

It was almost a relief when they were finally inside Kempe's tiny room. As he was turning the key in the lock Lotte looked around her, dazzled by the naked light bulb. The room was simple, almost spartan – bright, but cold. Looking down on to the bed was the obligatory portrait of Hitler in his high military collar. Lotte looked into the painted eyes and prayed for courage and the ability to carry out her duty.

Kempe had gone to his locker and pulled out a scruffy holdall, from which he produced a half bottle of schnapps. He waved it towards Lotte, who had retreated to the window and was standing there shivering, as far from the light as possible.

'This'll get you going,' Kempe promised, taking a quick swig to test the validity of his words. He tipped a generous measure of the precious fluid into his toothmug and pressed it into Lotte's trembling hand.

'Prost!' he said. 'Try it!'

Lotte raised the glass to her lips and flinched as the fiery liquid touched her tongue. She closed her eyes and gulped. Her whole mouth went numb. It was horrible. When she opened her eyes again Kempe was grinning down on her. He nodded encouragingly.

'Now all we need to fix is the light.'

He took a handtowel from the washbasin and tied it over the naked bulb so that the room was filled with a rosy glow.

Lotte felt the gooseflesh creeping up her arms. Kempe flopped back on the bed and raised the bottle to Hitler's portrait.

'Cheers, you old bugger! Here's to Lebensborn!'

Lotte was trembling with anger. 'Are you all like this – so

lacking in respect and drunk – and,' her voice quavered, 'so irresponsible?'

Kempe raised himself up on one elbow. 'What's that mean? We fight and die for the Führer, and now we've got to deal with you.' He got off the bed and walked unsteadily to where she was cringing in the corner of the room. Suddenly his arms were round her and he was crushing her so that she couldn't breathe. His hand slipped up her jumper and roughly took hold of one small breast, pinching the nipple until it hurt. Lotte gasped and tried to pull away, but his mouth came down hungrily on hers, his tongue forcing apart her reluctant lips. But her teeth remained obstinately clenched. Kempe opened his eyes in surprise to see Lotte staring up at him, panic and nausea in every line of her face. Suddenly he was very sober, very cold. He released his hold on her and they stood quite still, looking into each others faces. Lotte was breathing heavily, fighting against tears. Slowly Kempe raised his hand and gently, very gently, touched her cheek. Then he turned, flicked the towel from the light bulb, and went out.

Lotte stood there alone, suddenly blinded by the giddily swinging light bulb, tears streaming freely down her cheeks.

Chapter Four

Klaus was walking aimlessly through the well-tended grounds, his head sunk low on his chest, his hands thrust deep into his pockets.

Suddenly a shadow fell across his path. Two desperately pleading eyes shone out of the night.

'Klaus,' whispered Doris urgently. Her voice sounded pathetically lost. She stretched out her arms timidly towards him.

They stood facing each other stiffly, like strangers. The young man's face was deathly pale; the girl's eyes shining with tears.

'Klaus, please say something.'

He suddenly swayed forwards so that his face came close to hers and she flinched in fear.

'So it was for this,' he hissed, 'for this that you saved yourself up. You refused me for this!'

The girl turned her pale face up to his and for a split second Klaus realised that he had never seen her so beautiful. Her eyes and lips were closed and he looked away quickly, choking down the bitterness inside him.

Then he turned and walked away, as if she didn't exist.

She stood for a moment rooted to the spot, then she ran after him and caught his arm.

She began to speak, to plead, to explain. Horrified, she realised that there was no explanation for what had happened. Every sentence was a trap.

Klaus stopped abruptly in his tracks. He broke a twig from a tree overhanging the path and absently began to slash it against his tall leather boots.

'Save yourself the trouble,' he said. 'Did you come to this place voluntarily or not?'

Doris looked up at him wordlessly.

'Well, then,' he concluded calmly, his voice cold and triumphant.

He turned to go and Doris walked on beside him.

And you, Klaus, thought Doris – how did you get here then? You see, you can explain it no better than I. But she didn't speak her thoughts out loud, because her love was clear and strong enough for both of them. She hung her head.

They had reached the Adolf Hitler Oak, a scrawny sapling planted in honour of the Führer and watered in the vain hope that this symbol of Nazism would one day reach the sky. Here Klaus stopped again and fumbled for a cigarette to gain a little time. If he was honest with himself, he was looking for a bridge over his hurt pride.

She stood next to him like a homeless waif and begged him with her eyes to take her back, back to the paradise they had lived in only half a year ago, so they could begin again and do everything differently this time.

'Klaus,' she said quickly, 'I love you.' A tentative smile hovered on her pale lips.

Klaus looked at her, and what he saw made him hate himself. His eyes burned and his tongue was dry and heavy in his mouth. In his nostrils the autumn stank of decay.

'And I,' he said in a strange hard voice, 'I don't ever want to see you again, ever, do you hear?'

Doris didn't move.

'Get out!' he hissed.

And she went. As she walked unsteadily away from him, Klaus hoped she would stop. He gave a vicious kick to Hitler's scrawny oak tree and gave it an almighty push. All at once the stem gave way and it fell to the ground underneath his weight.

* * *

Doris lay awake in her bed weeping silently. Over and over again she tortured herself with the words that Klaus had last spoken to her: 'I don't want to see you again, ever, do you hear?'

She heard footsteps outside her door and raised herself up. She hoped that he would still come to her, but this might be somebody else trying to force his way into her bedroom – anything might happen here. Surely someone was standing outside her door?

From downstairs laughter and scraps of conversation drifted up. In the distance she heard people moving about. Again someone was at the radio. What can Klaus be doing now, she wondered, is he at least thinking of me? And what is the meaning of all this? Where is the sense in a system which sets out to humiliate young men and women by interfering in their natural feelings, in their private lives? How is it possible to force people to come together, to demand that they sacrifice their children to the state?

Suddenly she felt comforted. I understand you Klaus, she thought, that you want nothing to do with this. I wouldn't be able to love you if you felt differently about it.

This time there was no mistaking the footsteps and Doris sat up in horror. The door opened. For a moment she really believed it was Klaus, then light flooded the room and she looked in disappointment and relief at Erika, her room-mate.

'What on earth are you doing in bed?' she cried. 'I've been looking for you everywhere – we're having quite a good time downstairs!'

Erika plonked herself down on her friend's bed. 'Up you get – you can't tell me you're tired, Doris!'

But Doris just turned away.

'What's the matter?' Erika gave her a friendly push.

'Oh, nothing.'

'Are you angry with me?'

'No.'

'Doris, don't tell me you're letting all this rubbish get on top of you?'

'It's – it's something else.'

'I don't understand.'

'Listen,' said Doris, her pale lips attempting a smile. 'I can't stand it here any longer. I've got to go away – first

43

thing tomorrow – I can't bear it another day!'

'But you can't do that,' said Erika puzzled. 'Don't be silly, Doris, it's not half as bad as you make out – no one can force us into bed if we don't want to go, and if you think *I'm* going to give birth to one of Hitler's brats, then you're mistaken.'

Erika stood up. Her thoughts were back in the common room where everyone was laughing and flirting. 'Come on, up with you.'

'I can't.'

'Well, then, don't make such a fuss,' said Erika finally, and she switched off the light and clattered back down the stairs.

But the next morning, Doris was gone.

Chapter Five

Scraps of cloud chased each other across the sky and a cold sun was mirrored in the muddy puddles. Doris trudged across the marshy land, her earth-coloured cloak fluttering in the wind. In the vast emptiness of this monotonously flat landscape the girl was the only moving point as she plodded off into the distance.

She didn't notice the weight of her suitcase biting into her hand, or the water as it squelched into her shoes and splashed up her legs. She stumbled when she twisted her ankle on the stones, but forced herself further and further on, panting for breath. There were tears in her eyes, but they could have been caused by the wind.

Not once did Doris turn round. She wanted never again to set eyes on that house where her holiest, most precious feelings had been abused. She wanted to forget the lascivious face of Westroff-Meyer. At the thought of him her breath came quicker and she began to walk in earnest.

But her mind must fix on something on this endless journey between the milestones of no-man's land: on Klaus. On his cold eyes, his hard mouth. She had loved him too much, had kissed his soft lips too often to be able to bear the thought of losing him. And he never wanted to see her again.

On the horizon a church spire appeared like a warning finger and Doris' pace increased for the final sprint. Her legs were aching and she had a terrible pain in her side. Her thoughts were racing.

Where? Where shall I go?

Home – where else? And from the approaching railway embankment, Doris guessed the direction in which her parents' house lay. She imagined the reception she'd get there.

Her father, a tall strong man, his eyes lit with pleasure, would hug her to him and drink a toast to her homecoming. The brandy in the glasses shimmered with a golden light. It was first class stuff, her father was saying, brought from France by Klaus – Klaus!

Doris reeled, dropped her case, rested a moment. Her mother . . .

'What on earth are you doing here – run away, without leave of absence? My God, how can you have done such a thing?' The whining voice went on: 'How will I be able to face my friends – I shouldn't like them to know that my daughter . . . '

Doris picked up her case again, changed it from hand to hand. She felt the blisters on her skin. Her arms were as heavy as lead. She walked the last 100 m to the embankment, put down her case and sat on it.

Where should she go?

Back to the League camp? The angry, dried-out face of the spinsterish camp leader loomed in front of her face. Suddenly everything that she had believed in and held dear seemed to whirl in confusion before her eyes. Her home, Klaus, the League, the Hitler Youth Movement – nothing seemed to fit together any more, it was just a nightmarish jumble that Doris was too weary to sort out in her mind. She was too exhausted to reason with herself. She would rather believe herself a bad National Socialist than consider the fact that the standards which had been hammered into her were rotten.

Her fever cooled. The girl stood and stared at the railway line below with dull and lifeless eyes.

Suddenly a jeep appeared behind her, rattling up on the bumpy ground. The man at the wheel was wearing the uniform of the SS. Westroff-Meyer had sent him to fetch home the black sheep.

'Get in!' barked the man.

'I . . . I wanted to . . . ' stammered Doris.

'You can tell that to the Colonel when we get back. Now get in.'

Doris had to lift her case in unaided. Her weary body followed it and she crouched unhappily on her seat, not looking around her or saying a word all the way.

* * *

Klaus looked unseeingly at the peas and chestnuts on the schoolroom charts, which illustrated the theory of reproduction according to the precepts of racial hygiene. Why had Doris run away? Perhaps it was because of him? He felt an involuntary sense of pleasure. But what would they do with her when they got her back? Would she be sent to an armaments factory to work out her punishment? Be posted to some godforsaken place far away?

At lunch he sought out Erika.

'Are you a friend of Doris?'

'Yes,' said Erika. 'Do you know her too?'

'I – well, we were engaged, I suppose.'

Erika's eyes widened. 'So that's why she ran away – because of you.'

Klaus nodded slowly. 'I was mad at her for volunteering to give herself up like this.'

'Listen, nobody has to give herself up – I wouldn't do it if Hitler came to me himself.'

'But what about all the others?'

'I'm not bothered about them,' said Erika with an impatient wave of the hand. 'I've only got to look after myself. And if you're thinking of Doris, I can answer for her – understand?'

Klaus nodded, bewildered. 'What got you here then?'

'It was quite simple,' Erika replied. 'The first thing was: anyone who wants to render a service to the Führer, step forward. So we stepped forward. Then we were investigated, "chosen". And only then did we find out what the "service" involved.' Erika gave a sharp, mocking laugh. 'It was then that I stopped being a National Socialist.'

Klaus started. This was not the sort of thing he'd listened to with equanimity before, but here he was being comforted by this girl's treacherous words.

'I can tell you one more thing,' Erika broke into his

47

thoughts. 'Do you know what *you* are, Herr Captain!' She drained her glass of apple juice, licked her lips and enlightened him. 'An ass.'

* * *

Doris was waiting with a thumping heart for her interview with Westroff-Meyer. Behind his office door she could hear him thundering at his secretary. Suddenly he flung the door open and looked out.

'So it's you,' he blazed. 'In you come!'

She wasn't asked to sit down. His face contorted with rage as he launched into his tirade against her.

'You are a member of the League of German Girls. You were being trained as a leader when we selected you for Lebensborn. You removed yourself from this place without leave of absence. You deserted in a time of war.'

Doris pressed her lips tightly together. So this was what happened when you volunteered. This was the name of the game.

Westroff-Meyer sensed the girl's resistance. His voice climbed the scale and took on the hysterical staccato of Party speech.

'What got into you? Treachery! Desertion! Defeatism! You have betrayed the Führer, stabbed him in the back!'

Doris listened without hearing. From time to time she nodded her head pathetically as if to give him credence, but it was only a reflex action to the reproaches that were being hurled at her.

The Colonel shook his clenched fist at her. 'Traitors should be exterminated! They ally themselves to the enemy – they are not worthy to be called German! In this battle for the future of our race – ' Before he ran out of breath, he ran out of phrases and was overtaken in mid-sentence by a fit of coughing.

When he had recovered he asked her lamely: 'What do you have to say to that?'

Doris felt as though everything was dragging her down. Some sort of reply was necessary, but she couldn't think what she might say. She was afraid of his small, spiteful eyes; she was afraid of the pent-up energy in his impatiently clenched fists. Her head drooped.

'I – can't join in here.'

He clasped his hands behind his back and sighed loudly. 'You of all people are in need of instruction,' he said tersely. 'Do you know the difference between F1 and F2 generations?'

'No,' answered Doris almost inaudibly.

'What do you know about nutrition, about germination?' Doris shook her head.

'You see how much you have to learn.'

'But I have personal reasons . . .'

'What personal reasons can make you disobey an order from the Führer?'

'I am engaged to be married.'

'And?' Westroff-Meyer's tone was impatient, threatening.

'My fiancé is here.'

'What do you mean, here?'

'Here in this house,' whispered Doris.

Westroff-Meyer's face brightened at once. 'Well, well! He's here on the course is he? And what's his name?'

'Klaus Steinbach.'

Westroff-Meyer grinned broadly, showing one gold tooth. Then he laughed aloud so that his head was jerked back and forward until tears poured down his face. 'Well, what a coincidence. Never heard anything like it!' He put his arm round Doris and squeezed her to him. She flinched away. He nauseated her.

'We'll have our first ever Lebensborn wedding! That'll be something to tell the Führer!' He looked down at Doris, but she was sunk in confusion. 'Off you go now and leave everything to me. I'll get flowers, champagne, the works.'

He squeezed Doris' hand and propelled her out of the room, calling to his secretary to send for Captain Steinbach. Doris ran quickly to her room, praying that she would not bump into him.

* * *

The afternoon was free and though most of the inmates at

Warthegau were lazing outside enjoying the last days of autumn sunshine, Lotte was upstairs in her room, examining herself in the mirror properly for the first time in her life.

Despite her relief that Kempe had withdrawn his attentions, she was haunted by the shudder of pleasure she had felt when he had touched her that first time in the park.

She was fiddling around with her hair. She undid the plaited crown and let the long blonde strands hang loose on her shoulders. She pouted to her reflection and turned this way and that. She approved of what she saw. Still, it looked a bit brazen. She fastened up her braids again and went downstairs. At first she hadn't noticed the way the others ignored her, but now it was beginning to hurt.

Lotte went to the reading room to choose herself a book. Sitting in the corner in an easy chair was a young major reading a propagandist periodical. Politely he stood up and introduced himself.

'Franz Lange. I've noticed you — you don't look as if you like it here much either.'

'No, I don't,' answered Lotte, surprised and flattered.

The officer nodded. 'I know exactly how you feel. It's so different from what one would imagine. Any Nazi must be disappointed to find out what goes on here.'

Lotte nodded violently and looked with new awareness at the man's face. It was gaunt and he had thin receding hair which made his forehead seem higher than it was. The black uniform sat tightly on his tall thin body.

'You take the movement as seriously as I do don't you?' said Lange. 'It's just sad to find there's a lot of chaff amongst the wheat.' He paused.

'Have you come from the front?' asked Lotte.

'Yes. Infantry.'

'Not the best place to be, I should think?'

'Someone has to serve the people.'

Lotte liked him immediately and felt herself blush. Again she looked into his face and discovered with pleasure that his appearance as well as his words had made a profound impression on her. She wished she'd worn her hair loose now, and started at the thought.

It was lucky she had forgotten Kempe, for at that

moment he was on somebody else's tail – he was after Erika, and he'd tracked her down in the music room.

'It's so dull in this place – how about having a bit of fun this evening?'

Erika wagged her finger at him. 'We're here for a serious purpose, you know.'

'Well, stuff that,' said Kempe cheerfully. He put his lips to her ear and communicated his secret. 'Listen, I've got some provisions – schnapps.'

'Sounds good.'

'Well, what about it?'

'What about what?' Erika raised her eyebrows.

'We could cheer ourselves up a bit.'

'We could – if we forgot the serious purpose we're here for.'

'How do you mean?'

'I tell you,' said Erika smiling, 'I'm not joining in this chicken farm.'

Kempe's face fell for a moment, then he laughed and slapped Erika on the back. 'That's the spirit, girl! I can see you and I are going to hit it off together. Let's make ourselves comfortable, shall we?'

'O.K.,' said Erika, 'but first I have to look for my friend.' As she climbed the stairs to Doris' room she was still smiling. Kempe's heart was in the right place. He might not be very sophisticated, but he only wanted to make the best of things. Erika liked him a lot.

* * *

Doris had spent the afternoon sorting out the clothes in her locker and trying to rearrange her thoughts at the same time. But they were impossible to order. She felt anger and despair, indifference and hope. Worst of all, she was afraid of what Westroff-Meyer's proposal would do to Klaus. Every word would be embarrassing and hurtful to him.

Then dusk fell and evening came, then night, Doris went outside as soon as the house began to liven up. Fifty pairs of eyes followed her out of the french windows. They were all curious to see the victim of the first Lebensborn wedding.

Doris began to walk aimlessly through the grounds. When Klaus appeared at her side, she was not surprised. She had known he would be there.

'I must speak to you, Doris.'

His face was white with strain. They fell into step and walked on silently. Klaus didn't know how to begin.

'I am sorry,' he said with a heavy heart, 'I . . . ' but no more words came. He no longer knew what he was sorry for. All his anger had drained away.

They stopped again by Hitler's broken oak. 'Westroff-Meyer spoke to me today.'

Doris nodded. 'To me, too.' Her eyes were glued to the wings of his pilot's badge, as though she was afraid the eagle would fly up and attack her at any moment.

Klaus clasped his hands behind his back and gnawed at his lower lip. 'Then you know I am to – marry you?'

Doris drew a deep breath. The night was cold and damp, but her blood was on fire. 'Yes,' she said, 'I know.'

Klaus drew a circle in the gravel with his boot. He looked at Doris' tightly clenched hands.

'And will you do it?' she asked.

He shuddered. He had pictured the moment when he would ask Doris to become his wife so differently. He moistened his lips. There was a bitter taste in his mouth.

'You always obey orders, Klaus,' said Doris, her voice hardly audible. 'Are you going to obey this one?'

He looked her full in the face for the first time. The calm tone of her voice made him realise how hurt she was. And I stood here, he thought, and told her I never wanted to see her again. 'Doris,' he said softly, 'would you do it?'

A fleeting smile passed across her face and a momentary glow flushed her pale cheeks. But she knew that how ever much she wanted Klaus, she could not take him in this way.

'No,' she said quietly.

Klaus' face was close to hers. He looked serious and sad. She felt his hand on her arm. 'And why not?'

'I don't want to be married to order,' said Doris, casting down her eyes. 'And least of all to you.'

The pressure on her arm increased. 'Forgive me,' whispered Klaus.

Doris nodded quickly and looked up at him, her eyes shining through her tears. She wished that this moment in the garden would last for ever.

Just then Horst Kempe came out of the house accompanied by a tangle of voices and a jangle of music and shouted in his rusty reedy voice across the park: 'Listen to me, you lot out there, come on back into the house. It's all happening in here. A riot in each room! Entrance free and the drinks on me!'

Kempe staggered drunkenly towards them. 'The bridal pair!' he shouted, fixing them with a bleary eye. 'On behalf of the Entertainments Committee I have organised a little celebration . . . ' He reeled back through the french windows on a wave of cheering, beckoning them to follow, but they turned smiling, with arms linked and wandered back into the darkness.

Lotte and her new-found friend, Major Lange, were the only other pair who remained oblivious to Kempe's boisterous party. They were upstairs in Lotte's room, where they had gone initially to avoid the others, rather than be alone together.

'It's scandalous, isn't it?' said Lange, nodding in the direction of the noise.

'Terrible,' agreed Lotte, who was sitting with her bare feet tucked up under her. She reached over shyly and touched his short wavy hair. 'Lucky you're different.'

'You are too.'

Lotte looked up at the major with large shy eyes. She wasn't thinking any more of the sacrifice she had to make, she was contemplating with amazement the miracle that she was in love. It was the first time in her life that she had loved anyone, and it made her soft and tender and thoughtful. It made her forget where she was and the purpose that had brought her there.

'Franz,' murmured Lotte softly.

'Mmm.' He turned out the light and put his arm round her shoulders.

'Do you – like me?' Her voice sounded lost and pleading.

'Of course I do.'

But he wasn't aware of the tenderness in her eyes, of her

53

soft and giving mouth or her loosely hanging hair. His thoughts were back on the battlefield. The devil, he thought, as bullets sprayed around him in the trenches near his dug-out. A cheer rang out in his ears. He shut his eyes tightly and ducked.

The major didn't touch Lotte's open face as she held it up to be kissed. His head was full of cries, grenades exploding. The Russian was holding the machine gun and he was look-ing straight down its barrel – a long, long tunnel. Why aren't I falling, he thought, falling . . .

'Franz, Franz?' whispered Lotte, but Lange heard nothing. He picked up his shovel. Now it was shovel against machine-gun. In a panic the Russian shot too high. There was a crunch of metal against bone as Lange let fly with his spade. Once with the flat; a second time with the blade. He went on striking for all he was worth – to save his life.

Lotte's hands were touching his neck, bringing him back from far, far away – from death. 'Franz, what's wrong?' she asked, small, fearful and alone.

His head drooped on to his arms. 'The machine-gun,' he groaned, Suddenly he came to himself, back to reality. He tried to excuse himself, to speak and think normally, but his mind and his body were still trembling elsewhere; the war was still raging inside him.

Chapter Six

The after-effects of Kempe's party still lay heavily on the air the next morning. Westroff-Meyer had been well aware of the disturbance, but he had been too busy himself to interfere. He had invited his new secretary to join him in a bottle or two of champagne. She was a slip of a thing with raven hair and eyes as black as coals who didn't quite fit the theory of racial purity. But he hadn't chosen his little Jewish girl with Lebensborn in mind.

Remembering the pleasures of the evening, he contented himself with a few well-chosen words of rebuke, and got on with the business in hand, which was an investigation of cross breeding.

Klaus had an appointment to see the Colonel after lunch. He had decided to tell Westroff-Meyer exactly where he and Doris stood, and as he waited in the ante-room he mentally prepared himself for a tough battle. But when the dark-haired secretary called him in, Westroff-Meyer welcomed him with a jovial smile. He was searching through a mass of papers on his desk.

'Haven't got much time old man,' he said, 'but take a seat.'

He shook a printed form free from the rest of the papers and waved it in Steinbach's direction. 'Here's your marriage licence,' he beamed. 'Everything's in order.'

'My commander will have to approve of the licence,' Klaus pointed out.

'Don't worry about that,' said the Colonel. 'I'm your commander now, and I'm going to organise a wedding that would make any garrison church green with envy.'

Klaus took a deep breath. 'I'm sorry, sir, but I can't go through with it.'

Westroff-Meyer clicked his tongue. 'Haven't you sorted it out between you yet?' He put a fatherly hand on Klaus' arm. 'I know that the girl's a bit difficult, but a fellow like you ought to be able to win her over – ' and he embarked on a history of his own successes with difficult members of the opposite sex.

Klaus interrupted the string of conquests. 'That's not the point, sir, Fräulein Korff and I want to get married, but not here.'

Westroff-Meyer took a step backwards and the smile faded from his face. 'I think you'd better explain yourself,' he said.

'I'm the old-fashioned type,' said Klaus quietly. 'I want to be able to look back on my wedding day and treasure the memory of it for the rest of my life.'

'Well?'

'I want to be married in a church, sir, not in a brothel!'

The Colonel supported himself against the desk. His voice was no more than a dangerous whisper. 'Interesting,' he said with a malicious smile, and with a casual flick of the hand he sent the marriage licence fluttering back to join the other papers. 'Very interesting, captain. You call Lebensborn a brothel. Lebensborn is a life-giving movement in which the noblest men and women of our race, the élite to which you do not deserve to belong – '

'It is a brothel,' repeated Klaus firmly, 'and I want nothing to do with it.'

Veins stood out on Westroff-Meyer's forehead. 'That is what you call this institution founded by the Führer? What sort of mentality is that, man?'

'I am an officer,' said Klaus between his teeth.

'I'll tell you something,' roared Westroff-Meyer, 'in my book you're a swine!'

'You will please withdraw that remark,' said Klaus quietly.

'Withdraw it? I'll make pet food of you, young man.'

'I'll see you damned first,' said Klaus under his breath.

Westroff-Meyer's face froze with hatred. 'I shall not let

this affair rest here. Proceedings will be taken against you. We make short work of the enemies of the movement.'

Klaus clicked his heels together and turned to leave. The new secretary watched in amazement as he strode resolutely away.

* * *

The inmates of the Lebensborn hostel could hardly believe the change they saw in Lotte. The awkward mousey girl with the almost embarrassingly fervent belief in the movement now walked among them with graceful confidence, her hair flowing loose and her eyes shining. She even wore a touch of lipstick. Everywhere she went, she was accompanied by Major Lange, for whom she showed her love naturally and openly, so that the others fell silent as they approached.

In the afternoons they walked in the park, enjoying the last light of the Indian summer. An enchanted silence lay between them. Lotte drew a deep breath. Her cheeks were burning with happiness. She felt as though she was walking on a carpet of roses, even if it was only dead and rotting leaves that rustled beneath her feet. She felt for Franz's hand, which tightened around hers, and believed him to be happy too.

But Franz Lange was no longer sure of anything. The difference between truth and falsehood and love and duty had become confused in his mind. He had been sent to this place to do his duty. He had been told that it was imperative and that he need give no further thought to the matter. The Führer would be doing all the thinking that was necessary. One man would think for all of them . . .

And now he looked into the trusting face so lovingly upturned to his and felt something like shame. For the first time in his life he was beginning to question authority. Carry out an order? Without knowing whether it's an armaments factory or a girl that you're supposed to be destroying? Take up your positions and leave the dead to bury themselves, that seemed to be the army's philosophy in all things. When marching on parade, he'd stamped his feet along with the rest without thinking what the soles of his boots might be crushing, but here his brain was working overtime, thinking about Lotte.

'We came here as free individuals,' he said.

'And found each other,' supplied Lotte with a smile.

Lange tried to find another beginning. In his frustration he squeezed Lotte's hand. She returned the pressure fondly.

'I mean,' he went on more roughly, 'we knew in advance why we were being sent here. What I mean is . . .'

Lotte looked down dreamily at the ground. 'I never thought it possible,' she sighed. 'I'm so very happy.'

There was so much she wanted to say to him, but her tongue couldn't keep pace with her happiness. She was grateful to the Führer for giving her the opportunity of meeting someone so wonderful. The miracle was that her love for Franz didn't interfere with her love for the Party, because this was something that they shared. Everything fitted together so well.

Tenderly, she put her arm round his waist. 'Franz,' she said. 'Do you know what would be the most marvellous thing?'

The man recoiled under Lotte's touch. He felt her weight clinging to him, dragging him down. He shook his head.

Lotte smiled and her eyes shone with longing. 'If, while we're here, we could . . . get married.'

Major Lange removed her arm from his waist. Two hard lines had grown round his mouth. Well, this is it, he thought. I shall have to tell her everything. He knew that Lotte would suffer no matter how gently he put it.

'No, Lotte,' he said stiffly, 'I'm afraid that won't be possible.'

Her smile faded and her shoulders began to shake. 'No?' she asked emptily.

He ran a dry tongue over his lips. 'You didn't rightly understand what I was saying before – that we always knew what to expect here.'

Lotte's face looked suddenly old.

'Come on,' said the Major with a stupid forced laugh, 'you understand that much, don't you Lotte?'

'No,' whispered Lotte, 'I don't understand it. I thought – I really thought you loved me.'

'Of course I do, but . . . '

'But what?' Lotte's lip was trembling.

Franz Lange's voice became strident, brutal : 'I am already married.'

Lotte nodded slowly, bravely. She closed her eyes and gave a long, shuddering sob. 'I – I understand.'

She turned to go. Drawing breath became more painful. One foot in front of the other, she told herself. Keep upright. It wasn't possible that the Führer could want a thing like this to happen. She dug her teeth hard into her lip until she could taste the blood.

Franz's arm was round her trying to hold her up. The ground was turning under Lotte's feet.

'Leave me,' she screamed and tore away from him and off into the park, dazed, defeated, shattered.

* * *

Doris heard the steps coming to a halt outside her door. It's Klaus, she thought. There was a knock and he came in looking strangely diffident. His gaze avoided her eyes as he looked round the room. He noticed the open locker with the neatly ordered laundry on the top shelf. The piles were edge to edge – it looked as though they had been measured with a ruler.

'Do you have anything for me to – read?' asked Klaus awkwardly.

'You want something to read?' repeated Doris with laughter in her eyes and went to search through a pile of books and papers. She was wearing a white towelling dressing-gown which Klaus remembered from happier days. His eyes bored through it.

She turned round smiling and holding up a copy of the *Illustrated Observer*. On the cover was a picture of the Führer laying his hand on the head of an innocent child. His eyes showed no emotion, but the moving caption underneath the picture left the reader in no doubt of his feelings. Klaus shuddered.

'Have you seen it already?' asked Doris.

'No.'

She looked up at him and the magazine fell to the floor with Hitler's face downwards.

'What is it then, Klaus?' asked Doris quietly.

He laid a hand on her shoulder and a shiver of desire ran through him. He hid his face in her blonde hair and breathed its familiar fragrance. Then he pushed her gently from him, afraid that he would lose control of himself, like he had done at home.

'Sorry,' he murmured, and bent to pick up the magazine.

'Klaus, isn't there anything you want to say to me?'

He thought how young and clumsy and stupid he was. Then she touched him tenderly. He had never felt such tenderness in his life. These were no longer the timid hands of his childhood playmate. They were hands that knew more than how to play, more than how to be tender – hands which could soothe and satisfy.

Klaus felt tears starting to his eyes. Doris touched him again and her mouth sought his lips, then his brow, then she dropped little light kisses all over his face. She kissed him slowly and consciously, bit by bit. Her eyes were wide open as though she was lying in a meadow on a summer afternoon watching the clouds sail by. Then she pushed him gently away.

'No one can destroy our love,' she said.

Suddenly Klaus' lungs were bursting with air. A rush of blood rose from his heart. 'Doris, help me – I want you so badly,' he murmured.

Doris lowered her head, breathing heavily. When she looked up again, her eyes were shining. 'We must not be afraid of each other any more,' she said.

They clung to each other and the miracle shot through them like a flame. The time of fear had passed; they loved each other and saw in that moment each other's love.

'Klaus,' whispered Doris, her breath caressing his cheek.

How often had she spoken his name. But never had he heard her say it this way before. Her voice was an invitation, a promise.

He undressed her gently. Each garment came alive under

his touch, offering up to him the flesh it covered. She stood before him naked, burning and sweet. He kissed her shoulders and cupped her breasts in his hands. Doris sighed and closed her eyes tightly, wanting touch to be the supreme sense. She threw back her head as Klaus took her swollen nipples in his lips. His hands fluttered over her thighs and she drew in her breath sharply as his fingers slid between her legs.

With quickening urgency and trembling fingers, she helped him out of his clothes and pulled him down upon her. A brief moment of pain and they were moving wildly together, conscious only of the fire within. Their release came quickly and they lay locked in each others arms as their passion ebbed from them.

'Happy?' murmured Klaus.

'Mmm. Are you?'

'Very.'

'For ever?'

'Longer than that,' whispered Klaus.

Doris raised herself up on one elbow and laughed with sheer joy and relief. 'Don't be silly! You can't have longer than for ever!'

'We can have anything,' answered Klaus softly.

'They will worm their way between us,' said the girl, burying her face against his shoulder.

Klaus took her face in his hands and his blue eyes looked into hers. 'The Nazis will not touch us,' he said firmly. 'Do you hear me?'

Doris nodded and he drew her close.

'We will get married soon,' he said.

'Yes,' whispered Doris joyfully.

'What can happen to us then?' His mouth spoke the words into hers. 'We'll leave this place. We will erase it from our thoughts. It'll be as though we never came.'

'Yes,' said Doris. But her voice was full of uncertainty.

'Then we'll be together for ever.'

Doris nodded. Her eyes glistened.

'We'll have our own home, and you'll never have to go back to that work camp again.'

He pulled her hands up to his mouth and kissed her finger-tips one by one.

'And then?' asked the girl softly.

'And then –' murmured Klaus, but nothing more occurred to him.

'I'll tell you,' said Doris, her voice trembling. 'You'll be fly-ing missions again.' Her eyes were full of tears. 'Please, Klaus, don't go back – I couldn't bear it without you.'

'But the war will soon be over, my love,' said Klaus, with more conviction than he felt.

'Perhaps "soon" will already be too late . . .'

Doris's eyes glowed in the dark. Her voice was desperate and she clutched at him with frightened hands. 'Klaus, they'll wait until you've gone back and then they'll do something to separate us, I know it.'

He pressed his fingers to her lips. 'That's just your imagination.'

She moulded her small body tightly to his. 'Couldn't we go away tomorrow?' she begged.

'We won't be able to,' he answered heavily.

'But these people here –'

'What have they got to do with us?' asked Klaus bitterly. 'We have nothing to do with the goings-on here, nothing to do with the home and nothing to do with Westroff-Meyer.'

'But he can do what he likes with us.'

'Nonsense,' hissed Klaus. 'When we leave this place we are finished with Lebensborn for good.'

'But, Klaus, think what they'll do to us.'

'They won't do anything to us. What do you think will happen when the armed forces get to hear about this and the people find out what crazy things they're trying to do in this place?'

'But how will they ever find out?'

'Something like this can never be kept a secret,' said Klaus with conviction.

'I hope you're right,' said Doris anxiously.

Then night folded them once more in her embrace and his lips sought hers. Words became meaningless; illusions faded;

slogans crumbled. Suddenly they had eyes that could see, and ears that could hear.

At some time in the night Doris awoke and saw Klaus' shadowy figure beside her. He was as dear and familiar to her as if they had always lain side by side. She sat up carefully and watched him sleep. Her love stood guard.

Chapter Seven

The next morning began as usual in the lecture hall, where the thundering words of Westroff-Meyer lent justification to the irresponsible acts of madmen. He screamed of mass madness and race madness. The chalk in his fingers grated across the blackboard in the effort to make the transgression of all the laws of nature understood by fifty young people. The Colonel's teaching was as simple as it was false. Marriage was a chance contract, he declared, and could be destroyed just as easily as it had been made. The purpose of marriage was superior to the contract, and the purpose of marriage was procreation. Procreation, and the future of the race, should not be left to chance: selective breeding equalled progression.

The Colonel hurled his words into the room: 'In a hundred years' time the Nordic race will be the only race in Europe. Elements not belonging to that race will have been absorbed into it or annihilated . . .'

You bloody idiot, thought Kempe with a grimace, why don't you make a start with your little Jewish secretary. Or better still, coward that you are, volunteer for my pioneer company and see how the Russians manage to absorb *you*. Who the hell is going to take all this drivel seriously, anyway?

'We're going to produce a race of fairhaired men and women,' lectured Westroff-Meyer. 'We'll lead our people back to their original racial purity and eliminate blood of inferior quality. We will be a nation of leaders!'

Klaus drew his lips together in contempt. Why didn't somebody stand up and shut his face for him? – why don't I do it? he asked himself, and was suddenly filled with shame

64

because he didn't dare. With a sigh of resignation he leant back in his chair. He's trying to strengthen his theories by weakening our brains, he thought. Then he looked sideways at Doris, who was sitting next to him and in whose face he could read the incredulity that she would always feel from now on when she heard Nazi rhetoric trying to subvert human reason.

'Your children,' shouted Westroff-Meyer, 'will be our secret weapon in the historical process which will make Germany great!'

Major Lange nodded. They must finish what they had begun.

'If you find your conviction wavering, if in your humility you cannot grasp the greatness of our destiny, then think of Adolf Hitler! He wakes when you sleep; he fights when you retreat.'

What else do they expect us to believe, wondered Erika, casting her eyes to the ceiling.

'And so let us pray for the faith to follow in his footsteps,' concluded the Colonel triumphantly.

Lotte, who usually sat forward and devoured the magical words in wide-eyed belief, was following today's speech in a stupor. She didn't even look up. The world which had first dawned for her in this home had been shattered. In the moment that she had learned to love, she had had to give up everything. Her feelings had run too high for her to be able to bear the fall.

Again and again, almost as if by hypnotism, her eyes flew to Major Lange. Since yesterday's conversation in the garden, Lotte knew that her girlish dream of a shared future had been destroyed. The man didn't love her, he was only obeying a command. He wasn't free – he had a wife already.

She was burning with shame and humiliation. And the longing swept over her, longing for a man who had never and would never belong to her. Never.

I must speak to him again, thought Lotte. I only want to know what he feels, whether I mean nothing to him. If I mean to him only a fraction of what he means to me, then . . .

Lotte unconsciously allowed her hopes to rise. She sat

5   65

through lunch as though in a trance. Mechanically, she returned to her room and tried to rest, burying her head in her pillow. She got up again and walked numbly into the garden.

Suddenly the Major was coming towards her. When he caught sight of her his pace quickened. He wanted to make her understand.

'Franz,' said Lotte softly, 'can I ask you a question?'

He nodded and looked past her. He wanted to say something but his tongue stuck to the roof of his mouth.

'Have you been ... married a long time?'

'Three years.'

'And you love your wife?'

'Of course.'

'Children?'

'Two.'

'And what about you and me ... ?'

'What about us?'

'There may be a child,' she answered hesitantly.

'But you know all this. It will be taken care of.' He didn't understand her despair. He looked at her and her skin seemed old and sallow. What on earth had attracted him to her in the first place, he wondered. He could find no word, no look to bridge the gap between them.

'And what will happen to us?' Lotte made a last desperate bid for affection.

'We still have a whole week together.'

'I see.' Her voice was strangely calm. 'And if we happen to meet up again later – we won't know each other?'

'Well, of course we'll know each other.'

'I see,' said Lotte again. A wild smile flickered across her lips. 'Then I must be grateful to you, mustn't I?'

'What's got into you?' asked Lange warily.

'Nothing,' answered the girl. And she walked on.

She was tempted. A thought had crossed her mind, taken root and became an obsession. It was driving her to her destruction. She turned back and saw that the man was hurrying off as if he couldn't wait to be rid of her, and then she walked on without knowing where she was going. She was filled with an overwhelming longing to get this whole thing, this life, over and done with.

She ran back into the house and felt her way stumblingly up the stairs as if she had lost the use of her eyes. The smile on her bloodless lips turned her face into a ghostly mask. Bits of leaf and twig were clinging to her coat.

On the landing she bumped into Erika, who smelled strongly of lavender. She looked her dishevelled friend up and down in surprise. 'Where on earth have you been?' she asked.

Lotte's smiled faded and her eyes flashed wildly. She said nothing, but pressed herself against the banister as if in fear before running off down the corridor. When she came to the end, she tore open a door and went inside. It was Franz Lange's room.

Erika watched her and laughed to herself. So that was what love did to you, she thought, and went on downstairs.

Major Lange was sitting in the reading room with a copy of Rosenberg's *Myth of the Twentieth Century*. Erika started. What's he doing in here, she thought, if Lotte's in his room?

'What's the matter with you?' she said. 'Lotte's waiting for you upstairs.'

He looked up from his book with irritation. He didn't like Erika. If he'd been one of the selectors, girls of her stamp would never have got into Lebensborn. She's got no class, he thought, no breeding. She isn't worthy of the nobility of our cause.

He made as if to read on.

'Hey!' Erika shook him by the shoulder. 'Don't you get it? Your girlfriend is up in your room.' He pulled a face. 'At this very moment she may be polishing your great big boots. You could at least go up and say thank you.'

The major glanced up hesitantly and shook his head. Erika sighed and left him.

Wearily, Lange snapped his book shut and climbed the stairs. He supposed he'd better see what she was up to. It all seemed very foolish to him. The door of his room was standing open. He quickened his pace and came to a halt on the threshold.

Lotte had gone. On the floor lay a handful of withered leaves. The door to his locker was swinging on its hinge and as he went to close it his gunbelt fell from its hook. The leather holster fell limply on to the linoleum. Lange looked at it in amazement. It was empty.

Where was his gun?

He ran from the room, along the corridor and down the stairs, four at a time, clutching the empty holster in his hand.

In the lounge a group of people had gathered. He scanned their faces hopefully, but Lotte's was missing. He dashed up to Erika who was laughing and talking with Horst Kempe.

'Excuse me,' he said breathlessly, 'but have you seen Lotte anywhere?'

Erika casually blew a stream of smoke into his face. 'Don't act more stupid than you are,' she said haughtily. 'I've just told you where she is.'

'She's disappeared,' said Lange anxiously.

'Find, boy, find!' mocked Kempe.

'And my pistol's gone too,' blurted Lange. He looked helplessly at Erika and his face crumpled. 'We have had words . . .'

Kempe shook his head and looked bemusedly at Lange, whose eyes were starting out of his head as if he had seen a ghost.

'Words?' asked Erika.

The major shrugged his shoulders. 'I'm married, you see,' he murmured ashamed.

Suddenly Kempe understood. 'Come on,' he said, jerking his head in the direction of the door. 'I'll come with you.'

Erika followed irresolutely as the two men went out on to the terrace calling Lotte's name. They searched the whole house. In vain. They scouted round the garden, but there was no one to be seen. By the main gate they came upon the Colonel's chauffeur.

'Did you see a girl running out of the gate just now?' asked Kempe.

'Was she blonde?' asked the chauffeur.

'Christ, everyone's blonde here!'

The chauffeur nodded dully. 'Now you come to mention it, I saw one a few minutes ago. She ran out across the stubble – towards that wood.'

The two men were away. Erika rubbed her palms thoughtfully against the coarse fabric of her skirt as she watched Lange's receding figure. I hope he breaks his legs! Lotte? Well, she had never really liked her. Not specially. She'd never thought she would be afraid for Lotte. Her hands clutched at her skirt and she strained her eyes towards the wood.

The men were running along side by side, panting.

'She'll hurt herself,' wheezed Lange.

'You're pretty sharp . . . what did you say to her?'

'I told her the truth of course.'

'Idiot!'

'Well, we're not here for our own pleasure. We're here at the Führer's wish.'

'Bullshit!'

They veered towards the wood, which was getting closer every minute.

'She's a staunch supporter of the movement,' whined Lange. 'She knew what she was doing.'

'For Christ's sake, save your breath.'

The wood came to an end and still there was no sign of Lotte. In front of them the flat plain rolled away as far as the eye could see. The only break in the monotony was the arch of a bridge as it spanned the canal.

'There she is!' Lange panted.

Two hundred metres in front of them the girl was stumbling across the fields. Kempe caught sight of her and they both shouted after her until their lungs were fit to burst.

Lotte turned round, but when she saw the two men behind her, she continued on her way more desperately than ever.

Kempe and Lange set off after her. The distance between them lessened and by the time she was reaching the canal they were only 20 m behind. Lotte reeled on to the bridge and grasped the railing for support. Then she turned to face her pursuers. The pistol trembled in her hand as she levelled the barrel at her head.

'Stay where you are,' she called shrilly.

Kempe stopped in his tracks immediately and grabbed hold of Lange.

'Lotte,' roared Lange, 'Put that thing down!'

The insane smile on Lotte's chalk white face grew wider.

She kept the pistol pointing at her head.

'No true-blooded German woman would do what you're doing,' howled Lange.

Lotte's lips tightened and the smile died. Her face convulsed with misery as she looked at the man who had robbed her of everything: of her faith in mankind, of her trust in her own feelings, of everything. And now he wanted to rob her of the chance to put all her losses behind her, wanted to rob her of her right to die.

Lotte considered no longer. Like a child that stamps its feet in anger, she pressed the trigger in wild defiance, in a gesture of supreme protest.

The shot rent the air.

Kempe threw himself forward, but his hand clutched at emptiness.

Lotte's body slumped across the railings, lost its balance, and fell with a splash into the still water of the canal. A handful of dead leaves drifted down after her. The white foam was dyed red.

Kempe was at the railings. Too late. He was filled with hatred for Lange – it was as much as he could do not to pick up the gun and use it on him.

'Yes,' he said with a heavy tongue, 'I hope you pass on your noble characteristics, you filthy bastard. We need more of your sort.'

And so, before Lebensborn had made its first addition to the numbers of the living, the first coffin was carried out. Operation Lebensborn had produced a corpse – not a good omen.

Chapter Eight

Westroff-Meyer had a problem on his hands. If he reported Steinbach's insubordination to the SS Central Office, the home might be investigated and he couldn't afford that because it would certainly mean losing his little Jewish girl, if not his own position.

So he decided not to punish the young officer for his disrespect. There would be time enough for that later, but meanwhile, he'd make use of him and his obstinate little fiancée. If he could get them to marry in the home, then they'd be Lebensborn's first bridal pair, and the achievement would be all his. It might even mean promotion. So he sent for Doris – he intended to break through her stubbornness.

When she entered his inner sanctum, he nodded curtly and motioned her to take a seat. She remained standing.

'Well, have you thought it over – about the wedding?'

'Yes,' said Doris, 'we have decided to get married.'

Westroff-Meyer smiled. 'When?'

'In a few weeks' time.'

His smile vanished. 'So he's infested you with his subversive ideas,' he spat. 'No wonder! That little jerk from the Luftwaffe – cowards, the lot of them!'

'Cowards?' asked Doris sharply.

His eyes avoided hers. He knew he had gone too far, nodded and forced himself to keep silent.

'Just so as you don't get the wrong idea,' he said, 'I could have your heroic little friend destroyed at the snap of my fingers. He has said enough here to make sure his neck gets broken – *if* I pass on the information. *If*,' he added with cruel emphasis, raising his hand.

Now Doris was frightened. Klaus had told her nothing about this.

'Now listen,' continued the Colonel more urgently. 'I want to speak openly to you because I know you're a sensible person. I want you to get married *here* and *now*.' He looked loweringly at her. 'Do me a favour and I'll leave this matter where it stands – have we understood each other?'

'Yes,' answered Doris in a small voice. She felt dizzy and full of a nameless fear.

'So you'll have a word with him?'

Doris lowered her head. 'Yes,' she answered quietly.

'I shall expect your answer tomorrow,' he said, closing the discussion.

* * *

The next morning, all the inmates of the Warthegau home gathered together to hear what Westroff-Meyer had to say about the death of their colleague Lotte.

'My friends,' he shouted, hands on hips, 'I have asked you to gather here so that we can all get clear in our minds what this hour demands of us.'

The men stood with cold, empty faces and the girls looked pale and drawn. In the back row someone sobbed and pressed a handkerchief to her mouth. Somewhere else in the house lay Lotte herself in a plain boxwood coffin.

'Sympathy,' roared Westroff-Meyer, 'is out of place here. Someone who sacrifices his life for a cause other than Nazism is not worthy of that life in the first place.' His eyes narrowed and focused on Kempe's face, where they suspected mutiny. The SS officer had his teeth clenched and his lips pressed tightly together into what looked like a malicious smile.

'That may sound hard,' Westroff-Meyer went on, 'damned hard. But we have no sympathy with those who lose sight of the goal.' His voice rose on a flood of emotion. 'Yes,' he thundered, 'this girl has betrayed the cause for an infatuation. She should have brought a gift to the Führer, and instead she wanted only to take for herself. Let the example of her fate be a warning to all you young German women here today!'

Erika's face was white with rage. 'Isn't there a man amongst you?' she hissed.

'Major Lange,' said the Colonel.

'Here, sir.' The blond SS officer stood to attention.

Westroff-Meyer signalled for him to stand at ease and allowed a friendlier note to enter his voice. 'I'm afraid I can't pronounce you entirely free of blame. You should have told me what was going on. You know that incidents of this kind can only damage our cause. Do you understand?'

'Yes sir!' Lange's voice broke and he seemed to sway on his feet.

'Coward!' said Kempe under his breath.

'We shall close our meeting with a triple Sieg Heil for our Führer,' cried the Colonel raising his arm.

'Sieg Heil! Sieg Heil! Sieg Heil!' shouted the gathering. But their voices were brittle and dull.

They trooped off slowly. As they went out, Klaus put his arm round Doris and drew her with him.

'This place is making me physically ill,' said Doris quietly.

'Me too,' answered Klaus shortly. 'Come on, let's get out of here. I don't know what I might do if I have to stay in the same room with him any longer.'

'Please be reasonable,' begged the girl.

'No,' he answered harshly. 'I can stand back no longer.'

They had come to Doris' room. She laid her hand on his shoulder. 'What do you mean to do, Klaus?' she asked anxiously.

Klaus spoke in a low, urgent whisper. 'Listen, darling, we can't stay here one more day. We must leave – immediately!'

'But that's impossible! You said so yourself!'

'I know. But we can't hold back any longer. We'll make ourselves guilty too if we stay. When I look at myself, I see a hypocrite,' he said angrily. 'I can't bear to look at myself any more.' He grasped the girl's hand so tightly that it hurt.

'I'm going into the town, to the post office, and I'm going to send two telegrams, one to your camp leader, the other to my Commodore. This – this – exercise,' he spat out the word,

73

'is voluntary, remember. Now we will take advantage of that fact.'

Doris closed her eyes. Never before had a man taken her life in such firm hands. And this was her man. How marvellous it was – and yet, she was afraid. She feared that Klaus was daring more than he could afford to risk.

'Wouldn't it be better if we got married first, Klaus?' she pleaded.

'Here?' He let go of her hand. 'Never!'

Doris lowered her head. 'But I have told him we would,' she said hesitantly. She didn't dare look him in the face.

'Told whom?'

'The Colonel.'

'Whatever for?'

'For your sake.'

'For my sake?' Klaus was baffled.

'Klaus,' said Doris, her eyes shining with tears, 'you let yourself be provoked. You got carried away and said something against the movement. He told me so.' Quickly she added: 'and if we get married here, he promised he wouldn't report you. Oh, Klaus, I'm so afraid for you.'

Klaus shut his eyes. 'So,' he said icily, 'he's pressurising us, is he?'

'So that's how it is,' he continued with enforced calm. He felt her hand on his shoulder and sensed her helplessness and her determination to be strong and do all she could to help him. For a moment he was tempted to give in to her and save himself in the haven of happiness she was offering. But immediately he strengthened his resolve. There seemed to be only one lifeline to pull them out of this mess – his squadron.

He stroked her hair tenderly. 'Doris, there's no need to be frightened,' he said, 'just leave it to me. I've always got out of dangerous situations in the past, and I'll get us out of this one too, you see if I don't.'

She watched him as he walked away. She should have been glad and filled with hope, but all she felt was a nameless dread. She thought of Lotte, her dead room-mate, and was suddenly afraid that they too might be taking a way out that would turn out to be no way at all.

The evening was as heavy as lead. The place was haunted

by the shadow of the dead girl. No one wanted to speak with Major Lange. The pioneer had become the outsider. The badly tuned piano remained silent. The propaganda posters in the recreation room had begun to peel off the walls. No one came to stick them back up. A ghostly silence hung over the house. Even Kempe had hidden himself in his room. Klaus had gone into town to send his telegrams and Doris was lying in bed trying to read.

In the basement Lotte was sleeping the eternal sleep of the dead.

Erika had fled into the garden. To avoid peeling potatoes in the work camp she had volunteered for the 'fun and games' of Lebensborn. Now she had learned the deadly nature of those games, she was longing to be back with her bucket and scrubbing brush. As she walked along, twigs caught at her skirt and she kicked aimlessly at the stones which lay in her path. She was thinking about Lotte, a girl whom she had never liked, but whom she was now mourning as a friend.

Erika wasn't alone in the garden. There were others who couldn't stand the air inside the former sanatorium. They were counting the days to see how soon they would be free again; looking at their watches to encourage the time to pass.

But the seconds dragged by as though the Third Reich was really the millennium and going to make the most of its thousand years. Time fell in tear drops of loneliness which splashed incessantly into their consciences. Even though Nazism annihilated God, did away with the family, abolished morality and exterminated millions of innocent men, women and children, it could not kill conscience.

Erika noticed that she was being followed. She wanted to be alone, and she quickened her pace. But the man behind her walked faster than she did and had soon caught her up. It was a Panzer lieutenant who had attached himself to Kempe.

'Hello, Erika, what are you doing here?' he asked.

'The same as you, walking,' answered Erika wearily. She walked on as if to shake him off, but he stuck all the closer.

'Why so alone today?' he asked. 'Where's your boy friend Kempe?'

'He's not my boy friend.'

'Good,' said the young man, grinning as he looked her up and down. 'Glad to hear it. Rotten about Lotte, isn't it?'

'Yes,' answered Erika distractedly.

'But life goes on,' he continued brightly. He tried to take hold of her hand and she pulled away sharply.

'Don't be like that,' he coaxed. 'I'd like you to come with me.'

'Where to?'

'Back to the house. We could go to my room . . .'

'Whatever for?'

'You don't need to ask that.'

'Oh, but I do.'

'Er, why are you here, then?'

'Because I didn't know what sort of pigsty this was going to be.'

'But listen,' said the lieutenant. He stretched his arm out towards her.

'Get away from me,' she hissed.

'No,' he breathed. 'Erika, you and I –'

She could contain her anger no longer. She swung round and hit out hard with her fist, catching him full in the face. He reeled back as her arm shot forward a second time. In confusion and anger she lashed out at the dumbfounded lieutenant. She struck out for Lotte, for herself, for Doris, for decency and reason. The man winced and cowered like a maltreated dog.

Erika walked slowly away, her shoulders hunched. Her face was burning and her knuckles were smarting with pain. I didn't mean to do that, she thought. He's only a young and stupid soldier. But suddenly she felt relieved, elated even, as if she had hit the face of Westroff-Meyer himself.

* * *

Klaus' Commodore acted immediately. He got in touch with the Luftwaffe HQ who cleared the matter with the SS and obtained the immediate release of the young squadron captain. Now, two days after he had sent the telegrams calling for help, Klaus stood for the last time in the Colonel's office.

The limpid-eyed secretary looked up from her typewriter

76

and recognised him from the time before. She knew what was going on and wanted to help, but she was afraid of the man who had taken her to be his secretary and his mistress. Quickly she turned round.

'He's in a terrible mood today,' she whispered pleadingly.

'It doesn't matter to me,' said Klaus coldly.

Eventually, after a quarter of an hour, he was let into the inner office.

'Ah, it's you,' said Westroff-Meyer, rummaging through his papers. 'Your Commodore has sent for you. You must be a first class pilot,' he sneered.

Klaus remained calm.

'In any case, you're useless here,' the Colonel went on settling himself comfortably in his chair. 'I can only hope that you conduct yourself as a soldier better than you do as a National Socialist.'

Klaus said not a word. His fists were clenched but they were bound by Doris's gentle hands.

'How come they need you so urgently all of a sudden?' asked the Colonel menacingly.

'I asked to be called back.'

Westroff-Meyer rolled his eyes. 'So that's it.'

'Yes. Fräulein Korff has also asked to be sent back to her camp. We are both leaving Lebensborn.'

'It won't come to that,' said the Colonel, a nervous tic jumping in his face. 'I'm *throwing* you out!'

'Thank you.' Klaus put his hands in his pockets.

'What's got into you, man? Stand to attention!' The medals jingled angrily on Westroff-Meyer's black-uniformed chest.

Klaus' stance grew more casual. 'I shall go to the Party and find out whether the armed forces stand behind this pig-sty – or whether indeed they even know of its existence,' he said.

'I'll finish you yet,' shouted Westroff-Meyer and flung Klaus' marching papers across the table at him.

Klaus picked them up and put them in his pocket. 'And where are my fiancée's papers?' he asked.

The Colonel pursed his lips and rubbed his hands together

in satisfaction. He had suddenly realised that he held a hostage in his camp.

'Fräulein Korff?' he mused, 'did your Commodore send for her too, then?'

'She has asked to be sent away from here, as I told you.'

'Splendid,' said Westroff-Meyer.

'And she's leaving with me tomorrow.'

The Colonel let out a contemptuous bark of laughter. 'You're a sly one; Leaving with you tomorrow, eh?' He walked across to the window. 'Everyone makes mistakes,' he said sharply. 'I happen to know that the League of German Girls isn't as badly off as the Luftwaffe. Your girl friend will stay here and do her duty.' He turned back to face Klaus. 'And you'll take yourself off, captain, if you please, at the double!'

Klaus turned and walked numbly away, cursing himself for not having realised what would happen. Doris would be here alone in the home, with no one to protect her from Westroff-Meyer, who was determined to get her into bed with someone else.

The door snapped to behind him just as the trap had snapped shut on his neck. He could still hear it snapping in his head. He felt like vomiting. He felt the pressure of his gun in the holster against his hip and the powerlessness of his own hands. He had got himself into this hole, and there was no way out of it. He prayed that he wouldn't lose his nerve.

I must see Doris, he thought. Then he stood still in the middle of the hall. He couldn't face her. What should he tell her? Should he let himself be comforted and consoled like a little boy? Should he repeat what the bastard had just said to him? Listen to her wordless questions: what will you do next? How will you get help now, Klaus Steinbach?

Klaus threw his coat around his shoulders and went outside. As he walked he turned over all sorts of plans in his mind, without finding any solution.

By the time he reached the town he had worked up a thirst, so he went into the nearest inn to be alone with his thoughts. He stepped into a swirling curtain of blue cigarette smoke and the smell of strong tobacco and watery beer hit him in the nostrils. Leaning on the bar was Kempe. Klaus wanted to steal out again, but it was too late – Kempe had spotted him already and was beckoning him over.

'Aha!' he grinned, 'here's the one that got away!'

Klaus forced a smile.

Kempe called to the dark-haired barmaid: 'Two doubles, and have one yourself.'

'I'm not thirsty,' said Klaus.

'Drinking makes you thirsty.' Kempe waved his arm around. 'It's my local, this,' he said. 'Isn't that right, Marie?'

The girl behind the bar nodded eagerly.

'See, everything's fresh here,' commented Kempe. 'Everything's natural – no artificial peas, here, get it? No dead bodies either.' He raised his glass. ' 'Nother double, Marie.'

Klaus looked closely at Kempe, who was staring past him, glassy-eyed, leaning heavily with both elbows on the bar. He was obviously drunk, but there was something very likeable about him even in this state.

Kempe ordered, and Klaus drank. They stood there in silence knocking back one after the other. As the barmaid went past, Kempe tried to untie her white apron, but succeeded only in knocking over a glass.

'That's how I am,' he mumbled, 'full of good intentions and nothing to show for it but cuts and bruises.'

The cheap schnapps burned in Klaus' mouth and thoughts of Doris burned in his head. Drinking made his dreams come alive. He stared at the flushed face of his companion, then he looked at his hard, strong hands – hands that held a pistol just as confidently as they made a grab at the barmaid's apron strings. Suddenly Klaus could see these great hands round Doris's slim waist. His thoughts raced and hammered against his skull: tomorrow I shan't be here! Tomorrow the way will be clear – and those hands will be on her waist.

'Another double?' asked Kempe.

'No, thank you.'

'What, no schnapps?'

'I've had enough, thanks.'

Kempe leaned across to Klaus and gave him a friendly punch on the arm. 'What's the matter with you now?'

'I'm leaving tomorrow,' said Klaus shortly.

'Good for you!' Kempe nodded his approval. 'Then you'll be rid of this shit house.'

Klaus shrugged his shoulders. 'I will,' he said dully, 'But Doris – she's got to stay.'

Kempe nodded thoughtfully. He reached for his glass, but it was empty. He knocked it on to the floor and it shattered noisily.

'Have you got any soda water, love?' he shouted to the barmaid.

The girl gave him a whole bottle. He poured some into his hand and splashed his face with it so that it streamed down his chin.

'I want to get her out, but I can't think how,' said Klaus hopelessly.

'You'll have to get her out,' agreed Kempe, 'and fast at that.'

Suddenly he didn't seem drunk any longer. He drained the soda bottle in one. 'That's how it is,' he said breathlessly.

'And all this shit comes from the SS.'

'Don't give me that – no one in active service in the SS has anything to do with it.'

'Who does then?' asked Klaus harshly.

'Listen here, pilot,' said Kempe menacingly, closing his giant hand around the soda bottle as though it was an enemy's throat, 'that sort of talk could make me get nasty, I'm warning you.'

'And what sort of uniform does Westroff-Meyer wear, then? It's the same, isn't it?'

'Ah, he's different. You don't know where you are with types like that. You don't know whether he's coming at your throat or about to knife you in the back.'

'But when he gets Doris alone, he'll . . .'

'He won't do nothing, I tell you, nothing, as long as old Kempe's here, understand?'

'No,' said Klaus glumly.

'But we're pals, aren't we?' Kempe stretched out his hand to Klaus, the hand that had threatened to knock him over moments before. 'I'll look after your girl – but not perhaps like you're thinking. I'll be her personal protector – no high-rankin' fool's going to lay a hand on her – and none of the others, either, for that matter.'

Klaus took a deep breath. 'You're drunk,' he said.

'An' what if I am?' grinned Kempe. The funny thing is, I always remember what I say when I'm drunk. Have another schnapps?'

Klaus's face relaxed into a smile. 'O.K.' he said. He was moved by Kempe's unexpected gesture of friendship and felt instinctively that he could trust him.

'Well, then,' said Kempe, slapping the drinks down in front of them, 'everything's fine and dandy, ain't it?' He propped himself up on both elbows, looking thoughtful for a moment. 'I may be thirsty all the time, but here it takes a lot of serious drinking to drown my sorrows, because no man can take this sort of shit. Anyway, you can count on your Doris, and on me.'

And with that the problem seemed to have been solved, for the time being, at any rate. Kempe beckoned to the dark-haired barmaid, gave her a good-natured hug and said contentedly: 'This is the life for me.'

And so, after another hour of drinking, they walked back to the home, their friendship cemented.

* * *

The dusty airstrip in northern France welcomed Klaus as if he'd brought a breath of home with him. As for Klaus, his heart lifted when he saw the Messerschmitts on the runway – in his eyes they weren't hawks bent on destruction, but birds who soared gloriously through the freedom of the upper air. The mechanics waved to him, and he waved back, glad to be with his squadron again.

Then his jeep screeched to a halt in front of the barracks. He went straight into his room, tore open the cupboard, and feasted his eyes on his flying suit as though it were made of cloth of gold. Then his eyes lighted on the photograph of Doris. The glass had got dusty and he wiped it off absently as he thought again of his parting from her at the Lebensborn home.

The remembrance of that moment made him want to

throw everything in again. Doris was smiling a sad, faraway smile, as though he had already gone. Love spanned the distance between them like a bridge over a precipice into which they stared, horrified. Their hands met and Klaus felt Doris tremble.

'Do you want me to stay?' he asked, tight-lipped.

'No,' she answered bravely.

'You don't feel . . .' his mouth hardened.

'No, I know . . . you don't have to say it.'

'I'll get you out even if I have to engage the whole squadron to help me,' he vowed.

Doris smiled her lost smile.

'Don't think that I don't mean it,' said Klaus earnestly.

'But I don't.'

'Afraid?'

'Not – much.'

'I'll stay,' he said, without much conviction.

The girl smiled tenderly and shook her head. She traced the lines of his face with her fingertips – his nose, his brow, his mouth. Abruptly he pulled away from her, turned to the door.

'Do you want to go like that?' she asked softly.

'No, I don't want to go at all.' And so saying, he took the first steps that led him away from her.

Doris followed him with her dark-circled eyes. She wanted to go with him to the door.

'Please don't,' he said.

'Can't I come down with you?'

'Please don't,' he repeated. 'It's difficult enough as it is.'

'Can't I wave?' she asked.

'I don't want you to say good-bye.' Doris stood rooted to the spot as he went down the stairs. Then she heard the car drawing up, the one that was to take him into town.

That was two days ago, and now?

The adjutant broke in on Steinbach's memories. 'Glad to see you back,' he said, holding out his hand in welcome. 'The Commodore's waiting to see you.'

'I'll have to change first.'

Captain Albrecht laughed. 'Since when have you been so formal? Come as you are.'

Berendsen stood up as Klaus entered his office, strode up to him and shook his hand warmly.

'You've got here fast,' he said. Then he rummaged in his cupboard for the obligatory bottle of schnapps. The skin on his massive face had grown coarser, but his hand remained quite steady as he filled the two glasses to the brim.

'Prost!' he said. 'How was it, then?'

'I am grateful you sent for me.' Klaus raised his glass.

'You were in a fine old hurry,' said the Commodore. 'Didn't you like it at the kindergarten?'

'No, sir,' answered Klaus quietly.

Berendsen raised his eyebrows. 'Well, it's not much fun here, either. There're more and more English and fewer and fewer of us. Before I forget – there's not much left of your squadron.'

'What – shot down?' asked Klaus in horror.

'Not all of them,' the squadron leader assured him. 'Maier has been wounded – Hübner's in hospital – well, and a couple were wiped out. Come, have another drink.'

Klaus wondered who it was who had been wiped out, but he couldn't bear to ask.

'Well, you haven't told me what it was like yet.'

'I don't want to talk about it, sir.'

'It was that good,' grinned the Commodore.

'It was that bloody awful,' said Klaus.

'What did you do, exactly?'

Klaus shrugged his shoulders. Then suddenly he was overcome by the guilt at having left Doris behind. He could hold back his story no longer. At first the Commodore was impatient to interrupt his flood of words, but then he slumped back in his chair and listened in silence. His face became hard and cold. He forgot his schnapps.

Klaus told of innocent girls, amongst them his fiancée, carried away by their youthful idealism, who were being made to act like whores. He told how they wanted to breed children from parents who didn't love each other, children who would grow up orphans. He omitted nothing.

Berendsen stood up so hastily that he knocked over his chair.

'Why the hell didn't you simply lay one on this fellow

83

Westroff-what-was-his-name?' he demanded sharply.

Klaus was silent.

'It's all right, I know,' said Berendsen with a sigh. 'I'm sorry, Steinbach. You see, I am a soldier and I have got nothing to do with politics – this filth – I've seen a lot in my time that I didn't like, heard a lot too, and I've always managed to shut my eyes and stop my ears, but if what you say is true . . . '

'It *is* true, sir.'

'Do you realise what this means?' demanded the Commodore. 'For you, for me, for all of us? We're no longer fighting for our Fatherland, we're defending brothels!'

'You're right, sir.'

'We're perishing here – slowly but surely, so that a pigsty like that . . . ' he broke off suddenly and leaned heavily on his desk. His face was burning and his hands clenched the edge of the desk so hard that his knuckles were drained of blood.

'Right, Steinbach,' he said calmly. 'I'll not let this matter rest here.'

Klaus looked at him with silent admiration, but he never guessed how courageous, thorough and merciless Berendsen could be.

Chapter Nine

Lebensborn was dancing a spirited fox trot, blond heads bobbing above the geometrical patterns sketched by the feet. Pleasure was the order of the day and the instruction course was taking place on the dance floor, with Westroff-Meyer playing master of ceremonies.

Doris was whirling round in a chain dance. Hands stretched out to catch her, flattery caressed her ears. Arms tried to embrace her, other feet set the pace for hers. Every turn was torture, every step was a step further into danger. Since Klaus had been called back to the war she had isolated herself from the others as best she could. She only mixed with them when ordered to do so.

'Why are you so withdrawn?' asked one of the officers. Doris shrank back as his head bent to hers.

'Shall we go out on to the terrace?' asked the next partner. 'Or if you care to come up to my room, there's plenty to drink!'

'Ladies' choice,' bellowed Westroff-Meyer, looking round triumphantly at the company.

Doris sat out. She felt like an exhibit at the slave market. Kempe came up to her, a shy smile on his rugged face.

'Ladies' choice,' roared Westroff-Meyer again, looking menacingly at Doris.

'Rubbish,' said Kempe. 'Would you allow me to dance with you?'

Doris got up, her legs heavy. 'Of course.'

'I've been watching you the whole time. I know what they're trying to do to you.'

They stepped on to the floor and Doris let herself be whirled around unconsciously.

'You don't need to be afraid of me,' whispered Kempe. 'If you want,' he continued with a broad grin, 'I'll stay dancing with you for the rest of the evening.'

'What for?' asked Doris, startled.

'Don't get me wrong,' said Kempe seriously, 'Klaus is a great friend of mine. I like him – I like you – and you make a first class pair together. And that's all.'

'You're very kind, Horst,' said the girl warmly.

'I know – it's my only vice.'

They both laughed and the hour passed without further awkwardness – Doris could have testified that Kempe had taken his promise seriously, had she known of its existence. And so they became friends and the humiliating stares of the other men didn't bother Doris any longer.

But there was someone else who was pleased that they spent the rest of the evening together. When Doris went up to her room towards eleven o'clock, Westroff-Meyer smiled to himself and went over to Kempe.

'Well, Kempe, you old dog,' he said beaming, 'congratulations!'

Kempe grinned back. 'What on, sir?'

'On your new girl friend, of course.'

'No need to congratulate me.'

Westroff-Meyer put his hands in his pockets and leaned forward with a conspiratorial wink.

'How about some schnapps?'

'From you?'

'Why not? You don't think I'm teetotal, just because alcohol is forbidden here, do you?'

'Well, I'll accept schnapps from anyone,' said Kempe.

The Colonel led the way to his office. The air was filled with his secretary's sweet and sickly perfume. The radio was playing softly in the background and the cushions were dented as though somebody had just left. The Führer's glazed eyes looked down heroically on them.

Westroff-Meyer poured and handed Kempe a glass. 'Here's to the future,' he said, knocking it back in one. 'I've wanted to tell you for some time that I'm very pleased with you.'

'Oh, yes?'

'Yes. You're just the sort of man we need: healthy,

honest, direct – that's how Germany should be.' The Colonel poured a second generous measure. 'I have been very glad to observe,' he said, tapping Kempe on the shoulder, 'that the little Korff girl has at last fallen into good hands.'

Kempe wiped his mouth on his sleeve. 'How so?' he asked.

'You have my blessing,' the Colonel went on. He took a step backwards and looked Kempe up and down. 'You suit each other very well.'

Kempe slammed his glass down on the table. 'The girl's engaged and you know it.'

'Engaged! Just let me take care of that. You don't need to worry about a thing.'

'Why?'

'Because her fiancé's a traitor, that's why,' said Westroff-Meyer under his breath. 'And I mean to see him punished accordingly.'

'What do you mean by that?' asked Kempe sharply.

'Don't tell me you're sticking up for him? You wouldn't put his interests before yours, would you?' The Colonel's voice was harsh, almost threatening.

Kempe stood easily, his hands deep in his pockets. 'A traitor, you said? I'd like to know more about that – just what did he betray?'

Westroff-Meyer twiddled irritably with the radio knobs and the voice of a newsreader filled the room with a blurred rendering of the army report.

'What did he betray? His belief in the Führer! He's a trouble maker, a muckraker – practically a communist! He stood in this very room and betrayed his cause!'

Kempe smiled, tight-lipped. 'It's strange,' he said, pouring himself another glass, 'how the cowards are off to the front, while the heroes,' he raised his glass to the Colonel, 'while the heroes stay at home.'

Westroff-Meyer's nostrils flared with anger. 'What do you mean by that?' he barked.

'I want to tell you something, man to man,' said Kempe, his voice dangerously low. 'These theories you've been spouting at us – join my company and you can put them into practice, you can plant peas and beans to your heart's content and the Ruskies'll buy them off you. Here in this loony bin they stink, they're rotten and that's what Steinbach sniffed out, isn't it? And now you want to get him by the scruff of the neck just because he's got a sensitive nose!'

'What's got into you, man?' thundered Westroff-Meyer.

Kempe was unruffled. 'Listen, I haven't bowed down to anybody for a long time and I'm not going to start again now. And I'll tell you one more thing, you old hypocrite – you can roll in your own dirt alone here, but don't start plastering other people with it, especially not me!'

He got up and swept his glass from the table so that it shattered on the floor. On the radio the newsreader was embellishing his announcement that the war was being lost with several stories of success:

' . . . last night the enemy was unable to muster more than a handful of planes to fly across Germany . . . The flak shot down seven Anglo-American bombers.'

Kempe nodded. 'Good work,' he murmured.

' . . . while in the west,' continued the voice, 'Captain Klaus Steinbach succeeded in shooting down sixteen adversaries in an air battle in one day . . .'

Kempe picked up the schnapps bottle and turned to Westroff-Meyer. 'I should throw this in your face,' he said, and left.

* * *

As Klaus' Messerschmitt climbed higher and higher through the clear air, a feeling of elation at his release pulsed through his body. Way below him, shrouded in mist and shadow lay the earth. He was flying above the clouds, his world bound only by the infinite blue horizon. Somewhere beneath him, below the banks of dirty grey cloud lay his problems and his fears: the Lebensborn home; Colonel Westroff-Meyer. But the heavens were clear and he was free up here. For minutes at a time Klaus forgot the war which was growing more cruel with each passing day. Since operation Sealion, the invasion of the British Isles, had come to grief in the English Channel, war had raged in the skies over England. But the German Luftwaffe was investing blood and courage in those quarters to no avail. Soon their losses would force their retreat. And then the way would be open for hundreds, for thousands of death-bearing enemy bombers which would hover in swarms over a tortured Germany.

A retreating bomber squadron had given the alarm signal and Klaus scanned the blue desert around him. His sharp eyes picked out a stray Lancaster that had been left behind, probably because of engine trouble. He climbed down sideways towards it. His aircraft cannon split the fuselage in two. The machine tumbled lazily downwards in a stream of black smoke.

The first Klaus knew of the escorting Spitfires were the incandescent white lines of tracer shells passing within inches of his wing tip. He cursed softly and threw the plane into a spiralling dive. It gave him a few valuable moments to weigh up the situation.

There were two Spitfires above him – one was at his height and on his tail. He went into a sickening loop, the engine screaming like a banshee, and came up right under the tail follower. His twin cannons scythed across the Spitfire's belly, breaking off pieces of fuselage, and it banked away, its pilot either wounded or dead. At first it fell leaf-fashion and then it dipped into an earth-bound plummet.

This registered briefly in part of Klaus' mind – the part which bled and scorched and hurtled downwards each time he scored a hit – but all his senses now were straining upwards, right into the sun. That's where two avenging Spitfires would be coming from at any moment, and find him dazzled and unprepared. In a split second he weighed the risks and turned the plane right into the sun. His only chance was to do the absurd – his only advantage was the seemingly suicidal.

He met the first Spitfire almost immediately, and their relative speed of nearly 1650 kph gave neither pilot a chance to hit the firing button – they could only flinch their machines away from certain collision.

The other Spitfire was pulling out of the abortive attacking dive and levelling off. Klaus came down from above and behind – perhaps the other pilot saw him in his mirror before he was torn apart by the cannon fire – but it was unlikely.

Somewhere in the emptiness that surrounded him was the

other Spitfire, but he was filled with a sudden overwhelming indifference. His fuel was low now; it seemed a good enough reason to return to base.

Klaus landed on what was virtually his last drop of petrol. The mechanics surged towards him, wanted to lift him up on their shoulders and carry him off triumphantly to the mess, but he saw his Commodore waiting for him and pushed his way through them.

'Well done,' said Berendsen, his teeth clenched on the stump of a cigar. He spoke without joy or interest. For days he'd been going round with a long and gloomy face. Since Klaus had reported back from the Lebensborn hostel he had been trying to launch a complaint with the Luftwaffe about all this racial nonsense.

The General had proved himself quite useless in the matter. 'Look here, Berendsen,' he'd said, 'we're pilots and that's all. These tales about the SS are no concern of ours. Simply send no more of your people to Lebensborn, all right?'

'All right,' Berendsen had replied.

But it wasn't all right. Everything that he'd noticed and overheard before and kept quiet about came back to him now, and his blood rebelled against it. He was used to meeting his opponent in a head-on attack, but suddenly didn't know whether his enemy was in front of him or behind.

Klaus' success, which had been mentioned in the forces' report, was going to be celebrated that evening in the mess. On occasions like this, the officers forgot whether they were drinking to their own survival or to the death of the enemy. Perhaps the schnapps was an end in itself – it made the stars blurry and the morning thick with mist, befuddled conscious thought and replaced the lost faith in a German victory with the intoxication and glory of individual triumph.

They stood up as the Commodore made his entrance, nodded to them and took his place at the head of the table. At his right hand sat Klaus, and on his left was the adjutant, Captain Albrecht. Every last seat was taken – like every last bed in the hospitals at the front. The faces around the table were new in part, almost anonymous, like the embodiment of heroic death.

'Fill 'em up!' drawled the Commodore, reaching for his glass. His hand was trembling, but the more he drank, the steadier it became.

'Gentlemen,' he said firmly, 'I drink to the successes of Captain Steinbach!'

His hand went to his third button, his glass to his mouth. The company followed suit. Berendsen waited.

'It is customary,' he continued, 'to drink a second toast to our absent leaders.' So saying, he took his glass and hurled it against the wall.

Klaus started. So he was going to make his protest now, in front of everybody – he was going to ruin his career.

'Gentlemen,' began Berendsen again, pushing his Knight's Cross a little to the left. 'What we are doing here, what we are fighting against, I don't need to explain to you. But what I must tell you is what we're fighting *for*.'

Captain Albrecht looked down at the tablecloth in embarrassment and kicked the Commodore gingerly under the table, but it had no effect.

Captain Kirn, his body as straight and narrow as the parting in his fair hair, raised his head and looked out of his pale face into that of his chief. As often as he could he attended the military church, because he could no longer reconcile himself to the war. And very slowly the scorn of his comrades had been turning into respect.

Next to him sat Dietrichs, who was still flying although he only had one leg. Opposite him was Captain Gerber, both of whose brothers had fallen. Then came Kronenberg, a comparative novice, and Pflüger, who had twenty-one planes chalked up to his credit and had survived being shot down twice.

'Up until now, I haven't asked any of you if you are confirmed National Socialists or not. Your enemy won't ask you that either. In the end we are all something that I consider much more important: we are all Germans. We are airmen, not politicians! But,' he added, as he reached for a fresh glass, drained it and filled it again, 'if we fight for our fatherland, then we are automatically condoning the politics of its government.'

The Commodore squared his slightly drooping shoulders

91

and drew himself up to his full height. His face was hard, his expression cold and his hands steady. But his eyes were burning.

'We don't need to pretend here,' he continued, spitting out the words as though they were abhorrent to him. 'We have all seen and heard . . . things which were far from pleasant. And we have put all this behind us so that no doubt should creep in between us and our goal – final victory for Germany.'

Klaus was looking pleadingly at Berendsen, but Captain Albrecht knew his chief too well to hope that he would stop now. Different emotions were portrayed in the other faces around the table. Captain Kirn was nodding, heavy with understanding. Dietrichs was concentrating on the pain in his amputated leg. Kronenberg's lips were pressed together tightly in anticipation of what was to come, while Pflüger shook his head, dumb with amazement.

'As far as I'm concerned,' continued the Commodore in a more measured voice, 'these doubts have grown beyond all bounds. I cannot ignore them any longer. I had to send one of our officers to take part in something called Operation Lebensborn. The aims of the people there go so far as to want to increase the nordic content of our blood. In theory this is ridiculous, in practice criminal. Gentlemen,' said Berendsen, looking along the row of his officers, 'innocent and trusting young women from the League of German Girls are being tempted and threatened into Lebensborn homes where strange men, their appetites whetted by war, are set upon them. They are being used as whores to further the ideology of madmen!'

'Sir –' said Steinbach.

'No, Steinbach, now it's my turn to speak,' barked the Commodore.

The officers looked at each other suspiciously, their faces filling with growing horror. All eyes seemed to ask the same question: who would be the Judas, the traitor, who would denounce their squadron leader and hand him over to the Gestapo?

And automatically, all eyes were drawn to the young and sallow face of the novice, Kronenberg, who lowered his head in shame, knowing what was expected of him.

'They are trying to breed humans as they do rabbits to produce a so-called élite,' Berendsen went on. 'Our most intimate and natural act is being controlled to eliminate "inferior" blood, to kill off "impure" strains and cultivate the rest.'

His face was full of contempt. Breathing heavily, he leant forward and supported himself on the table.

'As far as I am concerned, gentlemen, I am not prepared to conceal what I know. I shall see this thing through to the end. That will be all.' He nodded to his officers and walked quietly out of the room.

In a matter of seconds the reaction of each man around the table had become clear. Some feared for Berendsen, others for themselves. While a few called him weak, the majority were shamed by his directness and courage in speech, which only equalled his ruthlessness and daring in action.

Captain Albrecht collected himself, cleared his throat and said quickly : 'We must naturally keep this to ourselves. The chief has been overworking and is in need of a holiday. Gentlemen, the honourable thing to do in this case is to keep silent.'

During the victory celebration which followed, the atmosphere in the mess did not recover. The jokes were lame and the conversation steered a wide berth around the topic that was at the front of everyone's mind. The evening didn't end with the last of the schnapps chasing away conscience and consciousness as usual. Today the alcohol tasted of alcohol, and its taste was the bitter taste of destruction.

* * *

On the gravel sweep behind the house in Warthegau stood the victims of Lebensborn's first experiment in human mass-production, who had gathered together to celebrate their return to the world. Major Lange had his hand ready on the rope and waited for the signal to lower the flag. The course had ended, its purpose fulfilled. The rest was up to nature.

The flag of the Third Reich flapped gloriously in the wind.

The men and girls, now standing at a decent distance from each other once again, turned their frosty faces upwards to watch the descent of the symbol by which they lived, for which they died, and, when necessary, even mated.

Colonel Westroff-Meyer gave his final speech. His words were torn from his lips by the wind and hurled away unheard.

'I would like to say,' he roared, 'that you are all pioneers. You have given our society a new structure, a new future . . .'

One of the girls in the third row pressed a handkerchief to her mouth. It was all she could do to keep on her feet. Opposite her on the other side stood the man whom she now loved. In his breast-pocket were his marching orders for the front. She would never see him again. He looked miserably at the lazily flapping swastika. The girl's face no longer held any attraction for him. Love was not what he hoped it would be.

Black and green lights swam before the girl's eyes; the world tilted and swung round to meet her as she fell to the ground at the feet of her comrades. Someone rushed up from somewhere and hands lifted her up. The voice of the Colonel droned on as she was carried back into the house.

In the hall it was draughty and bare. The officers' trunks were stacked on one side while the girls' bags huddled together forlornly on the other. The nuptials were over, but the wedding journey would not be taking place. The luggage was going on separately and its owners were united only in their loneliness.

Outside the rooms bedlinen lay in heaps and the cleaning staff was polishing the bedroom floors. Tomorrow would see the beginning of the next course and in between times the house would be aired and cleaned to make ready for the conception of the next batch of Hitler's children.

A chair was brought for the still semi-conscious girl, who sat with her head in her hands, dimly aware of Westroff-Meyer's voice booming on outside. A giggle escaped from the front row of his listeners – the rope which Major Lange was desperately pulling had got caught up. The flag was stuck, flapping pitifully at half mast.

The laughter became general and even Doris found herself joining in. She had no reason to be sad. In an hour her train would be leaving and that would be the last of her involvement with Lebensborn.

'And now let us sing,' barked the Colonel testily, and their voices joined raggedly in a marching song. And with that the Lebensborn course at the home in Warthegau was at an end.

The next day Doris and Erika arrived back at the League camp. They unpacked their luggage and put everything away in their lockers. Here too, a new course had begun. All around them were new girls, young girls with city faces.

'Where have you been then?' asked one of them, who had been given the bed of the dead girl, Lotte.

'Gathering roses,' said Erika tartly.

'I bet you've had a nice holiday, eh?'

Erika smiled ruefully at her locker door. It was still plastered with the gallery of heroes that she had stuck up on her arrival at the camp. She tore them down methodically and screwed them into little balls.

'I hear you were addressed by the Führer too, is that right?' asked their new room-mate.

Doris paused in her unpacking. 'Of course we weren't,' she said quietly.

'But we were told that you gave the Führer something,' the girl went on relentlessly. 'There's another commission coming tomorrow, you know – I'm thinking of volunteering myself.'

Erika shut her eyes tightly. 'Listen,' she said, her voice harsh now, 'if you have a spark of commonsense, you'll think of Lotte before you think of volunteering.'

'What happened to Lotte?'

At that moment the camp leader walked into the room smiling, holding out her dry, bony hands in welcome to Doris and Erika. 'Well, girls, how was it?'

'Wonderful,' Erika's voice was full of irony.

'What's happened to Lotte? There are rumours going round – there's been a lot of silly talk – couldn't you clarify the matter?'

She was looking at Doris. Doris took a deep breath and answered shortly : 'If you want.'

'Good.' The leader smiled encouragingly. Doris spoke in a loud, clear voice as though she wanted the truth to be recorded for ever. 'Lotte committed suicide because she could no longer bear to suffer at the Führer's command.'

'My dear girl, what are you saying?' cried the leader wringing her hands together.

A hush fell on the room. Doris's lips remained sealed. The leader's face crumpled. She had never thought of 'the sacrifice' in human terms before and what Doris had said came as a tremendous shock.

'But this is unheard of,' she shrilled finally, and not wanting to listen to any more, she made her escape, leaving Doris staring after her trembling. Erika put her arm round her friend's shoulders. 'Just be careful,' she said.

* * *

When his first assignment in Warthegau had come to an end, Colonel Westroff-Meyer went to Poland. It was an official visit, and its purpose made his previous activities seem harmless. He was on a mission for Lebensborn. He was hunting. For children.

He sat in the car, his body rocking with its rhythm as it rolled over the cobbled streets. Yesterday's champagne kept repeating itself. He'd been in Krakow, where the élite had been celebrating Himmler's latest speech, a singularly gruesome piece of work.

' . . . we must produce children of good blood for Germany, and if we have to steal them, then we will not hesitate to do so. We either have to absorb the wealth of our enemies or destroy it . . . '

Himmler had spelled out the way and Westroff-Meyer had been only too ready to read between the lines of his speech and to follow the inspiration which had flashed from his rimless glasses. So here he was travelling through Poland – a promoter of life doing the business of death.

Suddenly the car jolted to a halt. They were outside the headquarters of the SS occupation force in Lodz. Westroff-

Meyer strode into the building and got down to business at once with the seedy-looking major in charge of the outfit who listened impartially to what he had to say.

'Hmm,' he said at last. 'So you want to breed Pollacks, do you? You can't hope for much from the people hereabouts,' explained the major. 'They're all fat nosed Jews or scratching gypsies – that's what I'm here for.' He sneered. 'Somebody's got to take charge of the gas ovens.'

But Westroff-Meyer wasn't put off. He had his contacts, and that evening saw his first triumph. He and his henchmen sought out a house that they'd heard about from a Polish informer. A young blonde woman came to the door, drawing her dressing-gown tightly around her slim body and peered out suspiciously at them.

'Where is your husband?' asked Westroff-Meyer.

'He has fallen,' said the woman. He had been an officer. The woman's eyes shone with tears.

This is good material, thought Westroff-Meyer. Race, intelligence, pride, she had the lot.

'And you have a baby?'

The young woman nodded.

'And would you like to give your child the best upbringing there is, an upbringing in a German home, approved by the German government?'

The woman looked at him in horror.

'My baby is all I have left,' she answered in hard, broken German. 'I shall never give him up.'

'But I can make sure you do,' said the Colonel, pushing roughly past her into the hall.

'No!' cried the woman clasping her hands together.

'Please – don't make it difficult for us.'

'I beg of you – no!' She backed frantically down the hall and stood shielding a doorway with arms outstretched. It was a brave but pathetic gesture.

'Hand over the baby.' Westroff-Meyer said, 'There's a good girl.'

The woman was shaking with rage and fear. The Colonel called his two accomplices and they forced their way past her into the child's room. The mother threw herself in desperation over her baby's bed. Hands were trying to pull her away. But she was strong, miraculously strong. Westroff-Meyer, smiling condescendingly, moved forward to restrain her and she hit him in the face with the full force of her hatred. Blood spurted from his nose as the two police soldiers fell on the woman and pinioned her wrists in a cruel, vice-like grip. A pistol was levelled at her head. There was a dry explosion.

By now the baby was screaming, its face red and wrinkled, its blue eyes dark with fear. As the man picked it up, it arched its back and bawled with all the strength in its lungs, tears spurting from its eyes.

'Shut the brat up,' hissed Westroff-Meyer as they struggled down the staircase. 'Here, give it to me.'

As he took the baby in his arms, it suddenly stopped crying and stared up at him in disbelief out of horrified eyes.

Chapter Ten

A leaden cloud lay over the whole of France. For three days the weather had prevented the planes from taking off. The bank of low pressure which reached from the Azores to Iceland seemed to care more for the lives of men than the air marshals of both sides. Allies and enemies used the breathing space for writing letters home – they got bored otherwise, or slept.

The men in Berendsen's squadron lay low during this time, waiting in silence for their Commodore to be arrested. Whether they approved of his outburst in the mess or not, they all hung on his every action. They were all afraid of losing him – he was their only support in a war in which they had long lost faith.

A knot of tension crouched in Steinbach's stomach. He felt the terrible weight of his responsibility for the Commodore's fate pressing against his temples like an iron band. In the past few days he had made constant efforts to speak to Berendsen, to relieve him of the burden which he carried. But the Commodore was living like a hermit – he never left his room or let any of his officers visit him. He had stopped issuing commands.

It was nine o'clock in the morning and Klaus stood at the window looking out at the miserable day. It was strangely still and lifeless in the barracks. No rumpus – no cursing – no jokes. The silence was fraying his nerves – he'd sooner hear the alarm bell going off constantly than live in this morgue-like atmosphere. It was as foreboding as a calm sea before a hurricane.

Time after time Klaus had relived the scene in the mess – the flickering candles, the oppressive shadows on the walls, the almost unreal light on the face of the squadron chief. And then his words – Klaus didn't know any longer whether he had really heard them or only dreamed them.

He took his tooth mug from the wash stand and the Pernod bottle out of the locker. Two-thirds water. He counted out three aspirins and crushed them in the milky liquid.

Then he went to the shower room. The hot water needled his skin fiercely, but his blood was still sluggish and dull. He towelled himself roughly, and when that failed to bring the life back into him, he dressed and strode outside for a breath of air. Suddenly round the corner came Berendsen. He was in his flying gear. Klaus started. What was he doing dressed like that? What the hell was he up to?

Klaus dashed back to his room, pulled his flying suit on over his clothes and, losing no time, hurried out.

Berendsen was leaning against the sandbag walls of a dug-out. His mechanics were pulling the covers off his machine. The Commodore didn't budge as Klaus came panting up to him, greeted him and then stood, lost for words. Berendsen looked him silently up and down, then he turned away and growled: 'Morning, Steinbach. What's the rush?'

'Has there been an announcement, sir? Did I miss the alarm bell?'

'Not yet,' answered the squadron leader. He kicked a sandbag into place.

'Are you starting up, sir?' asked Klaus, hoping for the signal to do likewise.

'As you see,' retorted the Commodore. But today the sharp mockery with which he usually made his officers understand the banality of their questions was missing.

The ground staff lieutenant who looked after Berendsen's machine offered him a cigar. He refused it. 'How much longer?' he asked impatiently.

The lieutenant glanced at Klaus with an expression of bewilderment in his eyes. Klaus licked his dry lips, but before he could say anything, Berendsen tore off the cockpit hood, jumped on to the wing and swung himself inside the plane.

'May I take off too?' shouted Klaus.

The Commodore's eyes had a faraway expression, almost as though he was already above the clouds.

'What's on your mind, Steinbach?'

'I'd like to fly with you, sir.'

The stony face lit up for a second and their eyes met with awful clarity.

'Wait for the alarm.'

Berendsen was fastening his gloves. On impulse he leant out of the cockpit and gave Klaus his free hand. 'Cheer up. It's all right,' he said.

The chocks were pulled away, the propeller began to turn and the Messerschmitt taxied slowly out of its hangar, whining and spitting as it went. Klaus' arm, still outstretched in farewell, fell slackly to his side as the plane droned along the airstrip and disappeared into the distance. The lieutenant wiped his hands on his overall and stared after it with a puzzled expression on his face.

'Funny,' he said, shaking his head and turning the cigar case over in his hand.

'What's that?' asked Klaus.

'Well, he's never refused a cigar before. And he's never taken off alone, either. Not ever.'

Klaus strained his eyes across the airfield towards where the Messerschmitt was lifting up from the concrete runway and disappearing over the wood, climbing up and up through the cloud. Suddenly he realised that something was very wrong.

'Come on!' he shouted to the lieutenant. 'Get my machine ready!'

'I can't do that without orders.'

'Rubbish,' exclaimed Klaus. 'Do you want him to fly alone?'

Just five minutes later, Klaus Steinbach's plane was taxiing down the airstrip. Klaus hardly let her warm up, so strong was the impatience that gripped him. He's four minutes ahead of me, he thought. I hope nothing's happened. Why the hell should anything have happened? But it must mean something, him taking off alone like that. I suppose he might just want to go up for a joyride, though — we haven't heard that the enemy's approaching. He grunted with amusement. In half an hour Berendsen will probably land again, file a complaint against me and I'll be in front of the military court for insubordination.

But at that moment the sirens began to howl.

'A strong enemy contingent is approaching across the English Channel!' announced Klaus' receiver.

The wind tossed the clouds apart and a cold sun looked down on the mad world beneath. Klaus flew out of the blanket of cloud and his cockpit filled with light. 1000 m – 1200 – 1500 – the plane climbed, her whirling nose pushed higher and higher into the sky. Klaus peered out to the left, to the right, scanning the horizon on all sides. Then he levelled the machine and flew straight ahead. Blue sky. White clouds. A vaulted horizon. To search for Berendsen up here seemed like insanity.

He tuned the receiver and listened in to the alert being broadcast back at base. He nodded and clenched his teeth.

Then the radio station near Dieppe announced itself with a lot of crackling and interference.

'A single Messerschmitt is flying towards the enemy, due north, in the direction of the English Channel, at low altitude.'

Klaus calculated his moves in a split second: direction, altitude, speed. Impatiently he cut the engine and the plane dropped like a stone, gathering an ear-bursting momentum.

The receiver began to crackle again. He'd caught him! 'Steinbach here!' he shouted excitedly. 'Steinbach, Steinbach!' More crackling. Now Klaus was at 300 m. Houses, hedges, dunes, the beach. The water glinted and gleamed. The radio roared like breakers.

'You bugger!' said a voice very calmly. 'You bugger!'

Klaus smiled to himself, tight-lipped. 'Yes, sir!' he said.

'Go back home! This is my little war.'

'No, sir!'

'That's an order, Steinbach.'

Suddenly a stream of cold air caught the plane and hurled it downwards: hedges, trees, dunes, hedges. At that moment he caught a glimpse of the Commodore's plane. It was over the water, soaring up almost vertically into the sun.

And then came the announcements, one after the other.

The enemy was approaching. There were a hundred, two hundred machines – bombers and their escorts. Against them – two men. Klaus was emboldened by the sheer laughability of his situation. Its fatalism – its inevitability, coursed through him.

He stuck to his Commodore and refused to be shaken off, either by Berendsen's commands or by the tracer shells which began to flash past on all sides. He held on behind his chief's machine as it climbed steadily upwards, and climbed with it. At 5000 m both planes levelled off.

Now Klaus had a breathing space, he considered his position for the first time. He must be out of his mind. Would Doris ever forgive him for being so damned brave that he got himself killed on a hopeless mission? What the hell! What the bloody hell!

'Bomber squadron at 9 o'clock,' shouted the Commodore.

Klaus gritted his teeth. He could see the bombers lined up as if they had been drawn with a ruler. There were thirty or forty of them. Too many – far too many. This was madness.

'I'm attacking,' announced the Commodore indifferently.

Berendsen opened the throttle and hurtled towards the bombers. Once again Klaus heard his voice: 'Fly home, you bloody fool.'

Without any warning Klaus was flying into a frenzied kaleidoscope of wings, sky and sea. The thundering, unforgiving shout of machinery was all around him. The bombers tumbled past in graceful arcs, spitting tracer shells in contemptuous patterns. Suddenly Klaus was overcome with weariness. The whole thing seemed totally unreal; only imminent death was certain. Klaus hung on to this certainty ferociously and fought back his langour. He rubbed the sweat from his eyes and straightened his cramped toes. The instruments came into focus again and the whirling forms of the kaleidoscope steadied into targets and hunters. Death was still real, but not so certain any more.

He searched for Berendsen's machine – found it, lost it, found it again.

'Look out! Spitfires two o'clock high!'

Berendsen didn't answer or take evasive action but flew

directly for the bombers. The fighters slammed in on him from behind while the Lancasters spewed cannon fire from their nose guns – but Berendsen flew a charmed flight path. Klaus fired at Berendsen's pursuers and banked violently to shake off his own.

'For God's sake, Commodore!' But the receiver crackled uncompromisingly. Klaus's plane fell back into the mêlée of Lancasters, Spitfires and tracer shells, but he rode it out with his reason and fear levelling him like left and right ailerons. He tasted blood and registered briefly that his lip was bitten through. He soared for altitude and caught sight of Berendsen's unremitting plane.

Berendsen. A man who wanted to do nothing in the whole world but fly. The honour of the cause had provided reason enough to get him airborne in the First World War. He flew under bridges, slid along high-voltage cables, could demonstrate a free fall crash landing to within seconds of impact, cared little for death and nothing for vertigo. And now the Commodore was fighting the war on a different front; he was fighting his own doubts. He wanted them obliterated.

Without changing course, without a single movement of the tail fin and with a pack of fighters pumping fire at him, Berendsen roared straight into the lead bomber. There was an almighty explosion as tons of bombs went off. A fragment of metal or explosive hit Klaus' plane, and moments later the shock wave, throwing his machine out of control.

Below him there was utter chaos. The formation had completely broken up. Two more bombers had been forced down under the impact of the explosion and a third was losing height rapidly. Bits of fuselage rained through the air, parachutes opened, men fought clear of smoking machines – or were incinerated.

Klaus' plane tumbled like a leaf, drawing a trail of smoke behind it. The Spitfires allowed him to fall, believing him finished. His face taut with concentration, he swung to avoid one of the parachutes.

Klaus was losing height rapidly now, but he gained the coast and managed a crash landing. He climbed brokenly out of the wreckage. Frustration and despair welled up inside him and forced out dry sobs through his clenched teeth. The airman wept for his Commodore and for his lost Fatherland.

* * *

In Poland, Westroff-Meyer had neglected no way of adding to his collection of Arian children. The easiest method of rounding them up was by raiding the orphanages. There the kidnappers met with the least protest, the least unpleasantness.

Nevertheless, Westroff-Meyer had also succeeded in persuading suitable parents to hand over their children 'voluntarily' to be looked after and raised as one of the élite of the conquering nation. When his promises and lies failed to convince them that their children would enjoy a better future in German hands, however, he had to employ other, less subtle methods: the heel of his boot, a blow with a club, arrest, or simply a blast of machine-gun fire.

In his wake he left endless broken homes and weeping mothers, and he took with him a hoard of tiny screaming children who were damned with blue eyes, fair hair and nordic skulls. These forlorn creatures were rounded up and carted off periodically in trains heading for Germany.

But Westroff-Meyer had a fastidious nose, and the smell of blood offended him. Impatient of his own weakness, he had decided to rid himself of it by habit and accompany Major Klein's death squad as they went round on their daily business of exterminating the Jews and the gypsies. He made himself stand next to the rattling machine-guns and watch the bodies fall riddled with bullets. He waited behind the young SS officers who sent old men and children to dig their own graves. He learned to estimate how many bodies were lying in a heap and how much petrol it would take to burn them. His eye, his heart, his hand, his stomach all learned to take mass murder as a matter of course. Only his nose was still offended by the stink of decay.

Westroff-Meyer was standing with Major Klein in front of a small wall map divided by a criss-cross of black lines. Some squares were marked with a cross, others were blank.

'We're working there today,' drawled the major, pointing to one of the unmarked squares with his pencil. 'Partial liquidation – only 500 or so.' He slashed the toes of his boots with a little whip he carried. 'Are you coming with us? There might be something in it for your boys.'

Westroff-Meyer nodded and the convoy set off with the round-up team leading the way in cars. Next came the armed guard, marching in columns. The men were smoking and singing – they had been ordered to because it gave them confidence. All the lily-livered boys and the faint-hearted cowards had been weeded out of this bunch, and the ones who were left were the hard core of Hitler's men who could face any assignment and shoot down defenceless men, women and children without turning a hair.

Behind the marching columns came the major in an armoured jeep, and sitting next to him was Westroff-Meyer. As a Lebensborn official he was permitted to help himself freely from the well of death.

'Left, right. Left, right. Sing!'

They sang or mumbled several songs and managed to keep in step. In their hip flasks happiness gurgled: coffee heavily laced with cognac.

By the time the jeep had arrived in the outskirts of the village, panic was spreading like wildfire through the streets. Two barns had already gone up in flames. Shots echoed in the narrow cobbled alleys. Men, women and children dashed for safety, or threw themselves to the ground, raised their clasped hands and begged for mercy. For some of them it was their last gesture, others escaped to their homes unhurt. Machine-gun fire spattered the village and the villagers at random.

Westroff-Meyer climbed down out of the jeep and lit a cigarette.

'We'll soon be done with this little lot,' shouted the major over the uproar.

A blonde schoolgirl in a blue dress ran across the street. A machine-gun was swung round and aimed.

'Not that child,' shouted the Colonel.

The guard nodded. Another soldier raced after the little girl and dragged her, cringing and whimpering, back to Westroff-Meyer, who looked down at her with technical interest.

'Mama, mama,' screamed the child against the background of machine-gun fire.

'Where is your mama, then?' asked the Colonel, gathering the child into his arms. Suddenly her crying stopped and she pointed in the direction of the gunfire.

Westroff-Meyer gave a curt signal to the guard and the young SS officer who was lying on his belly in the middle of the square was told to point his machine-gun elsewhere. The women could wait.

'Now we'll go and find your mama,' promised the Colonel, studying the child more closely. Yes, he had been right – there was a definite resemblance! The same high forehead, the determined set of the jaw, the defiant little mouth. Doris Korff must have looked exactly like this child when she was younger! He smiled to himself. But this one would be different, he'd see to that. He'd take that determined streak and mould it the way *he* wanted. The girl would be a model Nazi, reared according to Himmler's programme. He ran his hand through the child's blonde hair. She began to scream again, for no apparent reason.

The major signalled for the firing to stop and walked over to the village green with Westroff-Meyer at his heels, the little girl still in his arms.

Under a tree stood a group of women who were clinging hysterically together, afraid for their lives, or worse. Suddenly one of the women detached herself from the rest and fell to her knees, stretching out her arms towards the child.

'Is that your mama?' asked the Colonel.

The little girl struggled to be free, but Westroff-Meyer held her tightly. He wanted to take a good look at the woman who could have been Doris' mother. Although she wore a large cloak wrapped around her, he could tell that her body was long and slender. Reddish blonde hair tumbled over her shoulders and framed a delicate oval face which at that moment was distorted with terror for her child. Westroff-Meyer's eyes moved downwards to her breast, and there they stopped, transfixed. She was wearing a star. The star of David.

'Jewish whore,' he spat and dropped the child as though she might contaminate him.

Freed, elated, exhausted, the little girl in the sky-blue dress ran stumblingly across the green to her mother.

The Colonel hawked and spat on the ground and nodded curtly to the guard behind the machine-gun who set down his hip flask, fastened the strap on his helmet and took aim.

The child ran into a hail of bullets and her little body jerked and twisted and fell bleeding to the ground under her mother's eyes. Their hands were stretching out to touch one another across the short space between them which death had made an eternity.

'Pity,' said Westroff-Meyer bitterly.

Chapter Eleven

Two months later, shortly before Christmas 1941, Klaus and Doris were reunited. They were to be married and they were welcomed back to their home town with every mark of affection and respect. Amongst the piles of congratulatory letters that awaited them was a handful of envelopes with black edges, so that the young couple received wishes for their own happiness along with testimonies of the suffering of others. Klaus and Doris stood before the wedding table looking with obvious emotion at the humble gifts and the many flowers, some of which looked suspiciously like garlic flowers – there was not much else available in wartime Germany.

Doris had again been forced to keep quiet about her experience at the Lebensborn camp, and had been moved to another camp to join other girls who had learned to keep their secrets hidden. Before her contact with Lebensborn she had volunteered for a special course for future leaders of the League of German Girls. Now she was fighting for her release from the organisation.

Klaus's squadron had been ordered east and so, luckily, he could claim four days' leave to be married. The fact that he had taken off after Berendsen without permission had not been brought up at all, because his companions had been up in the air only minutes later. They had shot down four enemy aircraft and lost three of their own machines. If Berendsen had not fallen, he would have lived to experience a further victory : not one of his company denounced him. They remained what he had made them : his men.

A few days later his replacement arrived, Commodore Prillman, a tall, sinewy officer who kept more to himself and drank less than his predecessor, and yet in other ways still managed to resemble him. He was a man of few words.

One day he called Klaus to his office.

'Listen, Steinbach,' he said tersely and tapped his pencil on Klaus' personal file which lay before him on the desk. 'I know you're an excellent airman. Now here's something I've had from the SS.' He picked up a piece of paper. 'It's a reprimand for a political offence, and I'll make no bones about it – it's pretty damning.'

'Yes, sir,' said Klaus.

'It's no concern of mine what your political views are,' continued the Commodore with a melancholy expression, 'but I only want irreproachable people in my squadron. Is that understood?'

'Yes, sir.'

Prillman took Westroff-Meyer's letter, tore it down the middle, and dropped it into his waste paper basket.

'How many copies there are flying around, I don't know,' he growled, and Klaus was dismissed.

So Westroff-Meyer's first attempt at revenge ended up in the rubbish basket. Klaus had learned to forget that he had made an enemy or that he had ever been to Lebensborn. Either he was flying or he was thinking about Doris.

And now here they were . . .

They were standing together in the church which Klaus had only ever attended if he had no excuse to get him out of going, and Doris, despite protests from her mother, was wearing a dark red tailored suit.

'Why don't you wear your uniform?' Frau Korff had whined. 'You should be proud to let people see what you are and what you're doing for the nation.' But Doris had been adamant.

The simple clarity of the gothic church held them in its spell. On the other side of the church portals, war was raging, but here was a sanctuary of peace.

Klaus stole a glance at his young bride. Her face was pale and intent. The long blonde hair, parted in the middle, fell smoothly on either side of the high, clear forehead. Her eyes drank in the ceremony, as though she wanted to learn it by heart and remember it for all time.

She turned to Klaus and their eyes met. And then the priest's words cut her like a knife: ' . . . until death you do part . . .'

Her lips narrowed. For a moment war had invaded even the church.

Klaus heard it too. Perhaps without Doris, things would be a lot easier. How would he ever be able to go into battle again? He saw a field of crosses, mile upon mile of them, stretching all around him as far as the eye could see. They were wooden crosses, fashioned in a hurry, the names on them written in ink. Crumbling, fading memorials . . . Führer, command and we shall follow . . .

And then the organ burst forth, powerful and solemn, and its music drowned out the thud of bombs, the blast of hand-grenades, the cries, the suffering, confusion, and death . . .

Klaus and Doris were together, alone.

'Only three days,' said the young wife.

'An eternity,' came Klaus' reply.

'Where are you two hiding?' called Doris' mother from the next room. She wanted to show off the young couple to her friends. If I'm not careful, thought Klaus, with a wry smile, she'll be asking them to feel my medals.

'I'm so glad we've done it,' said Doris.

'Well, did you ever expect anything else?'

'Never. And you?'

'How can you ask?'

Doris went to the window. She had filled out a little and it suited her. Her eyes glowed with happiness. Her skin and hair were radiant.

Klaus followed her and drew her close into his arms, pressing his lips to her forehead. She let him kiss her and then tilted her head backwards and looked him long and searchingly in the eyes.

'We won't be alone for much longer, Klaus,' she said softly and smiled to see surprise and joy chase rapidly across his features.

On the last day of his honeymoon, Klaus found his father alone in his study. Direktor Steinbach had grown old and wizened. He had never been garrulous, but now he kept his thoughts to himself almost to the point of silence.

Klaus went in and shut the door behind him. His father was sitting in an old green leather chair reading, and he motioned to Klaus to take a seat opposite him. 'Happy?' he asked, closing his book.

'Yes,' said Klaus.

'Happiness is very rare in wartime, I think.'

Klaus nodded silently. 'When I'm away – you'll look after Doris, won't you?'

'You know I will,' answered his father, smiling.

'But especially during the next few months?'

Direktor Steinbach looked questioningly at his son. His eyes seemed unnaturally large in his pale, almost lifeless face.

'Please, father, I can't tell you now, but I'll write . . .'

'That's all right. We'd arranged for some people to come round this evening, but I've put them off. I'm sure you'd much rather be alone with Doris.'

'Thank you – I would. I've got something else to tell you too. I went to the university today and enrolled – I'm going to study law.'

Direktor Steinbach stared wordlessly out of the window. It seemed as though he hadn't heard at all. Then slowly he turned round.

'I thought you were still in active service?'

'I am, but I don't want to stay that way.'

'Why not?'

'It's not the life for me. I don't want to spend my time in the service of destruction – killing and seeing others being killed – perhaps being killed myself. I've got quite a different view of things now. When the war is over, I don't want anything more to do with the Luftwaffe.'

'Are you sure?'

'Yes. I want a job which will satisfy me. I want to *become* something. I want a job where having broad shoulders isn't the only thing that matters. Father,' he went on hesitantly, 'have you ever had doubts about what I'm doing with my life – fighting this war, I mean?'

'Had doubts?' His father grunted scornfully. He laid a hand on Klaus' shoulder. 'As far as I'm concerned, Hitler's been dead for a long time – from the start, in fact. No doubt you'll be asking yourself why I've never told you this before. Well, it's something that everybody has to decide for himself. In the beginning you were too young to know – and later on – I didn't want to make it any more difficult for you.'

Direktor Steinbach looked into Klaus' face. The old man's chin was trembling slightly and tears stood in his eyes. Klaus realised that he had never been as close to his father before.

Father and son moved self-consciously away from one another as the door opened and Doris came into the room. Seeing their embarrassment, she asked: 'Have I come at an awkward time?'

'Couldn't be a better one,' said Direktor Steinbach. 'I've been talking to Klaus and we think that you should be released from the League any day now. I was wondering if you'd like to come and work for me at my office?'

Doris' face lit up. 'Yes, but –'

'No buts,' said the lawyer. 'My suggestion is a purely selfish one: I should like to have you with me as much as possible.'

He put his right arm around her and his left around Klaus and pushed them gently out of his study. He wanted to be alone, to thank God that his son had grown up.

There were still twenty-two hours to go, but time was moving relentlessly onwards. News bulletins told that in the east the march on Moscow had ground to a halt in the snowy wastes. Tanks were being blown up and waves of wounded Russians were banding together again and advancing for another onslaught. Armies of men were freezing or bleeding to death.

And Klaus was being sent to the east, where hundreds of thousands of German soldiers were being rewarded for their frost bitten limbs with the 'Eastern Medal', otherwise known amongst its bearers as the 'Order of the Frozen Meat'.

Then Klaus and Doris were standing together on the platform. There was nothing about the station which marked this day out as being different from all the others – its dirty windows had looked out on so many scenes of welcome and parting, on tears of joy and grief. No one who left that station could ever be sure that he would return.

'Doris,' said Klaus gently, 'you should never have come with me.'

'Then we would have wasted half an hour of our time together.'

'But this half an hour is unbearable.'

'That can never be, if we are together,' replied the young woman bravely.

Just don't cry, she told herself. When the train has gone – all right, but not now. I mustn't make it harder for him – it must be hard enough already.

'I'm glad I'm going out east,' Klaus said with more conviction than he felt. 'We're gaining ground there every day.'

'Of course, darling.'

'It's true – I'm not just saying it to cheer you up. We've got better machines than the Russians too.'

'Yes, Klaus.'

'In six months' time I'll be due for some more leave – and this time it'll be four weeks – a whole month – think of that!'

The loudspeaker shattered their dreams. The train was pulling in. The women on the platform stood on tiptoes to see the soldiers getting down from the train, or hid their faces for fear that their men might not be amongst them.

'Come back,' said Doris.

'I will.' Klaus pushed through the crowds and into the train. 'Now go.'

'No, I'm waiting,' said Doris firmly.

He found a compartment and squeezed his head and shoulders out of the window that he was sharing with four other soldiers.

And in those last seconds the same language was spoken by every soldier in the train and every woman waiting on the platform. Eyes, hands and lips expressed fear and pain, and the sadness of parting.

And then the wheels began to turn, faster and faster, until the noise was deafening: come back, come back, come back . . .

But the lilting, limping plea would not be granted to all those who were in the train . . .

* * *

On his way back from Poland, Westroff-Meyer visited a concentration camp and toured the gas chambers. There were children here too, although most of them were obviously not candidates for Lebensborn.

The camp commandant gave him an informal reception.

'I expect you'll want to wash away the dust from your journey,' he said, gesturing towards a bottle.

'Funny smell in the air,' commented Westroff-Meyer.

'Not so bad when you get used to it,' growled the commandant, pouring two large measures of cognac. 'It's the incinerators, you know. Prost!' They smiled at each other and knocked back their drinks.

'I'll do what I can for you,' said the commandant, 'but I don't suppose there'll be anything to interest you here. That's Jewish flesh you can smell roasting.' He paused to pour another drink. 'The buggers in there don't even know what's happening – don't even realise they're being gassed.'

Like hell they don't, thought Westroff-Meyer, grinning himself.

The next morning he breakfasted heartily, and the round trip of the camp began. It was the first time Westroff-Meyer had seen a concentration camp from the inside. With morbid curiosity he observed the emaciated figures in their striped uniforms. Their heads were shaved and their lifeless eyes sunken deep into their skulls.

There were the gas chambers – the outside of them, anyway. There was a railway line right next to them, and a goods train had just arrived. It screamed sharply to a halt so that the waggons thudded into one another. Armed guards tore open the doors. There was a screeching of unoiled hinges. People were streaming out of the train. Men and women with grey faces. You could hardly tell one from the other – they weren't really people any more. The train had come from Litzmannstadt. The loudspeaker announced: 'All clothing must be removed for delousing.'

Delousing! So that was it. Westroff-Meyer laughed to himself. That's how they got the clothes off them! Well, it must make their work much easier, the lazy swines.

'Now see if there's anything you fancy,' offered the commandant.

Westroff-Meyer examined the women who were undressing in front of their murderers. His eyes roved over them and on to the children. Hmm, girls with black curly hair. Boys with flaring nostrils. Children with great big eyes like ripe black cherries. They were clinging desperately to their parents.

There was nothing here of any use to the colonel. He wrinkled his nose in distaste. In the last but one waggon he discovered a little head of blond curls, it's mother was dark. Westroff-Meyer climbed over piles of discarded clothes to take a closer look. The little boy would be four years old at the most.

The colonel's thoughts juggled with the child's young life. The boy looked up at him out of blue eyes dark with fear, his head burrowing into his mother's skirts. Westroff-Meyer grinned broadly to instil trust into his victims.

'Popolski?' he asked.

The woman nodded. The SS officer laid his hand on the child's head in a fatherly way, but his fingers had a more sinister task than just reassurance. Excellent shape, this head, he thought. He took the child by the hand, but it still clung tightly to its mother. The mother looked at him wordlessly, her lips trembling. Westroff-Meyer took a step backwards.

'Well?' he prompted.

The guard stepped forward to do his duty. His bayonet glinted on the rifle at his side and he bared his teeth in a smile. 'The children are to be sent for extra delousing,' he said to the woman in Polish.

The colonel nodded gratefully. The mother shuddered. 'Go on, off you go, Matka, go with the gentleman.'

'He'll be all right with me,' assured Westroff-Meyer through his interpreter. 'I promise you that.'

Tears were streaming down the mother's face. Wildly, she tore the child once more into her arms and whispered fevered words into his ear. She was saying good-bye for ever.

'Got to get rid of the lice,' said the Colonel firmly and grasped the child's hand in his own. The boy neither looked at him nor turned round to look back. He climbed over the railway line and the piles of discarded clothing with short, sturdy steps. The wind ruffled his blond curls.

Music was blaring out of the loudspeaker and Westroff-Meyer whistled along tonelessly with it. The first consignment was already going into the gas chamber. It didn't take very long.

The second consignment went in – and the child's mother with it. The boy stopped, rooted to the spot, as though he had suddenly understood what they were going to do to her.

'Mama,' he whispered.

'Mama will be back soon,' said the Colonel with a comforting smile.

Gas hissed out of the ducts. The mother died. It took between two and five minutes. She died with a prayer on her lips for her child. There was no time to curse her executioners.

'Well, I didn't do very well out of that lot, but it was worth the try,' said the Colonel to the commandant, rubbing his hands together with satisfaction.

I'm human after all, he thought with a certain amount of cynical delight – I've saved one more child from a certain death.

And a blond one, at that.

Chapter Twelve

Doris was back at the League, her application to leave mouldering away in a drawer somewhere. She had been sent to a remote and secluded camp where the accent was not so much on scrubbing and digging as on light clerical work. The food was good and wholesome and the medical attention given to the inmates left nothing to be desired. The camp was administered by an elderly lady who had summoned Doris to her office soon after her arrival there.

'I have sent for you,' she began, 'because . . . because . . .' her hand flew to an imaginary curl straying from the rigid Germanic hairstyle. Amazing, thought Doris, how all these Walkyries look alike: hollow, bony faces, angular figures, grating voices and sallow skins that looked more like the colour of their uniforms every day.

Doris knew why she had been summoned. Her gaze didn't falter. On the principal's desk lay a medical report. The examination had taken place two days ago. Doris had known what they would find for a long time now.

'I have to tell you that you are with child, the principal announced primly.

'I know that.'

'You know?'

'I'm not made out of stone.'

The principal blushed and looked hurriedly at her papers. 'For the time being you will stay here with us,' she went on. Doris listened in silence, her eyes glowing. The principal noticed and disapproved. 'In this day and age you can't afford to celebrate just because you're pregnant, you know,' she sniffed. 'You are first class material and you will stay here. When your time comes, you will be sent into a maternity home.'

'Which maternity home?' asked Doris.

The principal ran her finger down the medical report. Her hand stopped when she came to a clause stating that a chosen proportion of the mothers would be sent to a special Lebensborn maternity home.

It was all the same to Doris where they sent her. Her life had a new purpose which made everyday problems seem almost negligible. Her smile grew.

'What are you grinning about?' asked the principal sharply.

'I am just grateful for all the trouble you're taking for me,' said Doris sincerely.

The principal glared furiously at her, her eyes glinting with envy or hatred, or both.

'Right,' she snapped. 'That's settled.'

Doris was dismissed. From now on her life would be measured by the heartbeats of the baby wtihin her, and by her letters from Klaus. Her whole appearance mirrored the resurgence of life within her: her face had grown more womanly, and her eyes shone with an inner light, were lively and alert. Motherhood would only increase Doris' beauty.

* * *

The maternity home was on the outskirts of a small town in Pomerania, not far from the coast. It was set in the middle of a great park studded with ancient trees. The low white-washed building was only just visible between their massive trunks. There was a wrought-iron gate at the end of the drive, and a bronze plaque on the wall which said simply: 'Nursing Home'. That was all.

Doris arrived in the evening. The sun's fiery ball hung low over the park and set alight the gate, burnishing it like gold. The young woman took a deep breath. It is beautiful here, she thought. She was alone and forced to carry her own luggage, despite her advanced condition, or perhaps because of it, since the Nazis thought the ability to suffer hardship a virtue.

Doris pressed the bell and waited a few seconds. Then a gloomy figure appeared in the doorway – a nurse in Party brown. The young woman hesitantly gave her name and the nurse scanned the visitors' list in her hands.

'You are expected,' she announced coldly.

She opened the door half-way and allowed Doris to pass without relieving her of her cases.

'Dr Jessrich will speak with you tomorrow morning,' she said as they marched along the corridor. 'It's too late now, he has already left the house.'

On the third floor, the march came to a halt. 'You will occupy this room only temporarily,' the nurse explained, then added: 'We also like you to refrain from private conversation while you are with us. The other house rules will be explained to you tomorrow by Dr Jessrich.'

Then Doris was alone in her room. When she looked around her it seemed as though she had never left the Lebensborn home in Warthegau. Everything was cold and bare and built for a purpose. There were two beds. In the left one sat a lady in a dressing-gown. She put down the book she was reading and stood up heavily. She was a large woman with ash blonde hair. There were dark rings under her blue eyes. Her smile was enigmatic – there was sympathy there and something else – sarcasm.

'I am Frau Grete,' she said. Her handclasp was strong and firm.

Doris smiled, embarrassed. 'My name is Steinbach.'

The woman put a finger to her lips and at once the sarcasm in her expression came to the fore. 'Better not tell,' she whispered. 'What is your first name?'

'Doris.'

'Frau Doris, then,' smiled the other. 'There are no surnames in this house.'

'Why not?'

Frau Grete shook her head. Unsuspecting angel, she thought. Ah, well, you'll know soon enough tomorrow.

Doris opened her case. On the top was a photograph of

Klaus. She picked it up and looked at it, the love lighting her eyes.

'You had better put that back where it came from,' said Frau Grete, 'or else they'll be taking it off you.'

'Whatever for?' asked Doris, puzzled.

At that moment she caught sight of some words stencilled over the door. Her eyes narrowed and she spelled them out through half-closed lips: 'It is tactless to speak of your child's father.'

The other woman smiled. 'It's a madhouse, isn't it?'

Doris' face was pale. 'I don't understand,' she said. 'What's that supposed to mean?'

Frau Grete looked carefully at Doris. 'Are you married?' she asked suddenly. 'You don't have to tell me – in fact you're not allowed to, but – '

'Of course I'm married.'

'It's not as simple as that,' explained Frau Grete. 'Not here, at least. Hence those words up there.'

At last Doris understood. I am back in Lebensborn, she thought. It's exactly the same, except that here the policy is reversed. Instead of wanting us to concentrate on nothing but the opposite sex, we're forbidden to speak of them. That's how little human relations matter! Well, the words over the door meant nothing to her, and nothing to her baby, either. She had no reason to hide her relationship with Klaus from the world, no reason to deny her baby its father. No, the words didn't concern her. She ignored them as she would have done obscene scribbling on a lavatory wall.

That Frau Grete had not been exaggerating when she had described the peculiarities of the home, Doris found out the next morning.

Breakfast was a communal meal, and it was here that Doris was introduced to the others by the matron, whose brown uniform was emblazoned with the gold sign of the Party.

'Frau Doris,' she said loudly. 'Frau Edith . . . Frau Frieda . . . Frau Hildegunde . . . Frau Bertha . . .'

Doris gave her hand to her half-anonymous companions, who looked at her searchingly or challengingly, with indifference or derision. Many looked as though they were carrying burdens they couldn't be rid of quickly enough.

'Frau Doris,' said the matron after the meal was over, 'you will please report to Dr Jessrich.'

She had to wait in the ante-room, where an assistant pushed forward a chair for her. The door to the surgery was ajar, so that Doris had no choice but to overhear the conversation that was going on inside.

'Everything's in order, Frau Ursula,' the doctor was saying. 'You are free to go now.'

'Thank God for that! And you think I'll be able to get back to my normal weight O.K.?'

'No doubt about it.'

'This business has done enough damage to my figure as it is –'

'Well,' said the doctor brusquely, 'all the best then.'

High heels came click-clacking across the floor and a young blonde girl hurried out of the surgery.

The assistant stood up. 'Your baby,' she said shyly, ' – wouldn't you like to see it one last time?'

'What for?'

'It's just next door,' pleaded the assistant.

'It's not my child,' said the girl, opening the door to go, 'it's yours. You were the ones who wanted it. Good afternoon, Fräulein.'

Doris got to her feet and Dr Jessrich offered her his hand and led her into his surgery. Under his white overall she could see his leather boots and his cheeks bore duelling scars. Despite this, he was a gentleman. His examination was short and to the point.

He nodded encouragingly at Doris. 'The baby will probably be along in about seven days' time.' His grey eyes looked penetratingly into hers.

'Frau Doris, I am not only the head doctor here, I am also the warden of the hostel.'

'Yes, I know,' murmured Doris.

'All our rules are designed for the protection of our mothers.'

'Thank you.' Dr Jessrich raised an eyebrow. 'All the children who are born here, or nearly all of them, belong to the state. They are Hitler's children.'

'I am married,' said the young woman simply.

'Until you are released, your child will remain in our nursery. But when you leave us, of course you will take it with you.'

'Yes, doctor, I know already. I shall obey all the rules, you can be sure of that.'

The doctor bowed his head in acknowledgement and Doris went back to her room. Frau Grete welcomed her with a smile.

'The doctors are pretty good here, aren't they? I should know – this is my third time. How about you?'

'My first,' said Doris.

'And are you – glad?' Her voice sounded ominous.

'Glad?' Doris smiled. 'Glad? I'm more than glad.'

Frau Grete clicked her tongue against her teeth. 'Some of them here feel very differently. As soon as the birth is over and done with, they're gone and never heard of again.'

'And what happens to their babies?' asked Doris.

'Oh, somebody adopts them, or they go to a sort of home . . . ' She waved a hand vaguely.

Doris was lying on her bed listening wide-eyed. Suddenly she began to shake and tears rolled slowly on to the pillow. She didn't know why she was crying – for her child, who had a mother and a father to love him, or for the thousands who hadn't.

Frau Grete leaned over her and stroked the soft hair back from her face. 'There, there, it'll be all right,' she said.

She went across the room to her suitcase, rummaged around inside it and brought out a photograph. She sat down on Doris' bed to show it to her.

'Look,' she said, 'I've got my husband with me too – he's an officer. If he had any idea of what was going on here, he'd go out of his mind.'

For politeness' sake, Doris took the photo. Suddenly her hand began to tremble violently.

It was a photograph of Horst Kempe.

Slowly Doris put the photograph down. She felt weak and dizzy.

'He's nice-looking, isn't he?' said Grete Kempe.

'Yes,' answered Doris faintly.

Grete sighed. 'He's the sort who'll smell out danger and rush into it at the best of times, and there he is out at the front, risking his neck every minute of the day. Is your husband a soldier too?'

'Yes, he's a flying officer.'

'I think we'll have a lot in common, you and I . . .'

'I expect so,' murmured Doris.

She lay back on her bed, but sleep didn't come. All sorts of horrors were haunting her.

Somewhere in the house babies were grizzling in their little cradles, lined up as if for a regimental inspection. Ironically enough, only a minority of them turned out as their breeders had planned – many had dark eyes or round heads. Nature had the last laugh on the Nazis.

The post was handed out the next morning after breakfast. This was the duty of the matron, who called out the names of the recipients – only their first names, of course. Doris put out her hand to pass on a letter. 'No,' shrilled the matron, waving Doris away. 'That is not allowed.'

Doris was slowly learning. She noticed that the envelopes were being handed out face-downwards.

When it came to her turn and the envelope was carefully turned over, she burst out: 'Thank you, but you don't need to do that for me. My name is Steinbach – it's my married name and I don't care who knows it.' Her eyes were alight with anger. The other women looked at her in amazement.

'I will pretend I didn't hear that,' said the matron sharply. There were hard lines around her mouth and an unhealthy flush had crept over her gaunt features.

Doris looked past her at Frau Kempe, who was shaking her head in warning.

'It is time now for your morning rest, ladies,' announced the matron curtly.

The french windows were thrown open. Outside on the lawn stood gaily striped deck chairs. The sun shone brightly through the trees.

Doris went out alone, choosing a chair that stood apart from the rest under a large sycamore tree. The others followed her slowly, whispering amongst themselves about the scene she had caused.

Doris lay back in her chair, feeling as though a great burden had just been taken off her shoulders. Her pride and her defiance were not just hers alone. She had spoken to protect her unborn child.

Suddenly someone was standing over her. One of the girls had broken away from the rest and come up to Doris, her face set and unfriendly.

'My name is Frau Edith,' she said, her voice sounding like an imitation of the matron's.

'Would you like to sit by me?' asked Doris, once again feeling right with the world.

'No, I wouldn't. I'm going to sit as far away from you as possible.'

'Why is that?' asked Doris calmly.

The girl curled her bottom lip in scorn. 'You're trying to provoke us, aren't you?'

'No,' answered Doris, her tone neutral.

'I expect you're very proud of your *husband*,' Edith continued, with a sarcasm that seemed to tread the concept of marriage underfoot. 'But you ought to know that we – ' she nodded in the direction of the other women – 'we have no husbands. We volunteered to serve the Führer and we're not going to let you insult us because of it.'

Doris turned her head slowly. The other inmates of the home had arranged their chairs into two groups, one of which was staring at her with unconcealed animosity. She realised that it wasn't only a garden path that divided the two camps, but the unbridgeable gulf between the married and the unmarried.

'Do you understand that?' came Edith's hard voice.

'Yes,' said Doris quietly. 'I was in a Lebensborn home too, you know. Only my case was quite, quite different. You see, I would never leave any child of mine alone in the world. My child is my husband's child, not Hitler's.'

It looked as though Edith was going to lunge at Doris, but her knees gave way and she crumpled to the grass. Burying her head in her arms, she gave way to violent weeping.

She had only just begun to understand the nature of her sacrifice.

* * *

Colonel Westroff-Meyer had returned to Berlin with bloody, but by no means empty hands. At the headquarters of the SS he exchanged more than 200 stolen children for a few choice words of praise. On the way he had his car stop outside a military tailor's to order his new uniform – he hadn't plundered the east for nothing – the suffering of the mothers he had robbed, the screams of the children, the gunfire in the villages and the smoke in the crematorium chimneys had earned him the title of General. And he wore his new rank as though he were a mannequin parading the latest fashion.

He marched up the steps at headquarters, down the corridor into his office, and rang for Ruth.

'Well,' he said, stretching out his arms towards her, 'aren't you glad I'm back?'

'Yes,' said Ruth without any conviction.

'So am I,' said the General. 'It was a terrible assignment. Poland's full of filth.'

'Yes,' she said, collecting her thoughts. 'Actually I was expecting you this morning.'

He tilted her chin upwards and looked into her eyes. 'But you know that my first loyalty is to my Führer,' he said benevolently. 'I had business to do this morning. But I've brought you a present.' He rummaged around amongst his luggage and pulled out a mink coat.

'That's for me?' she said, the life creeping back into her voice.

'That's right.' He draped it around her shoulders.

'It's beautiful.'

'I got it in Warsaw.'

'I bet it was expensive,' Ruth said with relish.

Westroff-Meyer shrugged his shoulders. 'Not too bad,' he said casually. He couldn't remember whether it had cost him in bullets or cubic centimetres of gas. Anyway, it didn't matter.

'That's not all, either,' he said, producing a small black box. He took out a diamond ring and pushed it on to Ruth's finger. It was too big because it belonged on another hand.

'Fabulous,' said Ruth, admiring the ring. 'I didn't know you could get such good stones in Poland.'

'If you know where to look, you can get anything.'

Ruth walked over to the mirror and examined her side view in the new coat. It didn't sit quite right at the shoulders, she thought, and the hem could do with taking up a couple of inches. And there, on the left sleeve, was a worn patch.

'It's not new of course,' said Westroff-Meyer, 'but it's in good condition.'

His secretary murmured her thanks.

'And that's a nine-carat diamond. It's worth a fortune.'

'You spoil me,' said Ruth. A wave of nausea flooded through her as she thought of the thanks that would be required of her that night.

Westroff-Meyer cleared his throat and returned to business. 'Give me the papers for the Warthegau home,' he commanded. Ruth produced the folder and he opened it and leafed through its contents: costs, a list of names, another list of pairs of names, medical reports, final results.

His finger ran down the list of names and stopped at Doris Steinbach. Ah, so she did marry him then, thought the General. And now she's in confinement at Mecklenburg. Well, it's time I paid her a visit – taught them both a lesson.

His finger went on down the names. Erika. Nothing to show for herself, that one. Next to her name was a query – would Lebensborn object to her being released from the League?

The General rang for Ruth. 'Listen. Get this Erika Baumann over here. I want to see her.'

'What for?'

'I don't know yet,' he said.

He looked at the mink coat still hanging round her shoulders, heard the firing squad that had been the end of its owner, reached for his glass and drowned the ghost.

* * *

The corridors in the maternity home gleamed with oppressive hygiene, the air was sterile, and all the inmates were allowed to do was rest. Despite the rules, trouble was always brewing beneath the calm and ready to erupt without warning. Although it was strictly forbidden to talk about private matters, they were virtually the sole subject of conversation.

Doris got on best with Frau Ingeborg, who had no idea at all what Lebensborn was. She had come from the neighbouring town and been sent to this place because all the other nursing homes were full.

She was curious, but she didn't rightly understand what she saw going on around her. She regarded the rules and regulations as the ceremonial of some obscure cult into which she, as an outsider, would never be initiated. And in a couple of weeks' time, she, like many other mothers who came into contact with Lebensborn by chance and through no doings of their own, would pick up her child and her belongings and walk away, never to hear another word about the organisation again.

Apart from her sort, there was, Doris recognised, another group – the one which surrounded Frau Kempe. These women were the minority group whose husbands were SS officers and who came to Lebensborn nursing homes solely to take advantage of the excellent medical attention they provided and which was offered to them free. These mothers did very well out of the system. They shook their heads and clicked their tongues over what was going on – some of them even wrote and told their husbands and had been overheard using violent and abusive language when referring to the Nazis, but nevertheless, the consciousness of belonging to an élite usually sufficed to allay most of their doubts.

The third group were the true victims of Lebensborn and had been on 'lecture courses' like Doris had. Either these girls were too thick and unfeeling to care, or else giving birth and losing their babies would break their spirits for ever.

And it took Doris a long time to realise that not even one fifth of the children born in this or any other Lebensborn home was born in wedlock. This organisation surrounded by bourgeois respectability was in fact a gigantic breeding ground for illegitimate children.

Not until after the war was it known that Hitler's children numbered tens of thousands. At the same time documents were found in the secret archives of the SS revealing that after the war Himmler wanted to abolish marriage altogether for members of the SS who had proved their worth. Plans for polygamy had already been drawn up.

This was the strange world that Doris had to live in. She forced herself to pay no attention to her surroundings, but to concentrate on waiting in hope and fear for the future.

She had received a letter that day from Klaus and she went up to her room where she could read it in private.

'Now I understand,' wrote the young captain to his wife, 'how you must feel when you are afraid for me. Because now I live in constant fear for you. Dreadful fear. If once the post comes without a letter from you, I begin to believe the worst. Yesterday I was so distraught that I nearly rammed the plane in front of me . . . '

Doris' body contracted with pain. She thought of Klaus as she doubled up in agony and unwittingly crumpled his letter to a ball in her fist. Slowly the pain ebbed away. She could move her lips once more. Her pupils were dilated, her eyes shone, but not for Frau Kempe, who had just come into the room. Doris looked straight through her and into the distance where the miracle was slowly beginning. A smile hovered on her lips.

Grete Kempe took one look at her and nodded to herself.

'It's time,' she said. 'I'll get help.'

Chapter Thirteen

At half past eight that evening Doris was lying in the labour ward of the home. The sheets on her simple bed were chalk-white and the metal reflector on the light overhead blinded her eyes.

Dr Jessrich bent over her. There were minute beads of perspiration on his face. He turned to the assisting nurse and shrugged his shoulders indecisively. 'There might be complications.'

Doris moaned. She wasn't lying on a hospital bunk. She was in a boat and it was tossing on the sea. There was a storm – she could hear it, and sirens. No one was coming to her aid. No one. Her head looked small and delicate as the doctor applied the gas mask to her face.

'Count,' said the nurse.

That's the witch, thought Doris, the witch out of Hansel and Gretel.

'Count.'

'One,' said Doris weakly.

'Go on,' encouraged the doctor gently.

'One . . . ' breathed Doris, but her voice faltered again. She groaned.

Dr Jessrich felt her pulse. He was juggling with life and death. It was either the mother or the child.

'It's against our principles,' said the nurse, anticipating his decision.

'I have a job to do.'

'Your job is to save the *child*.'

'Hopeless . . . ' said the doctor to himself. But Doris couldn't have heard if she'd tried. She was slipping into unconsciousness – her world was darkening . . . perhaps for ever. But suddenly she knew something quite plainly – it was terribly clear and close. Klaus had been shot down over Russia.

While I am lying here in labour, Klaus will die ...

And so Dr Jessrich began his desperate fight to save Doris' life.

* * *

Klaus had been flying in the east for some months now. His base was a desolate collection of barrack huts in the Ukraine. Snow and rain bombarded the roofs and armies of bugs infested the walls and the beds. An empty sardine tin that served as an ashtray stood on the roughly hewn table and next to it an empty vodka bottle held a candle. There was no electricity and very little post, hardly any sun and only occasionally something to drink.

There were some men whom Klaus had known with the squadron in France, but most of them were new. They'd all been thrown into this godforsaken spot and left to the bugs. Even the officers' mess wasn't free of them. The new colonel scratched his chest selfconsciously as he gave Klaus an introductory talk.

'You know, Steinbach, we're up against two enemies here, the Russians and the lice. The game is to destroy anything that crawls.' He smiled grimly. 'You'll live longer out here, but the conditions are worse.'

Their missions were mainly dictated by chance. It was just up to the individual – you could fly as long as there was enough daylight and enough alcohol to keep you going. Flying had become almost just a way of passing the time. If you felt like it, you squashed a few lice, otherwise you let them go. It was the same with the Russians. It wasn't a question of air battles any more.

Today Klaus was reconnoitring for enemy aircraft, although there was little hope of finding any. The visibility was poor and it was raining. But the cockpit was the only place where he could really get his thoughts together. Flying is the only thing that keeps me going out here, he thought. Just looking at those four stinking walls in the barracks is enough to drive you mad – that and the eternal rain these Russians seem to go in for. And thinking about Doris . . .

Russia disappeared beneath him. The plane was going smoothly. Klaus' eyes ran mechanically over the instrument panel. The needle of the fuel clock was trembling on the 'full' mark. He was suddenly tempted to turn round 180 degrees and head for the west, to fly for as long as his supplies would last. But what then?

Klaus twisted his mouth into a tired smile. Then they'd shoot him for worrying about his own wife. Or they'd call it cowardice in the face of the enemy.

He tried to see a clear path upwards through the clouds that surrounded him, but they kept massing together, so he wiped the steam off the inside of the cockpit and levelled off. He looked down. Woods, meadows, woods – coniferous, deciduous, all dark with rain.

Klaus saw the runway ahead of him and accelerated towards it, flying low. A column of foot soldiers split up and dived for cover. They were his own men, but they could hardly believe that the plane above them was German. Klaus smiled wryly to himself. To make up for it, he picked up the Russians a moment later.

Klaus locked the safety catch on his steering as he entered the next zone. A cursory survey revealed nothing, so he looped around. The meadows were steaming and hills loomed up in his path. The earth was heavy and damp. There was no one to be seen.

Klaus shook his head and retraced the course he had flown. There were tracks on the earth. He followed them until he came to a tank which had been stirring up the dirt. It was crawling along under Klaus' plane like a beetle scurrying home.

There were no markings on it and Klaus couldn't tell whether it was German or Russian. He flew around it two or three times to get a closer look when suddenly the thing seemed to take fright and scuttled off. Klaus turned and swooped, his machine whining through the air as he descended on the beetle that was growing fatter and fatter every moment. Now. Press the button.

The 20 mm shells fell like water from a sprinkler. A shower of death. The shot bounced like silver droplets on the steel plates of the tank. Klaus turned to strike again. The tank limped across the field and into the undergrowth. Klaus' stomach was churning as he saw it dying.

Enough, he thought, as the black monster began to turn in hopeless circles. One of the chains must have gone. He couldn't finish it off anyway, its skin was much to thick for that. So he climbed steeply upwards into the washed-out sky, got his bearings and flew off to zone three.

When he came out of the spiral he saw the artillery below. He fired, and though he could hardly hear his own shot for the wailing of the engine, he saw the Russian gunners leaping into their trenches, some covering their heads with their arms, as though that would do any good. Now they were in position and firing back. Klaus clenched his teeth and prepared to make his getaway. There was nothing else for it.

But he was too late. There was a sudden rattling and whirring, and the next thing Klaus knew, boiling oil was hissing all over his legs. The cockpit was full of smoke and the infernal stink of petrol. Klaus' eyes sought out his oil gauge through the fumes. The needle was jerking wildly back and forth indicating the critical loss of fluid from a severed artery. Then it dropped and hit the red danger zone on the dial. This is it, he thought.

In the next second there was an almighty explosion and the machine spat a trail of black smoke and began to plummet downwards. Klaus pulled desperately on the throttle – a row of trees leapt up to meet him. There was a great cracking and a wrenching as branches tore aluminium asunder. Klaus felt his legs being trapped and wedged in and it seemed as though a giant fist came up and knocked his head back into a concrete wall.

His consciousness exploded like a firecracker and all the time it hammered against his brain: I'm finished. I'm finished.

He never knew how he managed to free himself from the wreckage. His flying suit was in rags and his left arm was practically torn off at the elbow – only the bones held it together. Blood streamed into his eyes, blocking his vision.

He staggered through wet, waist-high grass. Mechanically he rubbed his eyes and forced them open. There was a terrible stabbing pain in his side and he was stumbling over his own feet. He fell headlong. Nearby on the runway an army truck screeched to a halt and Russian infantry spilled out. The grass was trampled under the feet of the Soviet soldiers.

The Russians were coming nearer. They were heading straight for him. Klaus crouched down in the tall, sopping wet grass as the Russians flattened the vegetation around him. With the hand of his good arm he tore his gun from its holster and pressed it tightly between his knees.

The crashing and trampling was coming nearer. Klaus raised his head cautiously and made out the Soviets' round steel helmets moving through the grass like the round backs of tortoises. Over there, 200 or so metres away lay the wrecked fuselage. The Russians were shouting something to each other. Klaus took his pistol in a trembling hand. His breathing was slow and laboured.

The Russians had reached the burning wreck. They approached it with their machine-guns cocked. The ruined plane was smoking lazily. Suddenly it happened – the sheer force of it took Klaus' breath away. It felt as though someone had got him in the back of the neck with a crowbar. The plane rose up like a phoenix and exploded as if in slow motion. Bits of metal flew through the air resounding against the trees or crashing into the undergrowth.

Klaus threw himself down on his face and covered his head with his arms as best he could while the ammunition in the plane went on banging and cracking.

The Russians let out a piercing falsetto cry. Klaus got to his feet and ran as fast as he could. Behind him the commotion was dying down. In a hundred metres he fell thirty times, and each time he seemed to fall straight on to his injured arm.

His face was contorted with pain. Poor old plane, he thought senselessly.

The next time he hit the ground he stayed down and pulled the bandage out of his pocket. Somehow he wrapped it round his bad arm and then lay there waiting.

When it was dark he stood up painfully. The wood

seemed unchanged. It was never-ending, and the pain throbbed still through his body.

Klaus groaned. All around him he saw flames, and when he closed his eyes, fiery wheels rolled in on his brain. Somehow he managed to keep going for what must have been a couple of hours, although it seemed an eternity.

Then the squat shape of a wooden hut appeared in a clearing. The wood was thinning out here and Klaus dragged himself from trunk to trunk, his teeth chattering with the cold. The hut lay black and silent in front of him. When he was only a few metres away, he dropped down on to his belly and crawled. There was no door, only a black gaping hole. Slowly and painfully he dragged himself through it. A whiff of hay tickled his nose. The hut was empty. Klaus lay down exhausted on the soft hay. It buoyed him up gently and dusk swallowed him in a dreamless sleep.

Suddenly he was awoken by a sharp kick on the shin. He tried to reach for his gun but the foot stepped on his hand. The flickering light of a candle blinded his eyes. Somewhere in the distance he could hear firing at the front.

Klaus blinked and looked up to see three women standing over him, broad-boned, flat-faced women. They were staring wordlessly at him from their narrow slanting eyes. They were unafraid. Their muscular bodies were hard under their poor matted clothes. One of them pointed to his arm and Klaus looked down and saw that the bandage was black with blood. He dragged himself to his feet.

Without knowing why he was doing it, Klaus fumbled in his pocket and brought out his wallet. Inside was Doris' photograph. She looked calm and serene and Klaus' fingers trembled as he held the print out to the Russian women.

It was an uncanny scene – outside the thunder of guns at the front and here in the dark hut a wounded German was standing in a circle of candlelight with three Russian women looking at the photograph with eyes that showed an inner calm – a calm which was the heritage of their vast homeland.

One of the women smiled. She nodded at Klaus and pointed to the picture.

Klaus nodded back.

Frowning with the effort of working things out, the woman turned to the other two and said something to them. They nodded their heads slowly in agreement.

Klaus bent down quickly and picked up his gun, but the women remained impassive.

He thanked them with his eyes as he set off again into the night.

After only a matter of yards, he stumbled over something and bent down to see what it was. A cable! It must lead to a radio station, but his life would depend on whether he found Russians or Germans there. His life hung by a thread more slender than the cable in his hands. By now he must be well inside German territory. Where were the Russian soldiers hiding? It was senseless to search around like this in the night. The fiery circles began to turn again before his eyes.

Suddenly he let go of the wire. He'd almost stumbled into a dug-out.

Everything went black and empty, then a bright lurid yellow. Klaus took a deep and painful breath and kicked open the door of the dug-out. It reeked of Machorka and the Russians had almost disappeared in their cigarette smoke. But Klaus recognised them immediately by their glittering epaulettes.

The Russian officer who stepped out of the gloom had a head like a billiard ball. 'Is it you, Towaritsch?' he asked.

Klaus raised the pistol that the Russian woman had left him so that he could fight his way back to the girl in the photograph.

Then all hell broke loose. Klaus was running for his life over barbed wire, holes blown in the earth, the graves of dead soldiers. Searchlights crossed in the sky and the glowing trails of hand grenades arched through the air into No-Man's-Land. And Klaus stumbled blindly onwards, his bad arm forgotten, his heart pounding and his lungs on fire.

He stumbled and fell sprawling to the ground. Then the ear-splitting rattle of a machine-gun and the deafening thud of a grenade near at hand. He spat blood. There was a pause in the firing.

'You bastards!' roared Klaus and spat fiercely. A fresh

burst of firing. He strained his ears. It was a German machine-gun!

He got unsteadily to his feet. 'German,' he panted, 'Ger – man!' He waved his good arm frantically in the air. 'Can't you hear,' he groaned, 'German!'

'What's the password?' called a voice in the night.

'Password be damned,' panted Klaus. 'I'm a pilot . . . shot down.'

The Russians opened fire again from behind and hell opened its ugly jaws once more. Klaus ran blindly in the direction of the German machine-gun.

'Mow him down,' said one of the soldiers.

'But he speaks German,' protested the guard.

'Fool! The one who threw those grenades into our camp yesterday could speak German. I don't want to die!'

He took aim, but Klaus was already upon them. He collapsed and fell headlong at the feet of the guard, who pointed a pistol at his head and pressed his face close up to the wounded man's.

'My God,' he said, 'who got you into this mess?'

'The Russians,' mumbled Klaus, ' – and you bastards . . .'

Unconsciousness.

* * *

The room smelled of ether – the perfume of sacrifice. Doris was unconscious. The scalpel in Dr Jessrich's hand glittered with the beating of his pulse. He was determined not to sacrifice the mother in order to save the baby, but he was not allowed to give up the baby in order to save the mother.

All at once the knife in his hand stopped trembling. In beginning to operate he had made the most difficult decision a surgeon could make: to try to save both mother and child, knowing that the attempt could cost them both their lives.

Doris slept soundly. Klaus was there. He was laughing, drawing her into his arms. They were at the swimming pool. The water was so lovely and cool. Blue sky. Blazing sun. The wind was whipping up little waves on the pool. The spring-board. Doris' long slim legs knifed into the water.

137

'Race you!' called Klaus.

He came up behind her laughing. She crawled up the pool, back again. But Klaus was swimming like a swordfish. He streaked past her.

Then there was no sun to be seen and Klaus had disappeared. And the waves were high, the water was getting rougher and rougher. Doris couldn't carry on any longer.

Her body arched, was forced down again. She was struggling for her life. Water – nothing but water – how much could a person swallow?

Doris tossed and turned. There was nothing there. Why don't they do something?

Her eyes shot open, still and expressionless. All she could feel was that she was breathing. Coming alive again . . .

But Klaus wasn't there.

Then she understood. She was floating back towards consciousness. Slowly – slowly. And there, next to her – but she couldn't turn her head. She strained her eyes and saw for the first time the third person – the baby – her son.

Doris drew a deep and sobbing breath of endless wonder and shut her eyes tightly. Great tears of happiness rolled from under the long lashes.

'My baby,' she whispered.

The baby was cradled in Dr Jessrich's arms. The doctor was as white as his patient, but he was smiling tenderly, shyly, gratefully.

The difficulty of the birth had made it necessary for Doris to stay in the large ward with all the others longer than was usual, but this didn't bother her. She was living in her own private dreamworld, only surfacing to reality when the baby was brought to her, and with him, the knowledge that her dream had come true.

She looked at the baby in wonderment, seeing in him a tiny replica of her husband. He's got Klaus' eyes, his nose, his determined chin, she thought, and he'll grow up to be just like his father.

Doris was oblivious to what was going on around her. She didn't feel the hatred, the jealousy of the others, only basked in their sympathy and understanding.

Next to her lay Inge. Inge didn't want to see her baby and

138

lived in constant fear that her parents might find out what had been happening to her in this obscure Lebensborn maternity home. On her right was Ursula, a League leader who had become a mother because she was ordered to and was accomplishing the task efficiently and joylessly, just as she would have carried out other orders to scrub floors or make beds.

On the other side was Jutta. All she knew about the father of her child was that he was in the Panzer division and that he liked marmalade and cream cheese for breakfast.

Then there was Edith, the girl who had screamed at Doris in the garden that day. She had suddenly fallen in love with her small daughter and wanted to keep her, look after her, protect her. And right at the back in the corner was Frau Kempe.

Although their characters were so different, Doris and Frau Kempe had been united by the bond of motherhood, and when they returned to their room, their days passed pleasantly together in quiet routine. The doctor made his rounds once a day; the postman twice.

'Nothing for me again,' said Doris helplessly. She was beginning to worry – it had been more than a week since she had heard from Klaus.

'It's often the way,' said Grete. 'You get nothing for days, and then four or five letters arrive all at once – and you don't know which to open first.'

'Yes,' said Doris, but she was not convinced.

'Perhaps I shouldn't tell you,' began the other woman cautiously, 'but you'll have to know sooner or later. My husband's coming – he's got leave.' Her face broke into a smile.

'That's wonderful,' said Doris. But she was near to tears.

And suddenly there he was bursting in at the door as big and beefy as ever and laughing all over his face. In one hand he grasped a bunch of flowers as if it was a spade. He bent down and gave his wife a smacking kiss on the cheek and said: 'You look great. Everything went off O.K. then?'

'Yes Horst,' said his wife, smiling fondly up at him.

'The other kids are fine too – I popped in home to have a look at them.'

'This is Frau Doris,' said Grete, introducing them from her pillow.

Horst Kempe turned and started with a shock of recognition. Doris slowly closed one eye. He understood immediately and gave her his hand.

'Horst Kempe,' he said with a broad wink. 'Pleased to meet you.'

He pulled over a stool and sat down between the two beds. 'Nice place you've got here,' he said, for want of anything better to say.

His wife shook her head. 'This is where I was the last time,' she said in a low voice, 'and I want nothing more to do with the place.'

'Well, you're a funny one,' said Horst raising an eyebrow.

'Horst, promise me that I'll never have to come into a home like this again.'

'All right,' he said in a gruff, good-humoured voice, 'but don't forget it costs nothing to come here.'

'The price is still too high for me,' said Grete seriously.

'Visiting time is over,' announced a nurse who had just appeared in the doorway.

Kempe stood up immediately.

'I hope you get on all right, then, Grete. I'll be around for a while and I'll look in now and then to see how you're doing.' He turned to Doris. 'And how is your husband?'

'He's at the front. I don't know . . . ' Doris looked down at her hands.

Kempe nodded. 'Stupid question,' he growled. 'Forgive me. Well, until tomorrow, ladies.' He ducked his head as though he thought he might hit it on the door-frame, and went out.

* * *

General Westroff-Meyer conducted his life by this simple rule : daytime for the Führer; night-time for me. He divided his favours just as fairly as he divided his spoils, and just as he himself lived in terror of the men at the top, so he inspired fear into those below him.

'Pull yourself together,' he screamed at his secretary Ruth as he rummaged through the papers on his desk. 'I've never seen such a mess! The Church has got wind of Lebensborn and they're kicking up one hell of a fuss.' He paused. 'We'll show them.'

He'd found it. It was a report from an informer who'd taken down a sermon in shorthand in the church where he'd heard it. 'I'm up to my neck in rubbish like this.'

Ruth did her best to calm him, but he raged on: 'People like this ought to be put down. And after the war is over, we'll have a good clear out – I can promise you that. We'll give them the same treatment we gave the Poles.'

'The Poles?' asked Ruth.

'That's right,' said Westroff-Meyer violently. 'We'll exterminate the whole lot of them.' The flat of his hand came down heavily on his desk.

For a few seconds Ruth froze, thinking of her fur coat.

He reached for the telephone and gave instructions to the Gestapo to have the priest arrested.

Shortly before midday, Ruth announced that Erika Baumann had arrived.

'Send her in then,' thundered the general.

He stood up to meet Erika and gave her his hand. 'We know each other already, of course,' he said with an intimate smile. 'Do sit down.'

'Thank you.'

'Well, by rights you should be somewhere entirely different at the present time,' he said glancing meaningfully at the calendar on his desk.

'I know.'

Westroff-Meyer smiled again. 'But the Führer can be served in other ways.' His eyes roved over her body. He had a very good idea how she might serve the Führer. She had attracted him from the beginning.

'I hear you want to be released from the League.'

Erika nodded.

'Now why is that?'

Erika shrugged.

'Well,' he said sympathetically, 'I expect they're a pretty boring lot. Not for the likes of you, I'm sure. What were you doing before you joined the League?'

'I was a book-keeper in a munitions factory.'

'Ah!' Westroff-Meyer nodded so approvingly that Erika wondered if he was the factory's major shareholder. 'I'll make you a proposition,' he said. 'I'm looking for a second secretary. How would you like the job?'

'Here?' asked Erika. She thought fast. If I say no, he's bound not to let me leave the League, and I suppose sitting behind a typewriter isn't as bad as cleaning lavatories.

She nodded almost imperceptibly.

'I always knew we'd get on,' said Westroff-Meyer.

Erika's lips were shut. You'd be surprised, she thought.

The General rang for Ruth. 'There's too much work here for one,' he told her, looking both girls up and down. 'This is Erika – say hello to one another – she's starting here next week.'

'But – ' Ruth protested weakly. She understood very well that he was putting a rival in her camp.

'No buts,' said Westroff-Meyer. 'And now will you get my papers ready – I'm going on a visit to the home in Mecklenburg.'

He dismissed Erika, who was unaware that her destiny had chosen this new job for her for a very specific purpose.

* * *

Klaus stood outside the door where the nurse had left him. Today was the first time he'd been let out of the military hospital and according to the doctor, he should still be in bed.

And now he stood outside her door, feeling overwhelmed that he had made it back to his girl in the photograph. He knocked – almost gingerly.

'Yes?' Doris' voice was soft, but full of anticipation.

He pushed the door wide open and stood rooted to the spot, amazed by her radiant beauty and the abundance of golden hair spread out on the pillow.

Doris just looked at him without saying a word. Then she stretched out her arms towards him. He'd never seen such a glorious smile.

He was vaguely aware that there was a second bed in the

room and that it was occupied. He walked over to where Doris lay and bent over her tenderly.

Suddenly she noticed the black sling on his arm and her eyes widened in fear.

'It's nothing,' he said gently, but as he said it, his eyes looked far away, through Doris and back to the No-Man's-Land where he had stood under a hail of bullets thinking of this moment, hoping for it. 'As long as you are here,' he said quietly, 'then everything's all right.'

Doris cupped his face in her hands. 'I'm glad it's like that.'

'It is,' said Klaus. 'I love you so much.'

'Us,' whispered Doris dreamily. 'It's us, now, darling.'

Klaus drew back shyly. 'Can I see him?' he asked.

The young woman laughed. 'He's beautiful, she said, 'but I'm sure you'll think he's very ugly. You see, he's still so small, and he's a bit crinkly.'

'He is the most beautiful baby in the home,' said a voice from the other bed.

Klaus looked round in surprise.

'I am Frau Kempe.'

Doris gave Klaus a tacit sign. He understood and fixed his eyes curiously on the stranger. The same direct manner, the same open friendliness as her husband, he thought. Klaus smiled and turned to Doris

'He's over the corridor,' she said. 'Right opposite. Second cot on the left.'

The cots were all behind a glass panel, but the nurse held up the baby for Klaus to see.

So you're the one, he thought wonderingly. The baby had Doris' forehead and her eyes. Suddenly it clenched its tiny fist and began to yell loudly. The nurse laid it back in its cradle, but Klaus had looked for long enough to realise that for his son he'd fight every battle, win every war.

Chapter Fourteen

The nurses and doctors were terrified of their visitor and recognising it, Westroff-Meyer behaved as patronisingly as the Führer himself at a baby show. As he marched down the parade of cradles, the sisters and the chief surgeon, Dr Jessrich followed at a decent distance.

What was amazing was that the General seemed to be oblivious of the fact that Nature had supplied in these babies the proof that she was not a Party member, and that on the whole, the babies had developed quite differently from the peas and chestnuts on his wall charts.

'How many babies have you here at the moment?' he asked Dr Jessrich.

'Sixty-seven,' answered the chief surgeon.

Westroff-Meyer nodded in satisfaction. Then he walked slowly on, lingering for a moment by a baby with dark, fluffy hair – well, the Führer's not so blond either, he thought. And by the next : even Rosenberg doesn't look too nordic I suppose.

In the office a snack was waiting, and the General ate it with the proper amount of enjoyment. Dr Jessrich offered champagne.

'Not at this time of day, thank you,' said Westroff-Meyer. 'I must say that I'm very satisfied with what I've seen of this home. I shall see that you are rewarded for your services.'

Dr Jessrich clicked his heels smartly together, although his heart was sinking.

The General sat down on the desk. 'I believe you have a Frau Steinbach here with you? Do you remember her?'

'Indeed I do, sir,' answered the chief surgeon. 'Hers was a

very difficult birth and it's a miracle that she and the child pulled through.'

'Well, I have special plans for her. You understand that you are to carry out all my orders without enquiring into the whys and wherefores of my decisions?'

I'm doing that every minute of the day here, thought Dr Jessrich. But he answered quickly: 'Yes, sir.'

Westroff-Meyer liked the feeling of power. Here comes the reckoning, he thought. He had waited a long time for his vengeance, but it had never been far from his mind. Because two young people had dared to defy him, he had to destroy them. And now he had the means of doing so. His boots would trample them just as easily, just as cruelly, as they had trampled the mutilated corpses of the Poles.

'I think I might just have that glass of champagne now, doctor.'

'At once, sir.'

Dr Jessrich went to the cupboard in his clean and gleaming consulting room and from amongst its sober and practical contents, he brought out a bottle, already chilled.

'So,' Westroff-Meyer went on, 'you know Frau Steinbach, do you?'

The doctor nodded stiffly.

The SS officer watched the golden liquid foaming into his glass and smiled contentedly. He raised the glass to his lips, but paused before drinking. 'The Steinbach baby is to be sent to a state home along with all the rest. Is that clear?'

Dr Jessrich was puzzled. 'But the baby's mother **is** married.'

Westroff-Meyer took a gulp of champagne and wiped his mouth with the back of his hand. His lips were thick and wet. 'I've told you what must be done with this baby. You will fill out the particulars of the usual forms and send duplicates to me. The General savoured the taste of his words and licked his lips.

The eyes of both men met. The doctor felt a chill run down his spine and his fingers tightened on the stem of his glass, spilling some of the champagne on to his white coat.

'And why is that, sir?' he asked in a brittle voice. 'Without adequate reasons I cannot effect the transfer. And then

I need permission from the Lebensborn HQ in Munich.'

'Reasons?' asked Westroff-Meyer, draining his glass. 'I will give you a reason, my dear doctor.' His eyes became hard and stony. 'The reason is that the parents of that baby are not true National Socialists!' He brought his fist down angrily on the table. 'They are enemies of the state, traitors – and they'll make a traitor of that child too if we don't stop them – Germany cannot afford to lose the support of her children. Do you understand now? Is the reason adequate for you?'

There was a froth of champagne on the General's mouth and his eyes were yellow with hatred.

The doctor's thoughts were in a turmoil. He steadied his hand to refill the glasses, as the white walls of his consulting room closed slowly in on him.

'I cannot do what you ask,' he said at last with hard finality.

Westroff-Meyer started with surprise, put off his guard for the moment by the determined set of the doctor's jaw.

'No?' he asked. 'You can't? Or you don't want to?'

'I am a doctor,' said Jessrich in a cold, hard voice. 'It is my job to cure suffering, not to cause it. What you wish me to do, sir, is nothing less than to abduct a child – and for that sort of offence you go to prison, even in Nazi Germany. If that wasn't so, I would not be wearing this uniform.'

Westroff-Meyer raised an eyebrow. 'Don't talk nonsense, Jessrich – what we're doing is not abducting the child – we're *saving* it. But we're not here to discuss morality. What I want to know is, whether you are going to carry out my orders or not?'

'Not this one,' said the doctor coolly.

'Would you prefer to work at the front?'

Dr Jessrich nodded to himself slowly and thoughtfully. Now I'll pay for my impertinence, he thought.

'Yes,' he said quietly, 'I should prefer to be sent to the front. And I should rather go today than tomorrow.'

'In that case I will find a suitable post for you immediately,' barked Westroff-Meyer.

When he had gone, Dr Jessrich didn't move for a long time. Then he pulled off his white coat and dropped it to the floor.

It was over.

But there was one more thing to be seen to before he left.

* * *

On the day Erika began her job in Berlin, Westroff-Meyer was away on business. Ruth let her in with a mixture of sullenness and indifference.

'I'm to show you the way we work here,' said Ruth. 'You'll be in this room with me.' Her voice told Erika in no uncertain terms that she barely tolerated Westroff-Meyer's new arrangements.

Erika went to her desk. There were new things to get used to here like in any other office job. There was a list of abbreviations to be learned, for example. You wouldn't get quite these words in any other office, though, thought Erika. 'Ill' for illegitimate, how ironic.

'When the boss is away,' explained Ruth, 'we work on the backlog of material that has collected and bring everything up to date.'

Erika nodded.

'These envelopes have been hanging around for God knows how long – all you have to do is type the addresses on them – you'll get them from the letter headings inside.'

'O.K.' said Erika.

She took out one of the stencilled letters and read the text: 'We acknowledge your letter of the . . . but under the circumstances we regret that we are unable to give you any information at the present. Heil Hitler.'

Erika put the letter back into its pile. She'd have opportunity enough to be horrified and amazed at this place.

Ruth stole a covert glance at her intended rival and swallowed hard. She saw the expensive pullover, the well-cut skirt, the bright eyes, the dimpled cheeks. She bit her lip and bent over her typewriter, knowing exactly how her boss was going to react to these attractions.

Erika threaded envelopes in and out of her typewriter, tapped out the addresses and stacked them in a neat pile. Those that had been underneath were now on top – that was the only variety in this job, but she set to work as hard as she had once done in the munitions factory. There she had been working with grenades and cartridges, fuses and driving bands. And here?

She picked up a letter and read it. It was from a girl who had been sent to one of the Lebensborn homes like the one in Warthegau that Erika had been in. She'd had a child and lost touch with its father. The girl had fulfilled her side of the bargain and now the poor soul sent up her helpless plea:

'Could you make an exception in this particular case . . . although I am not married, I do so much want to have my child with me. I don't even know where she is . . . I was much too young to understand what it meant to give birth to a child and then to give it up. Please, I beg you to help me!'

From now on, Erika picked up the letters as though they were so many sheets of lead. She hardly dared read any more of them. She looked across at Ruth's indifferent face and shuddered to think that she might become just as blasé or uncaring.

At midday they went to the canteen to eat. They told jokes over lunch and laughed. Ruth was making eyes at every officer in sight.

Erika ate quickly and escaped back to the office, where she started sorting papers, reading names. Suddenly she froze in her seat at the sight of a familiar name: 'Klaus Steinbach, son of Doris Steinbach, née Korff – to be sent to an institution.'

The paper trembled in Erika's hand and just then Ruth walked in and hissed at her: 'How did that get on to your desk? That's a secret document!'

'Secret?' repeated Erika vaguely.

She had already made up her mind to give in her notice, but now she knew she had to stay, because of Doris.

* * *

Doris had gained strength quickly and she and the tiny Klaus were flourishing. Her beauty had mellowed with her deepening love. A tender smile hovered upon her lips as she lay back in the soft pillows, relaxed and happy, dreaming of the time when she would take the baby home.

Three times a day little Klaus was brought to her and she talked to him as though he could already understand what she was saying. And then sometimes in the afternoon, Klaus and Kempe came on a visit and the four of them would enjoy an hour or so of conversation, dreaming of what they would do when the war was ended.

Kempe was the first to have to go back. He took leave of his wife with the stolid fatalism of the front soldier. Everyone in Germany had learned by now how to say good-bye, with the knowledge that it didn't necessarily mean 'auf wiedersehen'.

Horste Kempe shook his wife by the hand and said, 'Good luck, Grete.' And off he went as if he were going no farther than a day trip in the country.

It was harder for Klaus. He stood looking out of the window and said : 'Soon I'll be getting my sick leave and we can use that time to get our flat set up.'

He turned and looked at his son. It was amazing to him how this baby had so quickly and inevitably become part of their lives. He'd always thought he'd be hopeless as a father, but this baby with the great round eyes made it seem natural, somehow.

Klaus Steinbach had left without looking back.

And now Doris was waiting to be sent home. Another doctor was looking after her by now – Dr Jessrich was still in the house but no longer practising. Rumour had it that he was going to be sent to the front as a punishment for some offence or other.

Doris and Grete Kempe were still talking softly to one another one night after lights out when they heard footsteps outside their door. It was Dr Jessrich.

He stood outside the door and knocked cautiously, looking round to make sure that he was unobserved. His heart had been in his mouth since Westroff-Meyer's visit, but soon he would be at the front, and the awful weight of guilt that he bore could be atoned for. At the moment, he was more afraid of what awaited him inside this room than of anything that he could meet at the front.

He went in and switched on the light. Frau Kempe raised

herself up on one elbow and said : 'What's wrong, doctor?'

'Excuse me for disturbing you at this late hour – '

The look on his face had frightened Doris and she waited for him to go on.

'Listen, Frau Kempe,' the doctor began, 'what I have to say concerns only Frau Steinbach and it could be fatal for me if – '

'I'm already asleep,' said Frau Kempe, turning over and pulling the sheet over her head.

'Is it – the baby?' asked Doris fearfully.

'Yes,' said Dr Jessrich, 'but it's not what you're thinking. He's a fine, healthy child.'

He sat down on Doris' bed. She tried to sit up, but he pushed her gently back on to the pillows. His smile had frozen on his face.

'Please be still and listen.'

She searched his face. 'Is it my husband?'

'No,' answered the doctor and added quickly, 'Please trust me, Frau Steinbach.'

Doris nodded. Her eyes were wide and dark.

'I'm not here as a doctor,' he said hastily. 'Just as a person who wants to help you.'

'What is it?' Doris asked, her voice trembling.

'Please stay calm. I must warn you . . .'

'Warn?'

'Yes,' said the doctor. This was even more difficult than he had feared.

'Against what?'

Dr Jessrich's eyes were rooted to the floor. 'They want to take your baby away from you and put it into an institution. I was to sign the transfer form. I refused, but . .'

His words dropped into a chasm that was engulfing Doris. 'Please,' she begged brokenly, 'tell me everything, doctor.'

'Recently we had a visit from someone high up in the SS called General Westroff-Meyer,' began the doctor.

And now everything fell into place. The bedclothes under which Doris lay rose and fell with her sobbing and the doctor gently stroked her hair until the young woman became calm, felt the strength flooding back into her body and along with it, the ability to think clearly and fast.

'What are you going to do?' asked Dr Jessrich.

'I'll go away tomorrow, with my baby . . .'

'Yes,' said the doctor.

'I shan't let them take him from me,' said Doris quietly.

'Then I wish you luck,' said Dr Jessrich. Doris gave him her hand. 'Do it quickly, Frau Steinbach.'

He stood up, was half-way to the door, when Grete Kempe sat up. 'I wasn't asleep, doctor. For Christ's sake, I wasn't asleep! That – what you said, *that's* what we're fighting for? *That's* why my husband has to risk his life every day – so that people have to run away to keep their own children?'

The doctor nodded.

Frau Kempe got up and went and sat on Doris' bed. 'I shall help you,' she said. 'You can count on me.'

* * *

The last hour passed feverishly for Doris. She waited until midday. At one the nurses went to eat. Frau Kempe had asked for a deck chair in the garden, where she was sitting keeping watch.

Doris got dressed secretly. A couple of times she had to sit down on the bed to rest – she was weaker than she had thought. She could feel her knees giving way underneath her weight and her scar was hurting her. But what did the pain matter compared to the fear of losing her baby?

At nine in the morning they had brought little Klaus to her and she had whispered a thousand promises in his ear and he'd gurgled back as if he'd understood.

Doris couldn't help crying when they took the baby back. She had to turn away so that the nurse didn't notice her tears.

Now she looked at her watch, gingerly practised a few steps forward and decided that she'd better leave her baggage behind. She'd have to carry the baby, so she'd take only the bare essentials with her. I wish Klaus knew what was happening, she thought, but I'll send him a telegram when we've got away safely.

At five past one, Doris crept across the corridor to the

babies' ward. The gong had rung for lunch. She managed to put one foot in front of the other, but the walk seemed endless.

Suddenly a fearful scream rent the midday peace of the house, so that the patients jumped from their deck chairs and the nurses from their lunch table.

They found Doris collapsed by her baby's bed – by the only empty cradle in the ward. She clung fiercely to the nurse who tried to help her to her feet. Her face was a pallid mask. Over and over again, she screamed the same words: 'Where is my baby? Tell me where my baby is! You've stolen my baby – tell me where he is!'

She went on yelling and screaming until her face was red and wet with tears of rage. The nurses stared at the floor in embarrassment and confusion while the matron tried to bring the situation under control and comfort the hysterical girl. 'Please calm yourself,' she urged. 'Everything will sort itself out.'

Doris took a deep breath and then thrashed out with all her might. The nurses shrieked and threw themselves on her, but it took three or four of them a long time before they could hold her down.

Then they dragged her down the corridor and bound her to a stretcher in the doctor's room. Her face was waxen. The matron got on the telephone and made call after call while three nurses were detailed to watch over the exhausted young woman whom they had forced into submission. One of them kept mumbling monotonously: 'Your baby is all right – he's all right – everything's all right.'

Eventually the assistant chief surgeon arrived. A syringe glistened in his hand. The tranquilliser flowed through Doris' veins and lulled her to an icy sleep.

And then the roaring in her ears became glimpses of light again. It was daytime and she was awake.

'I – I'd like to speak to Dr Jessrich,' she said.

'I'm afraid he's no longer here,' answered his assistant. 'For the time being I have taken over from him.' He knew the price he would have to pay for his new position.

Doris pressed her hand against her forehead, sat up slowly and looked at him long and hard. 'I understand,' she said icily, and lay back on her pillows. When he had gone and left her alone, she sat up again and swung her legs on to the floor. She stood up slowly and carefully, supporting herself on the iron rail at the foot of the bed. Her heart racing, she took a few steps to the french window and looked out. There was no one about. She tried the handle – the door was unlocked.

She took this as a sign and, pulling her shawl tightly about her shoulders, she stepped out into the grounds. If she got to the village she would send a telegram, then go to the police.

* * *

When Klaus had left Doris in the maternity home, he'd had to report straight to a specialist hospital, where he was asked to stay a couple of days for tests on his arm. Soon after his arrival the head doctor took him on one side and removed the bandage. He looked at the wound thoughtfully and shook his head.

'I suppose you must be pretty important?'

'Important?' said Klaus with surprise, 'whatever makes you say that?'

'Your unit has been asking for you.'

Klaus raised his eyebrows questioningly.

'I know that your arm's not healed up by a long way yet – but they want you to go back and serve somewhere in the interior.'

'In the interior?'

'It's all very hush-hush,' said the doctor and shrugged his shoulders. 'And then there's the sick leave you're entitled to – you'll be wanting to take that, of course.'

'Yes, of course.'

'Well, I won't send you back against your own wishes.'

'Has the Commodore himself been asking for me?'

The doctor nodded. Klaus didn't hesitate. It must be something special, he thought. They must need me. The idea sent a glow of pride coursing through his veins.

Two orderlies from the hospital staff helped him pack his bags. His marching papers had already been signed. Suddenly the urgency of it all worried him. What was it that they wanted him for?

Klaus had already left the vast building when a subaltern ran after him and called: 'Just a moment, captain – this has just arrived for you!' He handed him an envelope. Klaus ripped it open and the words danced before his eyes as he read: 'Westroff-Meyer has taken our baby. I have reported him to the police. Doris.'

* * *

Doris went into the detective superintendent's office and he looked up reluctantly from his newspaper. When he saw his visitor was a young lady, he smiled, introduced himself, and offered her a chair.

'My name is Steinbach,' began Doris, 'and I would like to bring a charge against someone.'

'Who would that be?' asked the police chief, settling back comfortably into his chair.

'SS General Westroff-Meyer,' said Doris, looking steadily into his shocked eyes.

'A – and what for?'

'For kidnapping.'

Worriedly, the policeman lit a cigarette. 'Would you like to tell me about it?' he muttered.

Doris told him. Her lips were dry and her tongue was heavy, but she spoke calmly and distinctly, staring all the while at a stain on the floor. The policeman fidgeted with his tie.

'Lebensborn, you say?'

Doris nodded.

'And that's where you had your baby?'

'Yes.'

'In that case, can you still call it kidnapping?'

Doris was silent for a moment. She forced all the bitterness out of her voice and said with a calm she didn't feel: 'What else would you call it when someone takes a child away from its mother, superintendent?'

'Hmm,' said the policeman. 'We'll have to make a thorough investigation to establish the facts first, of course.

What I'll do for the time being is take a statement from you and then – '

'Listen,' said Doris firmly, 'I want my baby back and a warrant for Westroff-Meyer's arrest.'

The policeman looked thoughtful. 'It's not in my power to draw up a warrant for arrest,' he said cautiously.

'Whose job is that then?'

'The magistrate's.'

'Then I'd like to go and see him.'

'Yes, that would be the best,' said the superintendent with obvious relief.

He stood up and gave Doris his hand. 'The magistrate is here in this building,' he said. 'I'll take you to his office.' When he had left Doris with the magistrate, he picked up the phone and called Berlin.

The magistrate listened to Doris in silence, then cleared his throat somewhat nervously and looked past the young woman towards the grey-painted wall on which hung the inscription: 'Jesus is the servant of the people.'

'Hmm,' he said. 'Lebensborn. Isn't that a political organisation?'

'It's that too,' said Doris calmly.

'What I mean is, doesn't that make it exempt in some ways?'

Doris shook her head. 'Even there, mothers are allowed to take their children with them if they wish to.'

'Yes, but I don't quite understand . . .'

'It seems quite clear to me,' said Doris. 'There is no law which allows anyone to take a baby from its mother. General Westroff-Meyer has taken my baby from me.' Doris looked up and forced the magistrate to meet her eyes.

He glanced covertly at the telephone. He knew that the HQ in Berlin would make the decision for him. Legally, the case was absolutely clear, like so many others. But should he risk his career, his reputation as a fair-minded man, his family and his pension by making what would probably be a vain attempt to help a mother in distress?

'I'm sorry,' he said in a thin, dry voice, 'I don't think I quite follow you. Most likely it's all a mistake and your baby will be returned to you in due course.'

Doris held her tongue.

'What you describe couldn't possibly happen in this State. You know that mothers have the full protection of the Nazi movement? You haven't done anything wrong, have you? You're Aryan, aren't you?'

Doris nodded. 'Yes, I'm Aryan.'

'And your family too? Your husband is of good German stock?'

'My husband is an officer.'

'Well,' said the magistrate, 'this really is a most odd affair.'

He stood up. 'I'll do what I can for you,' he murmured. He called his clerk and told him to prepare a report. First he dictated the particulars of all the people concerned, going into them with an irritating attention to detail. Then he began to formulate the charge. Here again he was painstakingly careful. He didn't get very far before the telephone interrupted him.

The magistrate leaped to answer it. 'Yes, sir, certainly! Exactly what you say – I'll do it immediately, you can rely on me. Heil Hitler!'

He put down the receiver and stood looking down into the street below. The clerk was chewing boredly at his nails. Slowly the judge turned round.

'You can go now,' he said to the clerk.

He fought with his shame, as he'd had to do so often before. It was the most noble sentiment left to him, but he was determined to conquer it. Looking at the well-polished floor he said : 'I'm sorry, Frau Steinbach, but it is my duty to tell you that you are under arrest.'

Chapter Fifteen

Klaus never knew how he made the journey back to his squadron in that military train. At first he'd sat stiffly and numbly in the corner of his compartment, and though the jerking and jolting of the train was causing his injured arm considerable pain, he never felt it. The wound no longer burned his flesh, it went much deeper than that – it was devouring his soul, eating away at his heart, weakening his powers of thought, tearing at his whole being with the rhythm of the train: 'They've taken your baby away.'

Then he came to himself again and got out at the next station to look for a telephone. The operator tried her hardest, but night had fallen over Germany and enemy planes had brought down the wires – it was impossible to get through to Doris. He dashed back to the train and tried at the next station. It was the same story – all night long.

Eventually he made it to his squadron and reported his arrival. The adjutant shook his hand. 'For god's sake, Steinbach, what sort of a mess are you in? You're in no state to start flying again yet; you'll have to take your sick leave immediately after this.'

'After what?' asked Klaus, bewildered.

The adjutant smiled. 'Congratulations,' he said.

Klaus shrugged his shoulders and shook his head to clear it of all this nonsense. The only thing he understood was that his son had been taken away.

'I have to speak to the Commodore straight away,' he said.

'Well, he's not available at the moment, but you'll be able to see him afterwards,' answered the adjutant. 'The squadron will be here in half an hour. The general's coming over for an inspection.'

Klaus walked off towards the barracks.

'Don't forget to change into your parade uniform!' the adjutant shouted after him.

A whistle shrilled out across the air base. The squadron was lined up for inspection, amongst them Klaus, present in body, although his thoughts were far away.

Then the rigmarole began. Shining steel helmets, harsh voices, whirling dust. The Commodore welcomed the General, his greatcoat flapping importantly in the wind. And suddenly Klaus realised what was going to happen – he understood the reason for the smiling faces and the premature congratulations. The Knight's Cross!

This was what he had believed in – what he had dreamed of – for this he had risked his life and entire units had perished in enemy fire with this thought in their minds – it made men forget their instinct for self-preservation – it whipped them towards certain death in the enemy trenches.

Klaus felt the earth turning underneath his feet. I have exchanged gold for iron, he thought. Given up my child for a medal. Empty, meaningless words droned in his head, gathered to a roaring crescendo. There was nothing left – no joy, no pride – this moment was blank, as was his future.

'Heil Hitler!' cried the General.

'Heil Hitler, Herr General,' came the response.

Klaus' voice did not join the chorus. As though from behind a wall of ice, he watched the General striding towards the ranks. He heard his name being called. He felt his neighbour's elbow in his ribs. He began to walk forwards, the envious eyes of his comrades boring into his retreating back.

The adjutant stood next to the General holding a small box in his hand. The General was tall, with technicolor blue eyes that made him look as though he'd just stepped out of a propaganda film.

'Captain Steinbach,' he said loudly, 'In recognition of your success . . .'

Klaus' arms hung limply at his side, his damp fingers touching the coarse stuff of his uniform. The strap of his steel helmet was strangling him.

' . . . the Führer has decided to bestow upon you the Knight's Cross,' bawled the General.

A murmur ran through the ranks. Klaus looked fixedly at the General's moustache while he took the box from the adjutant's hand. The Knight's Cross lay gleaming on its silken cushion. It swung towards him, dangling on its ribbon from the General's fingers.

Klaus bent his head to receive the order. Now the ribbon was round his neck, rubbing against his skin. A millstone. A chain with a leaden weight at the end of it.

He turned to go back to his place and saw the eyes of his comrades alight with envy or pride. But there were other eyes, other comrades, now beneath the ground. They were the real survivors – they had fought, paid the price and atoned for their guilt. They were the lucky ones. For a moment, Klaus found himself envying his dead comrades.

'Permission to report to the General,' said Klaus, but the General's eyes were already on the next man who was to be decorated. 'Report to me in ten minutes,' he barked.

In the meantime Klaus listened with deaf ears as the congratulations of his comrades flowed around him. A publicity man took his photograph, and the public would see the face of a lost man, his eyes watchful and sunken in their sockets, a faraway, unreal expression on his face.

The General had come back and tapped him good-naturedly on the shoulder. 'You're an odd fellow, Steinbach – aren't you pleased?'

'Yes, sir,' answered Klaus dully.

'Come and tell me what's on your mind.'

When they reached the barracks, Klaus said, 'I can't accept the Knight's Cross, sir'.

'Madness,' growled the General. Poor chap must be suffering from shell shock, he thought. 'Sit down and tell me about it.'

Klaus pulled the telegram out of his pocket and the General read it shaking his head.

'I'm sorry to hear it,' he muttered, 'but surely this has got nothing to do with your decoration?'

'On the contrary,' said Klaus firmly, and explained the background of the story.

The General looked up at him slowly as he listened, his eyes resting on the Knight's Cross. 'All right, Captain,' he said sharply when Klaus had finished. In the silence that followed he paced up and down the room. Perhaps he was thinking of Berendsen, the Commodore who had ended his life because he could bring himself to fight for the cause no longer. He'd never really understood what had happened, but now new light was dawning.

'I'll clear it up for you, Captain,' he said, 'you can count on me.'

'Thank you, sir.'

'I'll get in touch with the fellows at the SS today. I shall see to it that you are able to wear your Knight's Cross god-damnit!'

*　*　*

The young police inspector had come from Berlin. Neither his appearance nor his behaviour betrayed the fact that he belonged to the most feared department of the government of the Third Reich: Security HQ. On his jacket front were pinned the order of the Hitler Youth Movement in gold and the wounded soldier's medal in silver. His lips were thin and bloodless and his eyes strangely transparent.

He asked for Doris to be brought out of her cell: 'Frau Steinbach,' he began quietly, 'you could have saved both yourself and us this unpleasant experience.'

Doris was calm, even apathetic. Her face showed what she had gone through in the last forty-eight hours. In fact her guards had treated her well – it was her own thoughts that had tortured her.

'Your child has been claimed by the Reich,' the inspector went on. 'I admit that in your case the procedure is some-what unusual, but then you have only yourself to blame. The child will remain in a state institution until we have a guarantee from its parents that it will be brought up according to National Socialist principles. Is that understood?'

'But you can't ask me to do that.'

'We can do anything we choose to.'

Doris forced her hands into a gesture of supplication. 'Please, when can we have him back?'

'That is entirely up to you. As soon as you decide to reform, we will review the matter. We realise how hard the separation must be for you.'

Blackness swam before Doris' eyes and they filled with tears.

'Pull yourself together!' said the inspector. 'There is a way of recovering your son – it means obedience, loyalty and sacrifice.' Almost casually he added: 'I'm releasing you from detention. You will go back to your home town, but we won't lose sight of you. You must volunteer for war duty of some sort. If you don't . . .'

The young woman nodded. She had understood nothing. Klaus must help me, she thought confusedly. Only he will be able to do anything now.

'One more thing,' said the Security officer. 'Your case has been declared an official secret, therefore you will keep quiet about it – any indiscretion, whether accidental or wilful, would have the most severe consequences.'

Doris was free.

And alone. Infinitely alone . . .

* * *

The General kept his word. He set his people on to the personal staff of the Chief of the SS – on the phone, to save time – and a shocked adjutant had the query repeated to him three times before he could grasp what was being said. 'A mistake, quite definitely a mistake,' he spluttered.

And so the case was back in Berlin in the hands of the SS at the very time when General Westroff-Meyer was reporting there to his chief. His willingness to tackle any task, however distasteful, had brought him a long way in the eyes of the men at the top.

The expression on the field marshal's face was sleepily good-natured as he sat behind his enormous desk twiddling his pencil. 'Good, good, my dear Westroff-Meyer. I don't need to tell you how pleased I am with your work.'

'Thank you, sir,' said Westroff-Meyer.

'Do everything that should be done – yes, I can always rely on you.' He rummaged through his desk drawer. 'But you're a bit hot-headed at times, eh?' he asked from beneath his eyebrows.

'What do you mean, sir?'

'Well, you've overshot the mark on this one.' He waved a bit of paper vaguely in the General's face. 'I mean in this case about what's-his-name – Steinbach.'

'Ah, but –'

'Buts don't interest me. Steinbach has been decorated with the Knight's Cross.'

'That's a little plot cooked up by the Luftwaffe,' said Westroff-Meyer, incensed.

'That's as may be – but this young man seems to have shown remarkable valour in battle,' said the field marshal. 'We don't want any fuss with the Luftwaffe, understand?'

The general nodded his head.

'I've got the measure of those chaps,' he went on with a glint in his eye, 'and after the war –' he snapped his fingers and shut his drawer with a bang. 'But first we've got to win it!'

'So you have nothing as such against the steps I have taken, sir?' asked Westroff-Meyer cautiously.

'Why should I? I just don't want a scandal on my hands, that's all – no scandal at any price!'

The chief stood up. 'Well, my dear fellow, deal with this case as discreetly as you can and get the child back to its parents.'

'But the parents are enemies of the movement, they are traitors!'

The chief nodded thoughtfully. 'But Rome wasn't built in a day. We'll see to the Jews first – then we'll get round to the others. Don't be in such a hurry.'

'I'll see the affair's settled,' said Westroff-Meyer. Something had occurred to him. He smiled crookedly.

The field marshal smiled back. Here was a man after his own heart: obedient, but cunning. And ruthless . . .

He gave the general his hand. Westroff-Meyer clapped his heels together, but his thoughts were already busy elsewhere, planning a devious victory from what seemed like a plain defeat.

* * *

Despair became Doris' way of life. She lived in the half-darkness. In a matter of days the vibrant young woman had become a timid animal, living in fear of being struck down again at any moment. She wandered round their little flat, looking forlornly into the bedroom where her baby was to have slept, into the cupboard where the nappies and baby clothes were neatly stacked. The slightest noise in the house made her start and her heart pound with terror.

The League had released Doris without protest and she had been given a cool welcome back to her parents' house. She was bombarded with questions that she couldn't answer. She was unable to speak of her suffering and finally her family gave up asking. Doris' eyes were dry again, but only because there were no tears left to be shed. She withdrew into herself and lived as though within a shell. Mostly the blinds in her room were down. Even the light hurt her eyes.

Every moment cost her pain. Life was passing her by – a parade of figures and images that were misty and unsubstantial. Even Klaus seemed unreal – she knew that he had received the Knight's Cross and that his sick leave was due, but it seemed impossible that he might be coming through the door at any moment.

When the doorbell rang, the sound called forth no emotion in Doris. She walked dejectedly down the hall of the little flat that he hadn't yet seen. This could have been so different, she thought, and tears sprang again to her eyes.

She opened the door to three people – mere shadows in the half-darkness of the staircase.

Doris started with fear. 'What can I do for you?'

And then she recognised the uniform of the police. The second – a man – wore civilian clothes, and the third person was a woman – a nurse.

'Are you Frau Steinbach?' asked the plain clothes man.

Doris nodded, but her eyes were drawn compulsively towards the nurse, who was carrying a bundle in her arms, wrapped up in a blanket. Suddenly Doris' pulse began to race.

'I'm from Party HQ,' explained the man. 'May we come in for a moment?'

'Yes,' said Doris, supporting herself against the door frame. The nurse was the last of the three to step inside.

'We have a surprise for you,' said the plain clothes man smiling. He unfolded a letter.

' "It is my duty on behalf of the Party to return to you the child known as Klaus – " '

Doris heard no more. She let out a cry of joy and held her arms out for the baby, her whole body trembling. She pressed the bundle to her heart, buried her face in its blankets, laughing and weeping. The nurse quickly pushed forward a chair for her.

'You must sign here,' the policeman was saying, embarrassed at the show of emotion. Doris nodded, but her eyes and her ears were only for the baby. The nurse put out her hands to take the child while she signed.

'No!' cried Doris, drawing back instinctively. She wasn't going to let him out of her arms ever again.

'But Frau Steinbach!' protested the man from HQ. What on earth has got into her? he wondered. Why didn't she take the baby with her when she left the home, if she feels like this? Must be off her rocker.

Doris asked nothing, said nothing. She didn't want to know what miracle had brought her son back to her – she knew only one thing – he was back in her arms, and she would never let him go again.

As she signed her name, the small print swam underneath her eyes. She signed to say that she was in receipt of her child in accordance with Party wishes. She testified that it was her own. Even mother-love could not be confirmed without the correct bureaucratic procedure. But the immensity of her joy allowed her no room for other feelings. She didn't think to ask why her baby had suddenly been returned.

With tenderness and the utmost care, she cupped the tiny face on the pillow with both hands. The baby was grizzling.

I must change his nappy straight away, thought the young mother.

The men had carried out their mission and were eager to be off. At last she was alone. With a miracle – her baby, who had been lost and was found again.

One day is enough to bathe a grey life in radiant happiness. She undressed the baby and laid him in his little cot. Every so often she had to sit down, overcome by dreadful fears that something must be wrong.

Had something happened to him? Was he quite healthy? Not too thin? Why didn't he cry more?

A hundred times she crept to the cradle when the child was asleep and tried to remember how he was in the first weeks of his life. Was his hair that fair? Why, of course – his hair must have grown since then, and his lips, too – they had filled out quite a bit. He was growing and changing all the time. His nose didn't look quite as straight as before. A hundred doubts became a hundred certainties. Up and down she walked, backwards and forwards, her heart pounding violently.

In the evening Klaus arrived to find her distraught and weeping at the side of the cot. It was too much for her. Too much happiness. First the child – then her husband. Imprisonment, then release – she was alive again.

They clung to each other, and when Klaus had kissed away her tears and told her the story behind the baby's return, they stood together in silence, looking down at the sleeping form of their little son.

'He has grown,' said Doris, breaking in on Klaus' thoughts.

'Of course,' Klaus smiled. 'Children grow very quickly in the first weeks, we read that, don't you remember?'

Doris shut her eyes. 'Oh, God,' she whispered, hiding her face against Klaus' shoulder. She suddenly felt so relieved and happy. 'I'm so thankful,' she said quietly.

Four weeks together – just the three of them. Four weeks without worries, fear or pain, just as they had always imagined.

* * *

Erika knew that her boss was back today, but nevertheless she started when she heard his footsteps echoing in the empty corridor outside and bent determinedly over her typewriter.

He tore open the door and a smile cracked his face at the sight of his shapely blonde secretary.

'Working so late?' he chuckled.

'I've got a lot of catching up to do,' explained Erika, without looking up.

'Glad to see you're taking the job seriously.' Westroff-Meyer offered her a cigarette and Erika inhaled deeply on it.

'Do you like it here with us?'

'Like it?' said Erika. 'I'm here to work.'

The General laughed and a gleam appeared in his eye as he remembered his plans for this evening. Erika saw it and an unpleasant shiver ran down her spine.

'I'm very pleased to see you working,' said Westroff-Meyer, 'but you can't carry on non-stop. I think it's about time that we – you and I – got to know each other a bit better.'

Erika nodded. This was what she had expected. He took the typewriter cover and threw it with a flourish over Erika's machine. Then he got out the schnapps.

'Would you like some?'

'Why not?'

He poured out two generous measures and knocked his glass against Erika's, sending a jet of the golden liquid splashing over her hand.

'Can you dance, Erika?'

'I don't know. I think I must be a bit rusty, it's so long since I tried.'

'Well, let's see, shall we?'

'But it's wartime,' said Erika hesitantly.

'Pooh! There's a little place I know where you can do all sorts of things nobody does in wartime,' said Westroff-Meyer.

'A place frequented by the cream of society, no doubt,' said Erika tartly.

The general nodded and tapped himself proudly on the chest. He picked up the telephone and called for his driver who took them to the side entrance of a luxury hotel, reserved for the favourites of the regime, dignitaries who were too good for the heroic death they preached to others.

The head waiter came to meet them, and bowing low, ushered them into an intimate corner.

'Champagne!' called Westroff-Meyer impatiently.

After the second bottle of champagne and a couple of dances in a little room off to their left, the General leaned across to Erika and asked if they might not call each other by their first names.

' . . . of course when we're back in the office we'll be formal again.'

His arm reached out and slid round her back. At his touch Erika felt a whiplash of revulsion. Then his fleshy lips told her of the treasures he had plumbed from Poland and which could be hers.

'The officers at Warthegau weren't for you, my dear, you need a touch of class, someone with rank and position.

He thought for a moment. 'Talking of Warthegau, weren't you in the same batch as a girl called Doris?'

'Doris Steinbach?' offered Erika, suddenly concentrating.

'Yes, that's the one,' said Westroff-Meyer lightly. 'You'll be glad to know I've ruined her for her impertinence. I won't be crossed, you know. I've had my revenge.' He reached for his glass and drank to his personal victory.

'But she's got her baby back,' said Erika, puzzled.

'Is that so?' chuckled Westroff-Meyer. 'She's got her baby back, has she?' And he threw back his head and laughed. 'You know me very badly, my dear. Very badly indeed, if you think that some fool from the Luftwaffe can order me around!'

He hotched nearer to Erika, but she was no longer aware of his hand on her shoulder.

'What do you mean?' she asked.

'She certainly got a baby back,' hissed the general. He put his mouth to Erika's ear. 'And do you know what sort of a one it was?'

Erika shut her eyes.

'I gave her a Polish brat – just think – a dirty, stinking Pole!'

Erika took a deep breath. 'And the right baby?' she asked, her voice hardly more than a whisper.

'It's in one of our institutions, of course – and Steinbach doesn't have a clue about it! Not a bloody clue!' His arm claimed the shocked and trembling girl. Erika stared into her glass and tried to collect her thoughts.

'Are you tiddly yet?'

'No.'

'Waiter! Another bottle! We'll have a few more drinks, then go back to my place,' he whispered.

But Erika didn't hear him. She came to herself only when the sirens began to wail.

Suddenly all Westroff-Meyer's enthusiasm for the evening's adventure drained away as he made quickly for the cellar.

Never had the unnerving night song of the sirens sounded so sweet in Erika's ears.

Chapter Sixteen

Shortly before Klaus was due to return to the front, he was examined at the local hospital. Dr Jäger shook his head.

'There isn't *much* wrong with your arm,' he said. Klaus looked at him questioningly.

'Well, I'm not altogether happy with it, but there's nothing a little electro-massage won't put right.'

Klaus nodded.

'Of course, there's no question of flying at present. Are you very eager to get back?'

'No,' said Klaus honestly.

'Well, then,' said Dr Jäger, 'you'll have to be treated as an outpatient, and we can do the job here as well as anyone else, so I'll sign you on.'

'Thank you, doctor.'

Dr Jäger was already attending to his next patient when he turned back and said quietly: 'Remember me to your father.'

Only when Klaus got outside did he see the connection: his father, the doctor, his arm, the extended leave . . . He walked on quickly. So there are still decent people about, people who aren't twisted or bitter, he thought to himself. He had his baby, he had his wife, and the war was granting him a breathing space in the paradise of his two-roomed flat.

'Doris,' he called the moment he got home, 'the doctor says I can stay!'

'Yes? That's wonderful.' Doris smiled up at him, but there was a touch of sadness in her expression.

'What is it?' he asked puzzled.

'It's nothing.' Doris put her finger to her lips. 'Shh! I've just put the baby to bed.'

It was a little while before Doris could bring herself to speak. 'Klaus, you know that the birth was a difficult one ...'

'Yes?'

'Well, I – I was at the doctor's today, too.' Her face was suddenly very serious. 'I've got something to tell you.'

Klaus's blood ran cold. 'What is it?' he asked numbly.

'We'll never be able to have any more children.'

'Doris!' Klaus smiled with relief and drew her into his arms. 'I couldn't be happier if I had six children, you silly goose.'

The treatment at the hospital still had eight weeks to go, and in the meantime, Klaus' unit was split up and divided between other squadrons. The more hopeless the situation in the air became, the more the Luftwaffe shuffled round its men. The bomber squadrons had discovered a new weapon: they hunted at night using two-engined machines from a base inside Germany. They took off after dark with the help of searchlights and were guided by radio. But their number was pitifully small, and never increased.

Klaus didn't hesitate when he was asked to take up active service again.

After a couple of weeks' training for night flying he was stationed in the neighbourhood of Berlin, and from then on the young officer fought his war from at home, for Doris and the baby went with him.

* * *

For the first time in her life, Erika found herself in a situation she didn't know how to deal with. Her first impulse was to go to Doris and reveal Westroff-Meyer's monstrous deception. But then she thought better of it. Even if Doris knew she had another child in place of her own she wouldn't be able to do anything about it. A battle was waging in Erika's mind between her courage and her conscience. But as often as she made up her mind, she rejected the decision and her own fears kept her from acting. She was burdened with a responsibility she had never asked for – the fate of another's child lay in her hands.

Eventually she realised that she couldn't make the decision herself. There was only one person to whom she could entrust that responsibility : the baby's father. The risk that she herself would be taking in revealing an official secret seemed small to Erika compared with this simple human duty.

Secretly she found out where Klaus was stationed, feeling horrified that he was so close and that she would be rid of her burden after a thirty-minute journey. On the day that she had set for herself she caught a bus to the barracks. Despite her determination, a shiver of apprehension ran through her as she spoke Klaus' name to the guard on duty.

After a couple of minutes, the tall young captain came striding towards her, whistling as if he didn't have a care in the world. 'Well, it's you,' he called from a distance. 'What a surprise! Did you know that Doris is in Berlin too? Where are you living these days?'

Erika swallowed. So Doris was here too. 'Oh, I'm in Berlin. Working,' she said vaguely.

'Where's that?'

'Just an office.'

Klaus could see that there was something the matter and suggested a cup of coffee. 'You ought to see the baby,' he said cheerfully as they walked to the nearest café.

Oh, God, thought Erika, this is worse than I ever expected. She sat down at the small formica topped table and fumbled for her powder compact, noticing to her horror that her hand was trembling. Her quivering reflection threw frightened, unnaturally large eyes back up at her.

'Tell me what's wrong,' said Klaus. 'Are you in trouble?'

Erika nodded and looked round desperately. 'Klaus,' she began urgently, 'it's not my trouble – it's yours – and Doris'.'

He pushed the coffee cup away. His face was tense. He nodded.

'You see, I've been sent to work for the SS. For Westroff-Meyer.'

'I see,' said Klaus quietly. A shadow fell across his face.

'I can't help it –'

'Please, Erika, just tell me what's on your mind,' said Klaus gently.

'Oh, God,' whispered Erika and hung her head. She sighed deeply and looked up into Klaus' troubled face.

'You must know – I can't keep this to myself any longer, but what I'm going to tell you will upset you greatly, and you must consider what will happen to Doris and the baby – to yourself too – before you act on it. Maybe after the war there will be a chance to put things right.'

Erika paused. 'The baby that was given back to you – it isn't your own.'

Klaus sat bolt upright and gripped the table firmly. And Erika went on to tell all she knew. Eternities passed for her as Klaus' face expressed his misery and defeat. He said not a word, only nodded to himself slowly, doggedly, as if to establish the hopelessness of his life.

'Doris must know nothing,' said Erika. 'She must never know. I know where your baby is and I will keep an eye on him. I shall never let him out of my sight. Please understand me Klaus, it is for the best.' She looked up and saw an expressionless mask.

'I – I'll tell you everything I find out about the baby but must promise not to do anything. There's no sense in it. You shouldn't even know this much.'

'Yes,' said Klaus after an endless pause. Slowly he came to, like someone who has suffered a bad fall and takes the first few painful steps.

He stood up and together they walked to the bus stop. He wanted to thank Erika, but no words came. Erika's lip was trembling, but she dug her nails into the palm of her hand and tried to remain firm.

Long after she got into the bus she could feel Klaus' hand stroking her hair and his words: 'Don't cry, Erika,' he kept saying. 'Don't cry.'

Klaus was off duty now and could have gone straight home to Doris, but instead he lay on his bunk and stared at the ceiling. At last he telephoned her. The receiver was as heavy as lead in his hand.

'I'm sorry,' he said, 'but I have to stay here. We're on alert.'

The lie was better than the truth. Anything was better than that. He was afraid that he would give way in front of Doris. He was afraid of seeing his baby again. *His* baby?

He laughed bitterly. But it wasn't the baby's fault. He wouldn't treat it any differently. It would never know. Nobody need ever know. One day he would be able to get the baby back. The two children would grow up together, like brothers. But when?

Klaus could hide from Doris no longer. The journey home only lasted a couple of hours. She was there.

'I was so afraid,' she said.

He stroked her hair sadly and she looked into his eyes.

'It's much worse now that you're in Berlin. Every time there's an alarm, I go mad with fear.'

'But Doris,' protested Klaus gently, 'you know I haven't been up yet. I'm still training in the new plane.'

'How much longer will it last?'

Klaus drew a deep breath. 'You know that you must go away soon, Doris,' he said, 'to Bavaria or the Tyrol – and that if you don't, I'll have to transport you there myself.' His voice was tired, strained.

Doris merely caught hold of his arm and pulled him towards the nursery and the moment that Klaus had feared so much was upon him. He stood before the cradle like a stranger, the effort to conceal his feelings only making him the more awkward.

'Look at this,' said Doris smiling. 'He's learned to grip already.'

The tiny arms waved in the air and the little fingers curled tightly around the rattle Doris held out to him.

'Very good,' said Klaus mechanically. He went to the window and looked unseeingly out at the street.

Doris bent over the baby holding the rattle again. 'Please come and look,' she begged.

Klaus didn't turn round.

'When he laughs, he's got your mouth.'

Klaus looked sharply over his shoulder. Doris was kneeling at the cot smiling up at him. 'Don't you think so?'

'Perhaps,' said Klaus distractedly.

173

Slowly Doris rose, looking searchingly at her husband's face.

'Is something the matter?' she asked.

'No.' The word hovered uncertainly in the air. Lying was something Klaus had yet to learn.

'You're not much good at being a father,' teased Doris affectionately.

'I – I think I'd better have a drink,' said Klaus quickly. 'Have we got any schnapps in the house?'

It's not fair of me to tease him when he's so worn out, thought Doris, noticing the lines of tension on his face. She went to him and put her arm round his shoulders. 'I only want you to be able to enjoy your baby too.'

'Oh, but I do,' answered Klaus vehemently, pressing his hands against his temples. He went to the sideboard and got out the schnapps, poured himself a glass and knocked it back. Doris noticed how his hand shook. His face looked strangely old.

A shiver of fear ran down her spine – she didn't know why.

*　*　*

The plane thundered on through the night. Klaus' eyes were riveted to the instrument panel, his headphones clamped firmly over his ears. A strange bluish light flickered through the fuselage of the Ju 288. Night flying was like going down one long black tunnel – you could only escape it by reaching the enemy. Today at 22.35 the enemy was two allied bomber squadrons flying towards Berlin.

Klaus' lips were thin with concentration. His thoughts were with Doris, who had been evacuated to Bavaria with the child that was fated to be theirs. Since their departure Klaus had felt a great sense of release. For one thing, he knew Doris to be out of the danger zone likely to be hit during air raids, and for another, he could give up this hideous pretence which made being together a strain and every word and gesture a falsehood.

Klaus tuned the receiver, idly watching the needle move across the waveband. Suddenly he bent forward and listened

174

intently. The receiver began to crackle and a faint voice was heard.

'. . . now there are three,' said the voice.

'Three what?' wondered Klaus.

'A third flight has flown in – in the south – nothing for us to bother about,' explained one of his crew.

No, thought Klaus, don't let's bother about the imminent deaths of hundreds of innocent people. And in his fear for Doris in the supposed safety of the south, his grip tightened on the joystick. The plane lurched and the next moment a pitch black shadow sped underneath them through the even darker night.

'Did you see that?' came the horrified voice of the sergeant. Klaus nodded. They had escaped collision by a hair's breadth. And the machine roared on, an angel of death, the four men inside it automatons united by a single objective.

The receiver crackled and whistled, its irregular staccato sound Klaus' only means of knowing the whereabouts of his enemy.

But Klaus' thoughts were elsewhere. He was back in the high-ceilinged office sitting opposite the lawyer his father had recommended to him. The lawyer was listening silently to what he had to say. His face was haggard and his eyes tired as he added the line: 'to be opened only in the event of my death.' Only then would Doris know the whole truth.

'Attention,' snapped the voice of flight control. 'You are over the target.'

The opaque glass panel in the radio flickered milkily. Now it was up to them. They were alone in the darkness as flight control cut out. Electric tension ran through the fuselage like a flash of blue light. Klaus peered out into the night straining his eyes for the flight of bombers that was about to materialise out there.

The air was sticky. Oil fumes hung in their lungs. The sergeant cleared his throat. Nothing. Three minutes. Five. The silence was louder than the droning of the engines.

Suddenly the fuselage was almost consumed in light. Klaus shut his eyes. The stabbing pain in them told him that they had been picked out by a searchlight. Volleys of gunfire echoed past the plane.

'Bastards!' cursed the sergeant, but there was fear in his voice.

Their own guns rattled. Death spat splinters out of their burning mouths. Klaus banked sharply and plunged downwards. The beam of the searchlight wavered behind them, but this time Klaus managed to avoid it. He took his bearings and set off on an easterly course. That's where they must be, he reasoned.

'We could always wait here,' suggested the sergeant tentatively.

'Whatever for?'

'Until they come back –'

Klaus shook his head.

'Listen, Captain,' came the unsteady voice of one of the junior officers, 'we've lost a lot of our ammunition already. Without ammunition we're done for. I vote we turn back.'

Turn back, thought Klaus bitterly. They'll never learn. If we turn back now a couple of hundred people will die down there.

Then the Ju sighted the first flight against the flaming background of Berlin. Its slipstream howled against the Ju's wings; the whole plane vibrated. Klaus ducked below and behind the flight and in the next moment he was gaining height again, zooming straight for the planes hanging above him.

Then the cannons were rattling and Klaus could see the silhouette of giant wings. The Lancaster was keeping to its course as if it was running on rails. Salvoes of shells landed like dying sparks in its great black belly and then an enormous blast rent the bomber – its own explosives shattered it to silver shreds of flying aluminium. The blast became a mushroom that grew and grew.

Klaus felt his safety strap digging into his flesh with the force of the explosion. Then a great reeling emptiness. Then silence, as though they were deep under water. The pressure on their ears was almost unbearable. Get back on course – get back on course! shouted a voice inside Klaus.

And the miracle worked. Only a few hundred metres above the scarred earth, the machine which had been blown away like a leaf in the blast managed to straighten out.

The receiver began to function once more. The night hissed and crackled with urgent commands.

Klaus was put on a new course. He couldn't fly over Berlin as the Germans were shooting down anything in the sky above their capital. The dance of death went north instead.

'Neustrelitz,' announced flight control.

The name sank like a stone in Klaus' stomach. Erika had told him that his son was in a home in Neustrelitz.

A weak shadow swam across the radar scan.

'We've got one!' shouted the sergeant jubilantly. The outline grew stronger as the Ju gradually caught up with the enemy plane. Klaus stared at the radar picture and his clammy hands felt for the press button.

'We're in luck!' exclaimed flight control. 'It's a lame one limping behind the flight!'

My son's down there somewhere, thought Klaus, imagining the enemy aircraft nosediving into the children's home.

The shadow became a black knot. The sergeant sat forward and peered out into the night. Klaus' hand trembled momentarily on the joystick. No reasoned argument could overcome this sudden panic fear. He let the radar scan lose the wounded plane – or was he so close that it couldn't register him anyway? Klaus couldn't tell the difference any longer.

'There he is!' shouted the sergeant, but Klaus sat as though turned to stone, his body damp with icy sweat.

'Shoot!' barked flight control. 'Shoot now!'

My son, thought Klaus, if I shoot, my son might die.

'Shoot!'

Klaus banked gently and the exhaust flames of the lame English bomber danced in the sky like glow-worms. Off they went, floating to one side, before they were swallowed up in the blackness of the night.

'What happened?' asked the sergeant, open-mouthed with surprise.

But Klaus didn't answer. Half an hour later the Ju landed back at base and Klaus left his men with his head hung low. They watched him walk away.

'Madman,' murmured the sergeant.

'Coward,' hissed the junior officer.

'Shit!' exclaimed the mechanic, whose fingers were running over the holes in the fuselage made by the bullets and splinters.

* * *

The beds stood in a row on the long terrace under the awning. Their bars made them look like little cages, and inside each little cage lay a child, the property of the nation, its life mapped out for it from cradle to communal grave. Officials like Westroff-Meyer had decided how many vitamins each child should have per day and when was the best time to start hammering propaganda into their little heads. Their rooms were already decorated with choice Nazi slogans like: 'Be hard as steel, tough as hide.' All this the babies absorbed as they lay there thoughtfully sucking their thumbs.

The place was well-staffed with nurses of the highest qualifications and altogether it looked clean and well-appointed. The home catered for every need.

Only one thing was missing – love.

Today's visitors were being shown round by a secretary from HQ in Berlin. They were people who had come to see the children with a view to adoption. The secretary was Erika. She had volunteered for this assignment so that she could give a father the chance to see his son.

Klaus sat rigidly in the car, his eyes staring at some invisible point in the distance. Since Erika had plucked up the courage to ask him if he wanted to see his child, he hadn't been able to think of anything else.

'Klaus,' she said, 'perhaps what I'm doing is very wrong, bringing you together like this. You must keep your feelings well hidden, because Westroff-Meyer must never find out that I've brought you here.'

Klaus nodded. The car had reached its destination and there was a screech of tyres as it came to a halt on the gravel forecourt. The matron hurried up to meet them, stretching out her hand in welcome. Her greyish plaits were wound tightly round her head and she wore a silver brooch of an old Germanic design pinned to her scrawny bosom.

They followed her into the home and she led them on a conducted tour of the children's rooms, the terrace, the kitchen. She showed them the toys, the neatly piled nappies, the cots, the empty beds with their name-tags : Siegfried, Kunigunde, Sieglinde – all the good old German names bestowed at the Nazi baptismal font.

Then they went into the dormitory where the newest arrivals slept. Klaus had to exert a superhuman effort to conceal his feelings. Anticipation took his breath away. Erika saw his confusion and put a comforting hand on his arm. He managed a smile for her, but was aware of nothing but the presence of his son.

A door was pushed open and there he was. His two little fists were gripping a white teething ring hanging over his cot. His hair was blond and had grown much thicker.

Klaus' lips moved silently and he looked round at Erika : it was a look that she would never forget. In his eyes was all the pitiable helplessness of a tortured man begging for mercy.

Erika suddenly felt that she had done wrong and began to reproach herself bitterly – she should have known how painful this would be for Klaus.

The matron leaned over the baby's cot. 'There, there, Klaus,' she cooed, 'let's see what a pretty boy you are.' And she picked him up and held him expertly against her shoulder.

Lines of tension showed in Klaus' face and he clenched his hands together behind his back.

'Please,' whispered Erika.

He turned and looked into her worried eyes and shook his head as if to reassure her. And then he saw his son smile and the sturdy little arms reached out towards him. He dug his nails into the palms of his hands.

'Say hello to your uncle,' drooled the matron.

Erika turned away, unable to bear the spectacle any longer, but the baby gurgled with laughter and strained towards Klaus.

'He must be looking at your medal,' explained the matron. Klaus' hands went to his collar and undid the ribbon which held the Knight's Cross. Now the glittering medal was swinging from his hand and he held it slowly out to the baby who shouted with joy and batted the air with his hands to catch the gleaming toy.

'If he likes it,' said Klaus quietly, 'then he can have it.'

The baby caught hold of the ribbon and Klaus released it. The matron looked from one to the other of them, open-mouthed.

'But captain,' she stuttered. 'You can't give that to a baby – the Führer gave you that.' There were worried red patches on her cheeks.

'Why not?' asked Klaus calmly, and then his voice grew harsh. 'I can always buy myself another – they're on sale all over the place.'

The matron fiddled nervously with the baby's shawl. 'But you can't do that,' she repeated lamely.

But the look in Klaus' eyes told her that he could, and that there was nothing she could do about it. She laid the baby back in his cot but didn't dare take the medal off him, although her eyes were drawn often enough to the place on Klaus' chest where it should have been hanging. He looked indecent, almost naked without it.

Klaus bent to take a last look at his son and met the baby's laughing eyes. Doris' eyes, he thought sadly, and turned to go.

Chapter Seventeen

The Americans had long since crossed the Rhine, and the Russians had reached that other great river, the Oder. The war was in its last phase and yet hundreds of thousands of German soldiers and just as many civilians, women, children, and old people, had yet to die before peace was declared. The Nazi empire collapsed as barbarically as it had been built up. It was choked by its own blood, the blood that it had let itself; it was burned in the fire that it had ignited and it was buried under the rubble of the buildings it had pulled down.

Doris felt the dying breath of Nazism as it blew across on the wind from the battlefields. For two years now she had been living in evacuation with the child on a farm in Bavaria. It was ten weeks since she had last heard from Klaus.

And the Americans flew low over the forgotten village. Each time they came, they flew lower, and they came back more and more often. Indifferently dropping bombs, they wheeled over the cluster of cowering cottages whose window panes trembled with fear. The tension was released by a series of sharp explosions which erupted to one side or other of the village like bubbles in a cauldron of boiling water – boiling water that threatened, sooner or later, to drown the villagers.

The nights that Doris spent there were filled with worry and confusion – the whole of Germany seemed to be fleeing to her village to take refuge and the darkness rang with cries and curses and the endless tramping of soldiers, the clash of metal and the roar of engines.

In the morning the farmyard was heaped with weapons and military equipment of all kinds. It was destined to rust and remain there as a milestone along the path of the thousands who fled.

Every night Doris watched over her baby's cot as he lay there, eyes tight shut, clutching his teddy bear. Her thoughts were with her husband and it was a double comfort to her to have the child now that Klaus was no longer with her. As she lay awake tossing and turning she asked herself continually: how will all this end? Will my husband come out of it alive?

Then the defence forces retreated to just beyond the village boundary. In the night the last infantry unit marched wearily into the village. It consisted of only twelve youngsters from the Hitler Youth Movement. The eldest was fifteen, and ready to die.

At the edge of the village they set up their defence. They built a wall of birch stems against the allied tanks and dug little mouseholes in the sand to protect themselves from the allied artillery.

The women of the village had congregated in front of the village hall, amongst them Doris, her son in her arms.

'Send those boys back home,' shouted the women. 'We don't want them dying on our doorstep.'

Inside the mayor was standing opposite an army official who was staring fixedly at his boots.

'What can I do?' the farmer asked the soldier.

'Do what you like,' warned the other, 'you won't be able to stop the Americans. They'll be here by tomorrow at the latest – the only question is whether they'll blow the village up first.'

The mayor looked down at his broad hands and at the fields outside that he had tilled all his life long. He went out quietly, taking two neighbours with him. The women made way for him, relief showing on their faces.

By the time Doris had laid her baby down to sleep that night the three of them had taken the boys' guns from them, cleared away the birch stems and told the disappointed 'defenders' to go back to the village.

Then they waited. But the Americans didn't come, not then, nor during the night, nor the next morning. Everything was unnaturally still and quiet. And then at midday, instead of enemy tanks, a German armoured car drove into the main street and a leather-coated official got out, followed by three soldiers.

Doris pulled the curtain aside with trembling hands. The one in the leather coat was speaking to the boys from the Hitler Youth. Hesitantly, the people came out of their houses. Doris went with them.

Suddenly, on the doorstep, she froze. She knew his face – it was one that was imprinted for ever on her brain – it was the face of General Westroff-Meyer. He was shouting something. Doris went straight back into the house.

Unlike his Führer, Westroff-Meyer had understood in good time that Berlin was not the place to be caught in when the war came to an end. So that when reliable murderers were sought to send deserting soldiers to the gallows and thus prolong the war, Westroff-Meyer was one of the first to volunteer. By tightening the noose on the necks of these German soldiers, he hoped he could save his own.

Here in the village street, he was setting up another court-room farce. He had his soldiers arrest the mayor and the other two men who had taken the boys' weapons away, while the teenagers themselves looked on sulkily.

'Did you or did you not hinder the Hitler Youth from their military duty?'

The mayor shook his head tiredly. 'It doesn't make sense any more,' he muttered.

'Sense? You are traitors, deserters!'

Incensed by the blank faces in front of him, Westroff-Meyer signalled to one of his men. 'That tree over there, and let's do it quickly.'

The lime tree was old and mighty – soon it would be in bloom and its fragrant scent would fill the air. Its boughs bent down gracefully, and the SS men fixed the noose firmly to one of them.

Old women were crossing themselves, children were crying with fear, and the toughest of the men uttered a prayer. One of the crowd threw himself forward, but the hangman caught him a blow on the back of the head with his pistol and he slumped to the ground.

'Hang him up first,' thundered the General, pointing to the inert body.

So the SS men dragged the man to where the noose dangled from the tree. But the branch was too high. There were a couple of milk churns standing nearby, and they took those and put them under the rope. The boys from the Hitler Youth had started to skulk away. Westroff-Meyer grabbed the nearest one by the shoulder and wrenched him round to face the tree.

'You're staying,' he said. 'I want you to see how traitors die in this country.'

Suddenly the milk churns were pushed away and the farmer's legs kicked once into empty air. The noose tightened and it was over ...

'Now the rest,' shouted the general.

The second man was strung up to the lime tree. The boys huddled together, their faces pale and tear-stained. The women had gone down on their knees, and their children hid their faces in their skirts. But there was nothing sacred about death for Westroff-Meyer, who stood and puffed on a cigar until the third man and the fourth had stopped kicking.

He nodded again to his men. He was suddenly in a hurry, but before he climbed back into his car, he gave one last order – that the bodies of the hanged men should remain in the tree as a warning to the rest of them.

It was later that day that the Americans arrived. The first tank stopped by the lime tree and a young lieutenant lifted the cover. What he saw appalled him and he spat with disgust.

Then the women and children came out to bury their dead husbands and fathers.

* * *

The river Oder was afloat with the bodies of German soldiers as the Russians marched on towards the West. The German Reich collapsed as they reached the outskirts of Berlin and the loudspeakers droned out the final victory of the allies.

In the morning of that last day, 400 men had drunk coffee in Klaus' unit. In the evening there were seventy-two left.

They stumbled and fell over the mutilated bodies of their companions. They clambered over the hulks of dead horses already swarming with flies. If they went too slowly, they would be massacred by the Russians – if they arrived too soon, they would be shot by their own military police.

Klaus was one of the four men still alive in his battalion. Behind them they had the Russians; in front was a low hill.

The hill was buttressed by deep runnels made by the recent rains and smashed in places by bomb craters. There were also intermittent clumps of tattered gorse, so the cover was quite good. But not that good.

Klaus squinted up towards the summit. Machine-guns spat indolently from time to time from a dugout on a crest just before the summit. German machine-guns. Safety. And in between lay 400 m of crater-strewn ridge. A shooting gallery to entertain the advancing Russians. He hawked some phlegm to dull the edge of the fire in his throat and wrenched back the bolt of his Luger. Klaus sighted his target – a bush 60 m away rustled concealing its impatient sniper. The Luger recoiled in his palm and the Russian fell back, shot through the neck.

But Klaus had given away his position now. He took a deep dry breath and summoned his failing resources. He made for the bomb crater, but although he ran like fury in his head, his legs hung like dead weights. The ground behind him broke into pieces with machine-gun fire. He dived into the crater and lay there panting. The temptation to just close his eyes and sleep was enormous. He threw away his Luger and made the next crater, and the next, zig-zagging up the broken hill, a figure in a gunsight.

Only 20 m to go and Klaus could see the men in the dug-out. They were calling something, but he didn't care. His will was smashed.

The hill had been a German stronghold. There were still soldiers up there – the remains of several shattered companies had gathered together and looked on paralysed with horror as four men tried to climb their hill and save their senseless lives. One of them looked as if he was going to make it. He got so near before he fell that you could see how his eyes had glazed over.

Suddenly one of the men could stand it no longer. A tall, rangy figure, he leapt over the barricade, grasped Klaus' hands and dragged him the few metres to safety. It was Horst Kempe. For some reason the Russians didn't bother to shoot them both down. Perhaps they were just too lazy, or perhaps they thought they'd let this one get away – after all he was the last survivor.

Klaus was unconscious, but they managed to feed him a good quantity of tea and rum from a bottle with a rubber hose attached, which they forced down his throat.

Kempe had been studying the dirt-streaked face of the man he had saved for some time. 'I know that man,' he muttered, nodding to himself. Then he pulled the rubber tube out of Klaus' mouth. 'Don't overdo it,' he said to his men. 'He gets pissed quickly. He's a friend of mine.'

He took another look over the barricade. His small company had virtually run out of ammunition, and were just waiting, like all the other defenders of Berlin, until the Russians came and slaughtered them. And now the Russians were advancing in wild hordes – the hill was seething with them.

'If only I had just one hand grenade,' groaned Kempe.

He shook Klaus violently until one swollen eyelid half opened.

'Leave me alone,' moaned Klaus.

'They're half-way up now, sir,' called one of Kempe's men.

Kempe smiled wryly. 'Better get ready to die a hero's death then, hadn't we?'

He took out his pistol. He still had four shots left. Three for the Russians and one for himself. He turned to his men and said laconically: 'When I give you the signal you can either sling the ammunition boxes at them or run for your lives.'

At that moment a messenger came running, holding his side and panting for breath.

'Retreat to Erkner suburb,' he shouted. 'There's ammunition there – provisions!'

Kempe immediately lunged forward and picked out three of the advancing Russians. His men followed suit and the short volley of firing, though it was their last, convinced the Russians that the war was still on and they flung themselves face down on the sand, expecting an onslaught.

'How are we going to get him out of here?' asked one of the men, pointing to Klaus. 'He can't walk.'

Kempe brushed him aside with a curse and hauled Klaus to his feet. Klaus was still semi-conscious and all his body wanted to do was lie down. So Kempe hit him. Hard. He gave him a quick left, a sharp right and a well-aimed knee until he was awake enough to give his rescuer a crooked smile of recognition and get moving under his own steam.

* * *

The wood which had hidden the children's home in Neustrelitz from the world for so long rustled with the news of Germany's defeat. In the reeds at the lakeside rusting steel helmets had been becalmed and through the wood trekked endless refugees, their carts groaning under the load of their possessions. Forlorn cries and stifled sobs were heard amongst the trees and from time to time a weary soldier would come to the home to beg for a glass of water.

The house seemed to cower in its clearing, fearful of being found out for what it was. When the matron heard the distant thunder of passing troops, she had all the blinds pulled down so that she wouldn't have to be witness to defeat, so that she could go on believing a little longer.

'We are doing our duty for the Führer,' she told the nurses staunchly. 'We will carry on doing our duty.'

And so she went on bringing up the children in the name of a man who was shortly to signal the end of her work by putting an end to his own life.

When that happened, the home virtually collapsed about the children's ears. First one nurse ran off, then another. Others followed suit until there were hardly enough nurses to look after the children. They were often hungry and neglected. The babies who had been bred to form a super-nation in a golden age were now a useless commodity in a time of poverty and need.

The last action of the matron before she too deserted her

charges, was to destroy all the documents recording their origins – thus ruining their chances of ever finding their way home.

And then the exodus began. A horsedrawn cart was laden with whimpering children and babies – the older ones, like little Klaus, watched horrified as they pulled away from the only home they had ever known and set off towards the station to catch the last train for the northwest.

Little Klaus hugged his teddy bear tightly to him as his small world retreated into the distance. His lips were pressed together and his eyes large with fear as they passed a troop of soldiers.

When they arrived at the station, the platform was crammed with people who wouldn't make room, so they had to wait huddled together, a good way off, with not much hope of getting on the train.

After a long wait the train arrived, its engine belching soot from what was left of the country's supply of coal. Before it came to a halt, people rushed at the carriages, which were already full, and fought each other to gain a place. The nurses held back in despair – there was no chance of getting the children on board.

Suddenly, the face of one of the little boys lit up with delight as he realised what was going on. 'Train!' he cried, and pulling free of the nurse who was holding his hand, he dashed out into the road. Before he could get any closer, he was mown down under the wheels of an army car. His thin scream was drowned by the tumult around the train. No one heard the screech of tyres or the crunch of bone on metal. The nurses cried out and hid their faces – his little body lay bloody and mangled on the road. He was dead. In anguish and despair, the driver packed the rest of the group into his blood-bespattered car, fighting off the people who had given up trying to get on to the train.

Klaus and the other children didn't understand what they had seen, it had all happened so nightmarishly quickly. Klaus cried only because the others were crying.

Then the car started off, nosing its way though the surging crowds, and the children were heading at last for safety.

* * *

Berlin was the melting pot of all the Nazi disasters, and the German soldiers who passed through its famous gates found themselves in hell . . .

The city was unrecognisable to Klaus and Kempe – transformed by fire and blood – and many of its beautiful buildings lay in ruins.

They had found the promised store of ammunition hidden amongst the rubble – but there was only one rifle between them and they had long since forgotten what they were defending. There were seven left of the thirty who set out that morning. Death had not yet taken its final toll – the last sprint was still to be run and many more would perish that day.

A group of soldiers suddenly appeared making their way through the rubble, straggling towards them.

'Thank God we've found you!' shouted the nearest one, a boy of about fifteen. 'We need help.'

'So do we all,' said Kempe.

'We've got to bust the waterworks,' explained the young lieutenant breathlessly, 'and we need you to help us do it.'

'You won't find me doing that,' said Kempe grimly.

'What the hell for?' asked Klaus.

'They think the Russians are trying to get in through the Underground tunnels, sir, so we're to flood them.'

Kempe's face turned white. 'For Christ's sake – the Underground is full of people trying to shelter!' he exploded.

The youngster's eyes mirrored his disdain for such considerations.

'If you touch the waterworks, I'll see you shot,' roared Kempe. 'Leave them alone and that's a command – from me!'

'We have a command from the Führer,' retorted the boy defiantly.

'No man can give such a command,' said Kempe between his teeth, 'not even a madman.'

The young lieutenant looked round and gave a sign to his men and they turned and started stumbling back over the rubble.

Kempe boiled over. He snatched the machine-gun from Klaus and levelled the barrel at the retreating lieutenant.

There was a loud click, but no explosion. The bullet had stuck. Frustrated beyond endurance, Kempe hurled the gun to the ground, threw himself after it and pounded it with his fists until they bled.

'The bastards!' he howled.

Klaus tried to calm him, but Kempe grabbed him by the collar and shook him. His eyes glinted wildly.

'We've got to *do* something, damn you,' he roared. 'We can't let women and children drown like rats! We've got to *do* something!'

Klaus' face was stony, his eyes dull, his back bowed with defeat. He didn't need to witness the tragedy in the Underground to be convinced that an insane criminal was goading Berlin to self-destruction. He wanted only to survive.

'Horst,' he said, 'I'm taking our men with me and I'm getting out of here.'

Kempe still clung fast to him, but it seemed he hadn't heard.

'It takes more courage to desert,' began Klaus, but Kempe flung him aside, put his head down and ran. His men tried to stop him, but he rammed his way through them and stormed off in the direction the young lieutenant had taken. He leapt over the rubble without heeding the Russian bullets whistling all around him and made it to the Underground, winded but unhurt.

He hurtled down the steps and found himself in that dim world of caves and tunnels to which the people of Berlin had fled to vegetate. He was choked by the stink of human waste and the foul air tainted by the fires that had raged above ground. When his eyes got used to the darkness he picked out the shapeless forms of thousands of people who had dragged their mattresses and a few other pitiful possessions below ground and were now lying huddled on the platforms, on the benches, between the railway lines. Their clothes were hung neatly on hangers from the signal wires, their pillows piled on the railway sleepers.

Kempe's face was white, his gaze fixed and staring. He looked like a ghost as he entered this gloomy cavern.

When he realised the immensity of the misery down there, saw that people had even been forced inside the distant railway tunnel, he didn't know any more whether he had the right to send them on a new journey into as yet unknown horrors. It might even be better for them to ...

'Listen to me, everybody,' roared Kempe at the top of his voice. 'The Underground's going to be flooded. You've got to get out now, before it's too late. Come on, move!'

He shouted his message three or four times and the shapeless forms roused themselves and people drugged with sleep and foul air shook themselves conscious. Women and children began to cry with fatigue and fright. Kempe's call was heard and passed on down the tunnels until the whole of the underworld was echoing with it. Panic rose and travelled those tunnels faster than any train had managed it. But it wasn't fast enough.'

The water came. Men and women rushed to the exits, each blocking the escape of the one behind him. The water rose. Within minutes it was waist deep.

Kempe gave up trying to get out and pressed himself against the tunnel wall. He stared at the roaring tide milling with dead and dying bodies. He watched the limbs writhing with agony and the contorted mouths gasping for breath.

A helpless child was being swept along thrashing desperately with her arms. She was just about to go under when Kempe reached out and caught her in his arms. The little girl clung trembling and panting to his shoulders.

'Poor little love,' said Kempe tenderly. He hugged the little girl and pressed his face against her wet hair. Suddenly he remembered that he had children of his own at home. They were supposed to guarantee the future of Germany, but they might have to perish for the Führer, like this little girl, before they were old enough to walk.

The little girl was sobbing bitterly and the water went on rising.

'Mister,' she said, suddenly quite calm, 'my feet are getting wet.'

'Never mind, love,' said Kempe, holding her up higher. He shifted her weight to one arm and felt in his pocket for his pistol. It still had one bullet left in it – the bullet that he'd intended for himself.

The water was now swirling round his chest – it was hard

191

to keep his feet on the floor. The air was stifling, and the little girl was crying again.

'Mister,' she sobbed, 'my feet –'

Her death was merciful compared to that of the struggling masses around. One must be totally inhuman, thought Kempe, not to feel the horror of such a terrible death. What sort of monster could bring himself to order it? Suddenly he wished that Adolf Hitler was standing beside him, listening to the cries of the drowning people, watching their last desperate struggles, hearing the last words of the little girl whose limp form he still held in his arms: 'Mister, my feet are getting wet.'

When the water reached Horst Kempe's mouth, he simply let himself slip under . . .

Chapter Eighteen

Westroff-Meyer had deserted. Between Ingolstadt and Nürnberg he'd strung up a few more traitors, but after that he'd decided to put himself at the top of his list of priorities and do the very thing for which he'd condemned so many others to the gallows.

He took the suitcase out of the car and returned the driver's grave salute. In the distance he could hear the rumble of American tanks. They would be on them in a matter of hours.

He hung around until the car was out of sight, then crossed the grass verge and crouched down to open his suitcase behind the cover of a clump of brambles. Inside the case were some old civilian clothes that he'd always carried with him in case his luck ran out. He tore off his uniform and stuffed his leather coat, his breeches, his jacket and boots into one of the bramble bushes, then slipped easily into his other clothes. He'd brought a battered old hat and he pulled it down low over his forehead. No one would ever recognise him.

The difficult part came next : finding shelter. He'd have to worm his way into the trust of some householder somewhere and lie low for a while.

Walking down the street, he heard voices coming from a nearby basement. The windows were inexpertly blacked out and light was filtering through the cracks. The general stopped and listened, but he couldn't make out what was being said. The front door was open, so he walked inside and down the steps to the cellar. The cellar door squeaked rustily on its hinges. Westroff-Meyer could see nothing, but he could hear women's voices. That was a good sign.

'Come in and shut the bloody door,' came a loud voice.

There were fifteen to twenty people in the cellar and none of them took much notice of the new arrival.

'Heil Hitler!' he greeted them.

An old soldier who was sitting on a rough wooden bench with two others playing cards turned round angrily.

'To hell with Hitler,' he spat.

Westroff-Meyer laughed, nervously and sat down next to the three soldiers, who were all worse off for a bottle of schnapps they were sharing. He offered his cigarettes, and they accepted, and went back to their cards, ignoring him completely.

A girl pushed her way past Westroff-Meyer and sat down on one of the soldiers' laps. She snatched the bottle out of his hand, tilted it against her mouth and drank till she was breathless. She looked round, her face flushed, laughing wildly.

'Who's he?' she asked, pointing the bottle at Westroff-Meyer.

'How should I know?' grumbled her lover.

'I don't like his face,' said the girl, pouting her painted lips.

'Nor me,' agreed the soldier. He threw his cigarette down, crushed it under his heel and said in a low threatening voice: 'You'd better get out of here before you offend us any further.'

'But comrades,' began Westroff-Meyer.

'Comrades!' sneered the soldier. He stood up, pushed the door open, hauled Westroff-Meyer to his feet and kicked him out of the cellar.

As Westroff-Meyer dragged himself painfully up the stairs, the house began to shake and plaster showered from the ceiling. The rumble of tanks was deafening. The beam of a searchlight darted across the street and he recognised the olive green uniforms of the GIs, their guns at the ready.

Relief flooded through him. The war was over, and Germany would be in the hands of strangers. He was free.

As he emerged into the street, an American soldier came up to him and shouted something he couldn't understand to his companions.

Westroff-Meyer took off his hat and bowed low to welcome the conquering heroes.

* * *

In the little village in Bavaria three months had gone by since the incident under the lime tree, and the wooden crosses in the cemetery that marked that occasion were showing the first signs of weathering. The war had come to an end, but peace was still uneasy and unreal.

The destruction of the great politicians had little effect on the lives of the villagers. Only when a soldier returned home, or when a mother learned that her son had fallen, did the outside world intrude upon this closely-knit community.

Doris waited, but she had given up hoping. She could have gone back home, but she was tortured by the thought that Klaus might come back here first, and find her gone – if he came back at all. She had had copies of his photograph made and sent them round to be pinned up on notice boards everywhere alongside hundreds of thousands of other photographs. A whole nation was looking for its sons.

Whenever demobbed soldiers passed through the village, the inhabitants gathered round them and asked pointless questions. The soldiers shook their heads sadly and wearily and looked away towards the open country, as if they were fearing more shots, despite the peace, when they got out there.

Doris' baby could talk already. He was big for his age, a pretty boy with gentle, affectionate ways.

'When's daddy coming?' he asked continually. 'Is daddy coming today?'

'Soon,' said Doris when the questions got too frequent, and turned away.

She gave up standing at the window. She asked no more questions. Her waiting was silent and resigned. Time wound around her, cocooning her from the world and from her own feelings. The conversation of her neighbours, the everyday noises of the village, reached her only distantly – she was hardly aware of what was going on.

But one day she opened the door to find her husband

standing on the step. She just stood and gazed at him, unable to believe either that he had come back, or that this stranger outside her door was the man she had married. His face was ashen and lined with defeat. His eyes were dull and lifeless and his body emaciated inside the uniform that had worn and faded like its owner.

He gave his wife a brief, mechanical embrace and walked inside. He knew that that short moment symbolised the dearest wish, the only hope of every one of those millions of soldiers who had not come home, but who had enacted that embrace in their dreams as they were blown to bits or buried or burned alive. The kiss had to be quick, because it meant too much : it meant a return to life where others had died.

'Hungry,' said Klaus faintly and slumped into the shabby sofa which stood beside the kitchen fire. Doris brought him food, but he wasn't strong enough to hold the spoon and she had to feed him like a child. When he had eaten she sat down beside him. She had got him back – and she hadn't. She was frightened.

'Was it bad?' she whispered.

'Bad?' His eyes avoided hers. 'I'm home now,' he said finally, but it sounded as though he hardly believed it himself.

Suddenly he started at the scuffling of tiny feet outside the door.

'Mummy,' called a clear little voice.

'Is it him?' asked Klaus nervously.

Doris nodded, smiling for the first time since Klaus had come in. She went to the door and opened it, taking the little boy by the hand. He drew back suddenly, seeing the strange man.

'Mummy?' he asked, his voice full of apprehension.

'He's home,' said Doris gently.

Klaus sat as if rooted to the sofa. The weight of a year's old lie bore down heavily on his tortured nerves. He wanted nothing more than to sleep, and within an hour of his home-coming he was presented face to face with the cruel truth that he'd left behind.

'Daddy,' said the little boy, gulping bravely. His eyes were large and round and although he held back, his expression was full of nascent trust.

Klaus forced himself to look into the clear childish eyes. He raised a hand to shut out the vision and slumped suddenly backwards, burying his head in the cushions, as tears streamed unchecked down his cheeks.

'Off you go,' said Doris to the little boy. 'He's very tired.'

While her husband slept and in his dreams went over and over the journey from Berlin to the Bavarian village, past the hanged men rotting in the trees and the Russians, still begging for a fight, the villagers came to Doris to congratulate her on his return. She had to turn her face away to hide her tears. Tears of disappointment.

She tried to persuade herself that Klaus was just exhausted; that he was living in a limbo-world where there was neither joy nor sadness. Sleep had softened the haggard lines of his face, made him look younger, almost as he had looked before the war had begun to ravage his features.

But the next few weeks showed little change for the better. Peace was barbaric. Calories were the new currency, but hunger was more plentiful than bread and there were no coals to light a fire. The only thing that could buy food was American cigarettes. It was a terrible time, a time of scrounging and begging and going without, a time when marriages broke up and friendships collapsed and when the meanness of everyday life ate away at the last shreds of dignity left to mankind.

And still there was something not right in Doris' marriage. Every time she saw Klaus playing with their son, a cold hand clutched at her heart. There was something not quite genuine in the affection he showed for the little boy, Doris could sense that. Sometimes she caught him glancing sideways at her as if to reassure himself she hadn't noticed he was only interested in the child for her sake.

One evening Doris broached the subject with him.

'I wish you'd tell me what's the matter, Klaus,' she said.

He laid the newspaper aside, his eyes betraying his resignation. He'd known she would ask sooner or later.

'Please tell me,' she begged. 'You're so different somehow.

And then there's little Klaus. I don't think you even like him.'

He got up and looked out of the window. 'Nonsense,' he said, attempting to sound light-hearted. 'There's nothing the matter. Nothing at all.'

And Doris gave up asking.

But the next morning she found a note on the kitchen table: 'I'll be back soon. There's something I've got to do. You'll understand it all when I come back. Trust me, Doris . . .'

The letters blurred before her eyes.

* * *

The young GI didn't like the look of Westroff-Meyer, and he took his arm firmly and led him to a waiting jeep. At the HQ of the military police he was told to strip. There on his upper arm his blood group was marked – an obligatory precaution for all SS officers. The sergeant put through a call to American Intelligence straight away. Within hours they sent a lieutenant round to question Westroff-Meyer. His face was grey and haggard. He knew all about Dachau and Buchenwald. When he spoke he held his head on one side, cast his eyes to the floor and barely moved his lips at all. He gave the impression of laziness or indifference. There was a strange dead look to his face. His German was excellent.

'So you were in the SS?' he began.

'I was a reserve officer, yes,' answered Westroff-Meyer.

'What rank?'

'Major.'

'And what were you working on?'

Westroff-Meyer hesitated.

'You'll have to cook up your lies faster than this,' said the lieutenant, examining his fingernails. They were perfectly manicured.

'Lebensborn,' said the general in a low voice.

The lieutenant nodded.

'I had no choice,' blurted Westroff-Meyer. 'I hated all the organisation stood for – I had no choice.'

198

'Then you will perhaps be pleased to help us – wipe out these people?'

There were beads of perspiration on Westroff-Meyer's forehead. He nodded blankly.

'As you well know,' drawled the lieutenant, looking down once more at his perfect fingernails, 'the entire staff of the SS has dived underground. They have all got hold of false papers and disappeared somewhere – either abroad or to Bavaria . . . Well, these people interest me.' The lieutenant paused and then went on in a tired voice: 'The first thing I asked myself when I saw you, was whether you had any idea where they might be? And the second thing is – could you lead us to them?'

'And then what?' asked Westroff-Meyer unsteadily.

'Oh, we'll sort that out later,' said the American casually.

And so Westroff-Meyer became an informer against his own kind.

* * *

Klaus travelled hanging to the outside of overcrowded trains if he couldn't find a place inside. In his worn-out officer's great coat he was indistinguishable from the rest of the amorphous mass of Germans on the move that year.

Although he didn't know his destination, his journey had a very definite purpose: he was searching for more than just his son – he was hoping to find the happiness that he and Doris had once shared. And he knew that they would only find it again if he managed to bring back the boy.

At first he let his instinct guide him. All the survivors were fleeing to the north-west, so Klaus made for Hamburg. There he asked at youth centres and vicarages, at church hostels and orphanages. His questions were answered for the most part with a shrug of the shoulders. Once he was given a bowl of soup; another time he barely escaped being thrown into jail.

His shoes were falling apart and the light of hope had gone from his eyes. Klaus had no more money to buy food, but even less desire to give up.

So on he walked through Schleswig-Holstein. A vicar's

daughter slammed the door in his face, but as he turned to go, he met the vicar walking up the garden path. His head was stubbly, his body old and gnarled, his skin like leather. Only his eyes were still alive.

'Yes,' he said when he heard Klaus' question, 'I do know something about that.'

He began to fill his pipe thoughtfully while Klaus waited on a knife edge of expectation.

'A woman came here once,' said the vicar carefully, 'and asked if we could take in some children from the Nazi homes. Three and four years old, they were.

'And?'

'Well,' said the vicar round the side of his pipe, 'I didn't have room myself, but I've kept the woman's address.'

He copied something on to a scrap of paper and Klaus stuffed it into his pocket. The same thing had happened time and time again. Names and addresses – milestones in a meaningless journey.

'Seek and you will find,' quoted the old man. His words were carried away on the wind as though they no longer bore the weight of conviction.

So Klaus went on seeking. In Kiel. In Lübeck. In Hamburg.

In between the towns there were trains. Klaus sat with his feet drawn up underneath him, the roaring of the engine in his ears. There was a hole in his stomach and a hole in the roof of the goods waggon. The rain was pouring through it. Outside the bomb sites rolled by. Bodies were still buried under the heaps of rubble, and weeds had started to grow on top of them. Women came and carried away the stones, one by one. A golden age . . . Everywhere was infested with rats. There were chemicals to kill them, but that just made more dead bodies.

I wish I could go home, thought Klaus wearily. This search is pointless and I can't lie any longer. I will have to tell Doris the truth and she will have to share my burden.

That bit of paper the vicar had given him was still in his pocket. He took it out and had another look. Hanover – he was on his way there. So the woman lived in Hanover? Erika had relations there too, but he hadn't been able to track them down, or Erika either. He read the words on the scrap of paper once more: Erika Vogel. Erika? Now that was strange . . .

When he arrived in Hanover, Klaus walked through the ruins to the address on the bit of paper. It was on the edge of the town and on the brink of collapse itself. There were fifteen families in a three-storey building. On the second landing Klaus read a notice: Vogel, ring three times.

Footsteps came to the door. The paper fluttered from his hand. 'Erika . . .' he said incredulously.

She had aged. Her golden hair was tarnished and her sensuous lips had grown sharp and pinched. She didn't smile.

'Yes,' she said. 'I was married. My husband's name was Vogel. I'm a widow.' She paused. 'And you must be looking for your son.'

Klaus nodded, his eyes full of pity.

Erika's face was wooden and expressionless as she said: 'I know where he is.'

* * *

The American lieutenant sat in the front of the jeep next to the driver. Westroff-Meyer sat behind. From time to time the lieutenant signalled to the driver to hand their passenger a cigarette or something to eat. Not a word of conversation passed between them.

It was always the same. The car stopped and the driver turned to Westroff-Meyer, who nodded. The lieutenant felt for his pistol and all three got out of the jeep and went up to the house. They pushed their way past the man or woman who opened the door, and made a thorough search from attic to cellar. And always they found the same despairing face with its wavering glance and its resigned nod of confirmation. And another one was caught.

After three weeks, Westroff-Meyer announced that he had delivered every one of his former colleagues into the hands of the Americans.

'Think carefully,' said the lieutenant. 'There's still one missing.'

'One missing?'

'Yes. The former SS general Westroff-Meyer. Do you know him at all?'

Westroff-Meyer shook his head.

'Oh, but I do,' said the lieutenant. 'And I hereby arrest you for crimes committed against humanity in Poland and Germany on countless occasions . . .'

And so Westroff-Meyer was hanged and the inhuman jerk of the rope that broke his neck was an act of humanity.

Chapter Nineteen

Erika went to the orphanage with Klaus. 'It's better if I come too,' she had explained. 'The people there know me. I've signed on as a sort of volunteer; I try to find homes for some of the children.'

'You are a very kind person, Erika,' said Klaus quietly.

Erika shook her head woodenly. 'I'm through,' she said. 'Through with everything.'

When they arrived at the home, Erika left Klaus in a sort of waiting room while she went to explain. After what seemed like an eternity, she reappeared with the warden. Klaus could read nothing from her expression.

'I'm glad to see you,' said the warden, a crabbed old man with tobacco-stained teeth. 'The more we can get rid of, the better. When do you want to leave?'

Klaus swallowed. 'Immediately, if that's possible.'

'Very well. The packing won't take long. The boy doesn't have anything to pack. You'll have to sign the official papers, of course.'

Klaus looked at Erika, but she was staring out of the window.

After he had finished signing the papers, he looked up to see a nurse standing in the doorway with a pale, thin little boy in an ugly grey suit that was far too big for him.

Klaus rose unsteadily to his feet and looked down at the drawn little face. 'Klaus,' he said softly.

The little boy screwed up his eyes and began to cry, burying his head in the nurse's skirt.

Klaus picked up his son very gently. 'Listen,' he whispered, 'you mustn't be afraid of me. I'm your daddy.'

But the word meant nothing to the little boy, and he went

on sobbing pitifully to himself as Klaus carried him out of the room. Klaus thought how ironic it was that a strange child should look up at him with love and trust, while his own son hid his face and wept. And with the weight of the child on his arm, he suddenly felt the full burden of the monstrous injustice that he'd borne alone for three years.

'It'll be all right,' said Erika, who had fallen into step with him. And she stroked the boy's hair gently.

When they said good-bye in the overcrowded station waiting room, the child was asleep on Klaus' lap. His lips were slightly parted and one tiny fist clutched hold of Klaus' jacket, as if he was holding on hard to all life had to offer.

Klaus put his free hand on Erika's arm.

'I can't ever thank you enough,' he whispered.

'No need to thank me at all.'

'Erika,' he began, but no more words came.

The young woman nodded. There were tears in her eyes. She bent once more over the sleeping child.

'Everything's worked out,' she said in a dull voice.

'We will all have to learn how to live again,' said Klaus brokenly.

'Yes,' whispered Erika. Then she turned away quickly and walked off into the crowd, her head hung and her shoulders bowed. She was thinking about Berlin, and how it was when the Russians had stormed the city, how six or eight of them had cornered her. She could see their flat, broad faces, their cruel, lecherous eyes ...

* * *

Eventually they were there. Klaus had seen Doris from a distance, but she had her back to them. She was bending down in the garden doing some weeding. Suddenly all Klaus' worries fell from him. He just wanted to run to her and take her in his arms. He lifted the child up so that he could see over the fence.

'Call "Mummy",' he whispered.

Doris turned round and saw Klaus. Her face lit up and she dropped her trowel and ran to meet him. Klaus bent to kiss

204

her, holding on tightly to his son, who was looking wide-eyed with curiosity and dread at this strange woman, his mother.

'So you're back,' said Doris quietly, her eyes shining.

'And this time for good. And not alone, either.'

Doris looked from the man to the child, and suddenly the muscles in her face relaxed. She opened her mouth to speak, but her lips were trembling uncontrollably. She just stood there transfixed and Klaus said: 'Take a good long look at him.'

Doris' eyes devoured the child. She tried to say something. Never would Klaus forget the first sign of recognition in her face – it made all the years of lying worthwhile to see the joy in her eyes.

'It can't be,' said Doris, as though mesmerised. It was a terrible, wonderful shock. She leaned on the fence for support.

'Klaus,' she said, 'it can't be. Please tell me –'

'But it is,' he said quietly. 'He is really yours – ours – aren't you, Klaus?'

'Yes,' said the three-year-old seriously.

Then Doris swept him into her arms. The little boy stiffened, then suddenly seeming to understand, he shouted for joy and put his spindly arms round the neck of his very own mother.

So Doris carried him into the house, and when Klaus followed them he found them in the hall, with Doris kneeling between the two children.

'Look, Klaus,' she said to both of them, laughing through her tears, 'you've got a brother!'

She stood up shakily and put her arms round her husband. 'Tell me how – all about it,' she sobbed.

'Later,' said Klaus, kissing her forehead.

Doris looked up at him anxiously. 'And they're both going to stay with us?'

'Both of them,' said Klaus firmly.

'And is that what you really want?'

'I have never wanted anything else,' said Klaus. He felt that he had now truly come home from the war.

'I couldn't tell you about it, you see, without making you terribly unhappy. That's why you didn't understand me.'

At that moment everything became clear to Doris: the burden that he must have borne for the last three years; the terrible sacrifice he'd had to make; the lies, the suffering.

And in that moment she was filled with a love she'd never known before and she pressed her body against his and buried her burning, tearful face in his chest.

It was the first real embrace since the end of the war . . .

* * *

In time things got back to normal. The mountains of rubble began to be cleared away. The wounds the war had left started to heal, but it was a painful process.

Klaus and Doris bought a small two-roomed flat with a garden, with the help of Klaus' father, and the two boys grew up like brothers. They called their adopted son Martin. Klaus followed in his father's footsteps and took up law, studying at the nearby university.

But they were to suffer one last blow. Late one afternoon while the children were playing outside and Klaus was poring over his books, there was a ring at the door.

A thin, tired-looking woman stood there. She had come a long way. From Poland.

Hesitantly, in her hard, guttural German, she told them her name. Klaus suddenly realised why she had come and ushered her gently inside.

'You have my boy. I have looked for him all over. For months. Please, give him back to me.'

'He's our son now,' said Klaus quietly. 'We have looked after him since he was a baby.'

The woman was sobbing. 'No one can take my boy away from me again. They stole him . . . my husband . . . dead . . . I have nothing, just my son.'

'Oh, god,' murmured Doris, her lips bloodless.

'Please let me see him.'

Klaus nodded. He went to the garden door and jerked it open. The two children looked up from their game at the strange-looking lady, who went instinctively towards Martin. He was frightened by the expression on her face, and ran and hid behind Doris.

'Please go now,' said Klaus firmly.

'I – I'll come back,' said the Polish woman. 'I understand.'

Doris stood as if turned to stone. Klaus tried to talk to her, to reassure her, but it was useless. She wouldn't listen.

In the middle of the night Klaus awoke to find Doris' side of the bed empty. He got up and went into the children's room. There was Doris sitting between the two beds, a sleeping child on either side of her. Her eyes were on Martin. She was stroking his hair and weeping silently. She knew that it was time to say good-bye. For ever.

'We're not going to give him up,' said Klaus vehemently. 'We have adopted him and we shall fight – '

'No,' said Doris softly, 'We must say good-bye to Martin.'

She turned round and her tearful eyes met his. Her voice was patient and brave. 'Klaus,' she said, 'we understand, you and I, what it means to have your child taken from you.'

Klaus took her tenderly into his arms.

'Yes,' she said. 'We must do it. If only it didn't hurt so terribly.'

The day came. The lady from Poland expressed her thanks and her joy in a language none of them understood. Martin was frightened and clung to Doris.

'You must go with this lady, Martin. She will look after you. I shall write to you, my son.'

It was the last time she would be able to call Martin her own – it was the last time she would ever see this child who had been hers from birth.

Martin's mother took him firmly but gently by the hand and led him off.

They stood at the window and watched as Martin disappeared from sight. Klaus drew Doris tightly to him, but she felt nothing. Tears had drawn a veil across her eyes. The Polish woman had wept too, and so had Martin, and little Klaus, the brother who had been left behind.

And so the symbol of that time touched them all – the one

bond that united people whatever language they spoke, whatever country they lived in, whatever crimes they had committed : tears, nothing but tears. They were an end – and a beginning.